WRITTEN *with* REGRET

The Regret Duet (Book 1)

ALY MARTINEZ

Cover Design: Hang Le
Photography: Wander Aguiar
Editor: Mickey Reed
Proofreader: Julie Deaton

Jamie,
I wish I had told you to live in the seconds.
And I wish I'd been there more often to experience them with you.
But most of all, I wish I had one more second to laugh with you.
Fly high, Jamison.
Love, Sassy Sasquatch

WRITTEN

with

REGRET

PROLOGUE

"Squeeze together," my sister ordered from a few yards away. She was holding the small disposable camera I'd gotten for my eighth birthday up to her eye.

It wasn't exactly what I'd meant when I'd asked my parents for a camera. But that hadn't stopped me from taking thirty-five sure-to-be-incredible pictures of my friends, my school, our iguana Herman, and even a few sneaky shots of third-grade heartthrob Brad Harris.

I'd always loved photography—or at least I'd loved what I could do with my mom's old thirty-five mm. I didn't know much about anything else. I'd been begging for a digital camera like the ones I'd seen at the electronics store, but it was never going to happen. My parents were old school to the core. If they hadn't had it growing up, we weren't getting it, either. And considering that our grandparents had been the original old-school parents, this meant no TV, no computers, and no cell phones. Short of a horse and buggy, we were as close to Amish as you could find in Watersedge, New Jersey—a sleepy suburb of New York City.

My father owned a bakery off Times Square, but according to him, the dangerous city was no place to raise a family. I didn't figure that the dozens of young children we saw on the occasional Saturday picnic in Central Park would agree, but there had been no convincing my parents otherwise.

My dad put his arms around my mom and me and curled

us into his sides. "I'm pretty sure this is as close as we can get without melding into one big Banks-family monster."

I rolled my eyes as my dad lifted his hands like talons and roared.

I loved him, but he could be such a dork.

My mom giggled, the sound as gentle as snowflakes on a tin roof. "Just take the picture, honey. I'm sure it will be great."

It wouldn't be great. Not at the angle she was taking it. I'd probably be cut out of the frame completely, but then again, that was more than likely her plan. What were big sisters for if not to torment you?

Whatever. I didn't particularly care if I was in the frame or not. The only reason I'd even agreed to a stupid picture in the middle of the mall food court was to finish my roll of film so I could get it developed. Film was a dying art—rightly so—and Sixty Minutes was one of the few places left in Watersedge that would develop it while you waited.

And, trust me, if you'd seen Brad Harris, you would understand why I was in a rush to get those pictures back.

"Say cheese!" Mom singsonged, no doubt through a breathtaking smile.

My mother was gorgeous in a way that made people stop and stare. Not in a sexy way. Not even in a traditional way. No, Keira Banks had a classic beauty that was all her own. Luckily, she'd passed on her red hair and green eyes to me and my sister. I hated my frizzy, orange curls most of the time, but she'd promised that one day they would turn into deep, rich waves of amber like hers. I wasn't sure I believed her, but I held out hope nonetheless.

I scowled at the camera, ready to get the dang picture over with and head to Sixty Minutes.

"You call that a smile?" Dad said, tickling my side. "I'm going to need something bigger than that, buttercup."

"Dad, stop," I grumbled.

Those were the last words I ever said to my father.

He fell face first, a gaping hole in the back of his head, before the sound of gunfire met any of our ears.

Chaos exploded. A symphony of screams and cries echoed off the white tile floors as the constant boom of a firearm played the bassline.

People ran. Everywhere. In all directions. Scattering and blurring past me in streaks of denim and cotton. I started to move, maybe to follow them, but some primal instinct inside me screamed at me to get down. Panicked, I looked at my mother. She'd know what to do.

She was standing only a few feet away, and our eyes locked just in time for me to see her body jerk from the impact. First, her shoulders, one at a time. Then her torso, her head snapping back from the sheer force of a bullet.

And then she fell, landing over the top of my father's dead body.

"Mama!" I screamed, diving toward her.

The gunfire continued, each shot bleeding into the last.

Dropped to my knees, I took her hand. "Mama, Mama, Mama," I chanted, hot tears streaming down my face. Blood leaked through her pale-pink sweater, and pure terror glistened in her eyes as she stared back at me.

I was only eight years old, and Hell was raining bullets all around us, but there was no mistaking the look on her face.

She knew she was dying—and she couldn't figure out how to make sure I didn't.

Suddenly, the gunfire stopped, and in a moment of clarity,

I popped my head up to look for my sister. But the only thing I could see was death and despair. The once-busy food court had been transformed into a graveyard. Bodies lay crumpled over, rivers of blood merging into pools, those pools joining to form a sea of red. The screams had turned into moans and the shouts into whimpers. The few remaining living souls were hiding under the tables or clinging to injured loved ones much like I was.

Only, when I looked back at my mother, she was no longer injured.

She was dead.

My shoulders shook wildly, silent sobs tearing from my throat. I needed to run. I needed to get out of there. But the fear and helplessness were paralyzing. I rested my forehead against my mother's the way she'd done to me so many times in the past, calming me after a bad dream.

I *needed* her—glassy-eyed and unmoving—to fix this. I needed her to sit up and tell me that it was over. I needed my father to rise to his feet and pull me into his strong arms, where nothing could hurt me. And I needed my sister to appear, take my hand, and tease me relentlessly for overreacting.

I needed this not to be real.

Suddenly, a man got up and darted toward the double glass doors. With one single gunshot, he dropped to the ground.

My scream mingled with the gasps and cries of others trapped and hidden in that war zone. Desperate, I scanned the area for help.

More death.

More blood.

More hopelessness.

I caught sight of a man around my father's age. He had his back to a flipped table, his face scrunched and his hands covering his ears as he rocked back and forth. With a thick beard and muscular arms covered in tattoos, he was someone I would have thought I could turn to for protection. The pure panic on his face made him more of a child than I was.

My stomach seized when another gunshot sounded followed by the thud of what I now knew was a body hitting the floor. I could have lived a lifetime without ever knowing what that sounded like. Yet, now, I'd never be able to unhear it.

"Anyone else want to make a break for it?" a man asked in a deep, gravelly voice.

I didn't know where he was, but I sucked in a sharp breath and flattened myself on the floor, hoping he wouldn't notice that I was still alive.

It was eerily silent after that. The only sound besides the thunder of my heart in my ears was the squeaking of his shoes against the tile every time he turned. They were slow, like he was taking his time surveying his damage. Or maybe they were deliberate as he searched for his next victim.

My stomach wrenched each time the sound got closer.

Then I'd shudder with relief when they faded into the distance.

It was only a matter of time though. My parents were dead, maybe my sister too. I would be next.

Lying as still as possible, I closed my eyes and prayed for the first time in my entire life. We didn't go to church and I'd never been taught religion, but if God was real, *He* was the only way I was going to survive.

Through it all, I held my mother's hand.

She would protect me.

Or, as it turned out, she'd send someone who could.

"When I say go, I need you to crawl with me," he whispered.

My lids flew open and I found a teenage boy, maybe fifteen or sixteen, with dark hair and the bluest eyes I'd ever seen staring back at me. He too was on his stomach, facing me with his cheek resting on the cold tile and a red baseball cap turned sideways to hide the majority of his face. How he'd gotten there, I would never know.

I shook my head so fast that it was almost as if it were vibrating.

His eyes bulged. "Listen to me, kid. He's pacing a pattern. Right now, he's down near the froyo place. After he makes his next pass, we'll have about sixty seconds to get over to the Pizza Crust. They have a door in the back we can escape through, but you gotta stick with me."

I blinked at him. Who was this boy? He was young but older than I was. And while he wasn't big and muscled like the tattooed guy, he was tall and could probably put up a fight.

"Did you hear me?" he asked when I didn't reply. "When I say go, you stay low and head behind the counter at the Pizza Crust. Okay?"

"He...he'll shoot us," I stammered out.

"That's why we have to be fast." He lifted his head and glanced around. "Shit," he muttered, putting his cheek back to the tile and closing his eyes.

I stared at his long, fluttering lashes for several seconds, debating if I was seriously going to trust this kid. I didn't know him any better than I knew the shooter. But he was all I had. Help in any form, even that of a lanky teenage boy, was better than nothing.

His eyes were still closed, his breathing shallow and his body completely still, when he suddenly reached out and used two fingers to close my lids.

"It's going to be okay," he whispered so quietly that, had he not been mere inches away, I wouldn't have heard him.

And for the first time since I'd seen my father collapse, I felt a spark of hope that maybe it would be okay.

Flattening my palm against the cool tile, I slid my hand over until I found the tips of his fingers. The footsteps were getting closer, but that boy didn't delay in moving his index finger to rest on top of mine.

It was such a small gesture, but it brought tears to my eyes.

For a terrified little girl, playing dead to hide from a madman, it was sweetest thing he could have done.

With nothing more than the pad of his finger resting on mine, I wasn't alone anymore.

I didn't know who he was or where he'd come from, but I knew without a shadow of a doubt that when he said go, I was going with him.

ONE

CAVEN

Fourteen years later...

"I wish I had more words. Well, honestly, I wish Ian had words. But, somehow, he always finds the back of the room."

"It's not by accident!" he yelled, causing everyone to laugh.

"I guess the only thing left to say is thank you. To all of you who helped us get here. And especially to all of those who doubted we ever would." Smiling, I lifted the bottle in the air. "To Kaleidoscope!"

The cork on the champagne sprang free, spilling bubbles all over my hardwood floors. A dozen of my friends, their dates, and a few assholes I pretended to like cheered as I tipped the seven-hundred-dollar bottle up for a sip before wiping my mouth on the sleeve of my blue button-down.

"Easy there, or you'll be worthless tonight," Veronica purred as she sidled up beside me, pressing her thin body and huge breasts against my side. Her golden-blond hair fell like silk over her bare shoulders, and her tight, strapless, red dress left little to the imagination.

However, after the way she'd been eye-fucking me all night, I didn't suspect she wanted me to use my imagination at all.

Smirking, I slid my free arm around her waist. We'd been playing the forbidden cat-and-mouse game for months. Her throwing herself at me. Me pretending that I didn't want to fuck her senseless. But, with the deal closed and the money in the bank, I was officially a free man. Well, not that I hadn't been a free man before. I'd been blissfully single for the majority of my life. But since we'd met three months earlier, Veronica had been off-limits. She was the personal assistant to Stan Gotham—billionaire owner of tech giant Copper Wire. Which happened to be the computer company that had just purchased my college start-up for six-hundred-eighty-six million dollars.

Hold on. Let me repeat that.

Six hundred.

Eighty-six.

Million.

Dollars.

No woman in the world was worth screwing up that kind of deal.

Eight years earlier, when I'd started Kaleidoscope with my best friend, Ian Villa, we couldn't even get his parents to invest in our facial recognition software. Companies like Google and Facebook had been lightyears ahead of us, but never underestimate two college kids with a fierce determination to avoid a nine-to-five. Turns out, not getting a job was the hardest job of all. I wasn't sure either of us had slept in years. But becoming multimillionaires at the age of twenty-nine had made it all worth it.

Kaleidoscope was revolutionary and had been used by federal and local authorities as well as hundreds of private businesses. Twenty-five pixels—that was all our system needed to identify a person. If an image or video existed on the internet or on a computer connected to the internet, our search engines would find it. This sucked for people applying for a job when they had a history in the porn industry. But for the hundreds of victims whose rapists, murderers, and abductors had not only been identified but also convicted, it was a miracle tool.

With an exorbitant amount of cash rolling in from licensing deals and millions more on the horizon, Ian and I had thought it was just the beginning of Kaleidoscope.

That had all changed a few months earlier.

No, Kaleidoscope wasn't perfect. We'd caught a lot of heat when DNA cleared a murder suspect our software had matched from a blurry security video to a Facebook profile. Definitely not our finest hour. However, we were cut some slack in the public eye when, two weeks later, a presidential candidate connected to an unsecure Wi-Fi network and our system found nude images of a missing underage girl on his hard drive. She was recovered along with three other girls from a sex-trafficking ring in Chicago.

In the wheelhouse of *no good deed goes unpunished*, that one image had changed the face of Kaleidoscope forever. By the end of the month, Ian and I had been called to testify in front of Congress, Zuckerberg-style. Thus beginning the greatest ethics and privacy debate our nation had ever seen.

News stations across the world were covering all things Kaleidoscope. People came out of the woodwork in support for the program, touting its successes in criminal investigations. Others wielded their pitchforks, holding protests and demanding that we be sentenced to prison time for creating such a powerful weapon. That was the week Caven Hunt and

Ian Villa had become household names. That was also the week we'd decided we weren't cut out for politics and had accepted Stan Gotham's low-ball offer to buy the company.

I hated to sell. Kaleidoscope had once been our passion, but our hands were tied. With a Supreme Court legal battle that would more than likely shut our search engines down for good, rich and devastated seemed a lot more palatable than broke and devastated.

So there we were—celebrating the finalized sale and a nine-digit balance in our bank accounts. And I was finally free to lose myself in a beautiful woman.

I passed Veronica the champagne. "What exactly do you think I'm going to be worthless for tonight?"

"Don't play coy with me." Smiling around the mouth of the bottle, she tipped it up for a sip.

"Who's playing?" I asked, absolutely being coy while sliding my hand down to her ass.

She cuddled in close. "What do you say we kick all of these people out and head back to my place?"

"Your place? That seems like a gross misuse of time what with my bed being fifteen steps down the hall."

"Your place is a dump, Caven."

I twisted my lips and glanced around my apartment. "Ahhh… Are we really calling this a dump nowadays?"

Her eyes twinkled as she peered up at me, her long—and more than likely fake—lashes fluttering innocently. "Yesterday? No. Now that you're loaded? Absolutely."

I'd been "loaded" by most people's standards since Kaleidoscope had first taken off, but I didn't spend enough time at home to justify forking over massive amounts of cash on an apartment that would serve as nothing more than a glorified hotel room. And I guessed when your boss was the third-richest person in America, my one-bedroom apartment, no matter how clean and spacious, probably did look like a dump.

"I'll start apartment hunting tomorrow."

She grinned, all pearly white and saccharin sweet. "Smart man."

Shaking my head, I tore my blue stare away from her to find Ian making his way toward us. His tall, lean body weaved through the chattering guests, but his stoic, brown eyes were locked on mine, disapproval carved into his features.

While I'd always been the consummate bachelor, Ian was slightly...well, boring. I loved the guy, truly. But while my weekends were spent mingling with socialites, his were spent at his house in the burbs, a book in one hand and, if his lack of female companionship over the last few years was any indication, his dick in his other.

Stopping in front of us, he shoved a hand into the pocket of his navy slacks and pointedly flicked his gaze to where Veronica's red fingernails were toying with a button on my shirt. "You two didn't waste any time."

"It's been hours since the funds hit the bank and we're both still dressed." I shot Veronica a wink and shifted her deeper into my side. "I'd say that's an unprecedented display of self-restraint."

Ian rolled his eyes.

Veronica giggled.

And I breathed, free and easy, as if it were the first day of my entire life.

Taking the champagne from my hand, Ian inspected the label. "Christ, are you chugging vintage Dom? This bottle could have paid our rent in college."

"Didn't you hear?" I leaned in close and whispered, "We're loaded now."

He kept his eye on the bottle, an unmistakable grin pulling at the corners of his lips. Yeah. He was proud of us too.

He lifted his gaze to mine, that subtle grin stretching into a full-blown smile. "Ah, fuck it." He threw the bottle up for a long draw.

I roared with laughter and my head filled with a high that had nothing to do with the alcohol.

Things were just…good.

Life had never been easy for me. Chaos had been following me like a dark cloud, looming and hovering, casting its shadow far and wide despite how bright the path in front of me should have appeared. After growing up the way I had, where happiness had been more of a privilege than a choice, I knew better than to believe that that moment would be anything other than fleeting.

And one second later, the universe proved me right.

My attention was drawn from Ian when the doorbell rang. People had been coming and going all night, not bothering with courtesies like knocking. I'd greased the palms of the couple who lived downstairs not to call the cops if things got rowdy. But it was only nine. Things were *far* from rowdy. Especially considering that Veronica was still wearing clothes.

The idea made me grin down at her, taking a peek at her cleavage.

"I'll get it," Ian said. "I'm heading out anyway."

"What?" My head snapped up. "You *just* got here."

"Yeah, and I'm *just* leaving. As very appealing as watching you get shit-faced before sneaking off to your bedroom sounds, I'd rather my ears fall off than be forced to listen to one more minute of Brandon's bullshit investment opportunities. Heads-up, he's waiting on you so he can pitch a dodgeball-brewery combination in Milwaukee."

"That sounds like a legal nightmare."

"My thoughts exactly. Now, I'm leaving, so it's your job to break the news to him. And I swear to God, Caven, if I wake up in the morning to find logo mockups for Fast Ball Brewing in my email, I will hunt you down and—"

"Yeah yeah yeah. Maybe on second thought, you should go." I took the champagne and passed it off to Veronica before giving him a shove toward the door. "I have six hundred million dollars to blow tonight. The last thing I need is your voice of reason in my head."

"Half," he grumbled. "Only half of that money is yours, asshole."

"Right. Right. Half. I'll try to keep that in mind while shopping for malted-barley-shaped dodgeballs."

He glared at me over his shoulder, a lip twitch giving him away as we made our way to the door.

It was March, but the city had been hit by a cold snap including a light dusting of snow, and we were expecting more overnight. While Ian got busy doing the abominable snowman routine with his coat, scarf, and gloves, I opened the door to see who had rung the bell.

A cursory check revealed an empty hallway.

And that's when I heard it: the sound that changed not only my entire life in the present, but my life for all future days to come.

At first, it was just a grunt, but as if that baby could feel my gaze, the minute my eyes made contact, it let out a sharp cry.

Confusion hit me like a lightning bolt, sending me back a step. I used the doorframe for balance as I took in the yellow blanket with a hole only big enough to reveal a pale-pink face.

"What the fuck?" I breathed. Glancing around the hall, I waited for someone to jump out and start laughing. When no one spoke up to issue a punchline, I took a step closer and repeated, "What the fuck?"

I was utterly unable to process the absurdity in front of me.

Of course, I knew the facts.

It was a baby.

On my doorstep.

Alone.

But the *why* in that equation was glaringly absent.

"Uhhh," Ian drawled, peering over my shoulder. "Why is there a kid at your door?"

"I have no fucking idea," I replied, staring down at the squirming and now-screaming bundle. "It was just there when I opened the door."

Ian shoved me to the side so he could stand beside me. "You're shitting me, right?"

"Does it look like I'm shitting you?"

He looked from me to the baby, then back again. "How did it get there?"

We were two incredibly smart men who had created a technology empire out of nothing. But, clearly, a baby was too big for either of us to wrap our minds around.

I swept an arm out and pointed to the kid. "I have no fucking clue, but I'm assuming it didn't catch a cab."

A light of understanding hit his eyes. He moved first,

stepping over the crying baby and hurrying down the hall, searching around the corner near the elevator before returning alone.

The party continued behind me, but even with the door open, the loud chatter was no match for the ear-piecing cries happening in that hallway.

Veronica suddenly appeared beside me, her body going solid as she stammered out. "Is that…a baby?"

"Back up," I urged, throwing my arm out to block her path as though the infant were going to suddenly morph into a rabid animal. And let's be honest, I knew nothing about babies. Anything was possible.

Ian dropped to his knees, scooping up the wailing child. Meanwhile, I stood there like a gawking idiot, paralyzed by a weight I didn't yet understand.

"Call the pol—" He stopped abruptly and reached into the top of the child's blanket. "Oh shit," he whispered, his wide, panic-filled eyes flashing to mine.

"What?" I asked, stepping toward him to get a better look at the kid. Only it wasn't that tiny baby cradled in his arms that made my heart stop and bile rise in my throat.

There, in my best friend's hand, was a folded piece of notebook paper that had been tucked into the child's blanket. From the looks of it, the paper was unremarkable in every sense of the word. Blue lines, white spaces, hanging remnants from where it had been haphazardly ripped from a spiral bound notebook. Even the crease was crooked. But it was my name scrawled on the outside in messy, black ink that made it the most remarkable paper in existence.

I snatched it from his hand and, with blood roaring in my ears, opened it.

Caven,

I'm sorry. I never meant for this to happen. This is our daughter Keira. I'll love her forever. Take care of her the way I can't.

Written with regret,
Hadley

The hall began to spin, my head feeling like every ounce of blood had been drained from my body. The thundering in my ears faded and the loud chatter of my guests, who were suddenly aware that something was happening at the door, roared to life.

And then the chaos finally found me all over again—the past playing out in my head like my life flashing before my eyes.

I knew Hadley. If that was even her real name. Or more accurately… I'd *known* Hadley—for one night. We'd met at a bar. She was stunning, with waves of thick, red hair that had caught my attention the minute I'd walked through the door. Upon approach, I realized that it was her eyes that made her the most mesmerizing woman I'd ever seen because they weren't the bright-green irises that flashed on the back of my lids every night as I woke up in a cold sweat. She seemed a little dry and serious, but she had a sharp, sarcastic wit. The physical attraction was mutual, and two drinks later, we were back at my apartment, naked, and fucking until we were on the verge of a coma.

Or at least *I* had been nearly comatose.

Hadley, on the other hand, had more than enough energy to ransack my apartment before taking off with my computer, iPad, cell phone, and wallet. The very same wallet that contained the only thing I'd had left of my mother.

I'd immediately called the police when I'd realized what she'd done, but short of a few red hairs left behind on the pillowcase, Hadley had all but vanished.

Until tonight.

"Caven?" Ian called. "What's it say?"

I sucked in a deep breath and looked at the baby in his arms. The blanket had fallen off its head just enough to reveal a patch of fine hairs, more orange than its mother's red.

I hadn't heard from Hadley in over eight months. It seemed awfully convenient that she'd reappeared long enough to dump a child she claimed to be mine on the night the Kaleidoscope deal had been finalized and the contents of my bank account had become public knowledge.

"Call the police," I declared, turning on a toe and walking back into my apartment, leaving Ian standing in the hall with Hadley's child.

Shoving through the crowd of concerned onlookers, I headed straight to the bottles of liquor lining the counter. I didn't bother with ice or even a glass. I threw back that bottle of vodka, hoping like hell the burn of the alcohol could numb the panic coursing through my veins.

Through it all, that baby never stopped crying.

TWO

CAVEN

"Do you have any reason to believe the child is yours?" the older, gray-haired police officer asked.

Avoiding his gaze, I stared blankly at the screen of my laptop as Kaleidoscope booted up, all the while fighting the urge to throw up or tear out of my skin and run as far away from that apartment as I could get—possibly both.

In the twenty minutes since we'd found the baby, I'd spent all of them thinking back on my night with Hadley.

I wasn't an idiot. When your sex life revolved around one-night stands or the occasional repeat performance, protection wasn't optional. I had a busy life, and if I didn't have time for a relationship, I sure as shit didn't have time for herpes or a toddler. I'd worn a condom every damn time I'd been with a woman for as long as I could remember. And that night with Hadley, I'd gone through at least four.

But it was the one time, when I'd woken up to her riding my cock, that was currently torturing my thoughts.

One time. One fucking time.

"Mr. Hunt?" the cop prompted.

Squeezing my eyes closed, I hung my head. "I don't know. Maybe." *Oh, God. Maybe.*

"Right," he muttered. "Well, do you happen to remember Hadley's last name?"

12

I looked up from my computer to scowl. "If I did, I probably would've mentioned that when she *robbed* me." I cut my eyes to the team of paramedics huddled around my couch, inspecting the baby. It was still shrieking to the point that I feared the soundwaves were going to split my head.

Christ. How had I gone from chugging champagne and celebrating a multimillion-dollar business deal to listening to a baby who may or may not be mine screaming its head off?

Everyone, including Veronica, had left. Turns out, having a baby dumped on your doormat was a real mood killer. Ian was still there though, quietly standing in the corner, typing away on his cell phone. Every so often, he'd pause to ask how I was doing.

I had no interest in conversation. I was too busy searching for Hadley all over again.

When she'd taken my wallet months earlier, I'd had no way to track her down. And trust me, I'd tried. Cameras at the small bar we'd met in were nonexistent. I'd spent an exorbitant amount of time trying to track down footage of us walking back to my place, but by that point, it had been over twenty-four hours and the whopping two businesses that had cameras aimed at the street had already purged the previous day's recordings.

My own damn building didn't even have working cameras.

It was a nightmare. That woman had taken close to ten thousand dollars in electronics. But I'd have gladly let her keep them all if she'd just returned my wallet.

I wasn't a particularly sentimental man, but inside that leather bi-fold was the necklace I'd stolen off my mother's neck while she'd lain in a coffin when I was ten. After months of watching the cancer crush her spirit and ultimately her body, my father hadn't even waited for her funeral to purge everything she had ever touched. My older brother, Trent, told me that it was part of Dad's grieving process. However, the morning of the service, when a woman showed up with a U-Haul, I'd figured the quick cleanup had more to do with her than it had the loss of my mom.

So, when I saw my mother, pale and lifeless, wearing the tiny silver heart she never took off, I pretended to lean in and kiss her just before they closed the casket. With a whispered apology, I snatched that necklace from her neck and tucked it into my pocket.

Short of two pictures I managed to hide under my mattress while my dad was ridding her memory from our home, that necklace was the only thing I had left.

I'd been livid when Hadley had taken it from me.

But, now, maybe it had been a blessing in disguise. Because, this time, I was ready for her. I'd added cameras to the front of my building. One image of her leaving after dumping the baby and I'd be able to identify her once and for all.

And then hopefully make her come back.

With Kaleidoscope open on my computer—my login thankfully hadn't been terminated yet—I scanned through the footage of the last few hours. I watched as all my friends and the other residents came and went in fast forward without the first sign of Hadley's fiery-red hair, and before I knew it, the police were rushing in on the screen, catching me up to the present.

Frustrated, I rewound another hour, not knowing when she had entered the building. For all I knew, she could have been hiding out there all day, waiting for her moment to spring her bundle of lies on me.

"Mr. Hunt," the cop called. "I need your attention up here."

The baby was still crying and my blood pressure was rising by the second, making my tone rougher than I had intended as I replied, "No, what you need is someone to find this woman."

He reached across the bar dividing my living room from the kitchen and pointedly closed my laptop. "Eyes on me."

I had negative amounts of patience left, and my six-foot-four frame swelled, shoulders taut, muscles thrumming. "Don't touch my computer again. Ask your goddamn questions, but keep your hands off my shit. Got it?"

Ian closed in on me. "Chill. They're here to help."

With that baby rupturing my ear drums, I had no chill left. I was coming apart at the seams.

Holding the cop's stare, I opened the top on my computer, daring him to argue. "Look, I understand that you're doing your job here, but I assure you I can find this woman before you can."

"Maybe, but Kaleidoscope is no longer legal to use in criminal investigations."

I ground my teeth. "Then I suggest you close your eyes."

He flicked his gaze to Ian in silent warning like he was my damn keeper or something, but I didn't bother with my best friend's reaction. I had work to do.

I hit play again.

"There." Ian pointed at the screen.

I paused the video and zoomed in on a brunette in a short, black skirt and heels, carrying a black oversized purse. Even if she was wearing a wig, her nose was too big, her legs too short, and her skin too tan to be Hadley. "That's not her."

He moved his finger down to the bag. "It might not be Hadley, but that's the baby."

My back shot straight as I leaned in close. Sure enough, there was the corner of a yellow blanket peeking out of the bag.

A wave of adrenaline surged in my veins.

If it wasn't Hadley, then maybe it wasn't even her baby.

Most importantly, if wasn't her baby, it was impossible for it to have been mine.

I blew out a ragged breath. I didn't give a shit if it was some fucked-up extortion attempt. At that point, I'd have been downright gleeful if someone was trying to scam me for money.

I just couldn't be a father. After the bastard I'd had for a dad, it was best for everyone that my genes were never passed down.

THREE

CAVEN

Fourteen years earlier...

T he little girl's finger trembled beneath mine. I shouldn't have gone to her. I was only putting her in more danger. But the damn kid wouldn't stop moving. If he'd walked by and seen her, that maniac would have put a bullet in the back of her head without hesitation.

As far as I'd been able to tell from my vantage point, he was killing anyone he could find with a pulse. I couldn't leave her there. She reminded me too much of myself as she lay on the floor, crying for her dead mother. I'd been there once, and I'd never forget her cold, lifeless body. It'd felt like I was going to die that day too, and there hadn't even been a gunman running rampant.

I held my breath as his footsteps grew closer. He hadn't made it deep enough into the food court to see us yet. Instead, he'd been staying close to the doors at the entrance. He'd eventually run out of victims up there, and when he did, I'd be the first to go. That little girl with the big, green eyes? Well...she'd be next.

I just needed a few more minutes. The police should have been there soon. If I could just get the two of us somewhere hidden to wait this out, we'd actually have a chance at making it out alive.

Another round of shots rang out and the kid jerked, a muted cry escaping as she shimmied over until she was flush with my side.

"Stop moving," I hissed, sliding my arm over her shoulders, bending my elbow so it covered both of our faces. Only then did I pry an eye open.

Tears were streaming down her cheeks even with her eyes closed, and her lips were quivering as though she were fighting back a scream—a scream that would get us both killed.

As the deafening cracks continued to ring in the air, I did the best I could to keep her calm. "It's okay. It's okay. It's okay," I chanted softly. "Just be still. It's almost over." Those words were as much for me as they were for her. The only thing louder than the gunshots was my heart drumming against the floor.

Everything fell silent again. But this time, it was truly silent.

There were no more cries.

No more gasps.

No more moans.

There was no sign of life at all except for the little girl crying under my arm, her body trembling at my side as she waited for me to give her a count of three so I could guide her to safety.

A safety I wasn't positive I'd be able to find for either of us.

But dammit, I was going to try.

I lifted my head up and looked around, barely catching sight of his back as he kicked a path through dead bodies. He was far enough away that he might not see us if we were quiet.

I looked back to the girl. She was on the verge of losing it. I had to get her out of there. Fast.

"It's time," I whispered.

Her green eyes flashed open, dread and second thoughts blazing within.

"We got this," I lied, praying with my whole heart that it was true. "Kick your shoes off so they don't make any noise."

Her forehead wrinkled, but she followed my direction.

"On the count of three, run as fast as you can, but don't make a sound. Got it?"

She nodded, but she didn't look convinced. I wasn't positive she was really with me at all. If I ran and she didn't follow, there would be no turning back for her. If she hesitated, even the slightest bit, I'd have no choice but to leave her behind.

We had one chance to get to that pizza shop and then out the back door. I had to make the most of it, and I hoped like hell I could make the most of it for her too.

Wrapping my hand around her wrist, I sucked in a deep breath and sent up one last silent prayer, but it wasn't to a god at all. It was to my mom.

And then, on an exhale, I whispered, "One, two, three... Go."

FOUR

CAVEN

Hope turned to sludge in my veins in the span of three hours.

The cops had tracked down Marina Chapen—a known working girl in the area. She told the cops that a red-headed woman had given her the baby and paid her to deliver it to my apartment. She was supposed to hand the baby to me directly, but she'd panicked when she heard all the commotion inside my apartment. Apparently, fifty bucks was the going rate to have someone drop a baby on a doorstep. A real bargain considering that Marina was now facing child endangerment charges and I was waiting on my eight-hundred-dollar-an-hour lawyer to meet me at the police station.

"What if the baby is mine?" I asked, pacing a path in the small conference room we'd been escorted to.

"Then you…take care of it?" Ian replied from his chair, cool and calm, his long legs crossed ankle to knee.

"You're kidding, right?"

"You allergic to diapers or something?"

I stopped and planted my hands on my hips. "This is not a fucking joke. You know the shit I lived through." I ground my teeth as the vise in my chest clamped down, making it difficult to breathe. "I can't raise a child… I just can't."

His voice got low and serious. "You're not your dad, Caven."

He was right, but that wasn't what scared me.

"I'm not saddling a kid with that. My old man's blood dies with me. End of story."

Once upon a time, my dad had been an amazing man. Or at least I'd thought he was. I remembered playing with him at the park and throwing a football in the backyard while he grilled burgers.

But then my mom got sick and everything changed.

And when I say everything, I mean, my *entire* life. Past, present, and future.

At first, he started numbing the pain with booze, but that only made him angry. Trent took the brunt of his abuse, but there was always more than enough left over for me. When the alcohol wasn't cutting it anymore, he moved on to pills. I'd never forget listening to my mother throwing up in the bathroom because she was in so much pain. Meanwhile, my father was passed out on the couch, high as a kite after raiding her stash of medications.

After that, she started hiding them. This enraged him more than anything else. According to several of his rampages, she was going to die regardless of if she had the medicine or not. He was the one being left behind to raise two worthless boys. Those pills belonged to him.

The woman was so frail that she could barely walk, but my father had no problems choking her unconscious until she told him where she'd hidden his next fix.

Honestly, I was relieved when he started disappearing for days at a time. Those were some of my favorite memories: sitting at my mother's bedside, talking about everything under the sun.

But the abuse didn't stop after she died. If anything, it got worse. Actually, it didn't stop until one day, seven years later, when *he* died.

But he'd made sure to drop me and my brother in Hell before he left.

I'd sworn to myself I'd never have a child. No shred of that man should ever be passed on to future generations. It was bad enough that I had to carry a piece of him like a boulder strapped around my neck. If I thought about it, I could feel the burn of his DNA inside me. At least I didn't look like him. Trent wasn't so lucky. But, thankfully for both of us, the apple had fallen pretty far from the tree.

If that child turned out to be mine, there wouldn't be a day that passed where I wouldn't worry that I'd put her at risk of being part of that rotten and decayed tree as well.

I laced my fingers together to hide the shake of my hands and rested them on the top of my head. "I can't do this."

"Maybe you won't have to," Ian said, plucking invisible lint off the leg of his slacks.

God, why hadn't this happened to him? He was the responsible one. Hell, knowing him, he'd have set up a nursery in his spare bedroom the minute he'd woken up and realized he hadn't worn a condom. Just in case.

Not me. The extent of my reaction had been to hit the doctor for an STD panel. A baby had never even been on my radar.

I shot him a glare. "We're currently panicking about what happens if it *is* my baby. Could you please keep up?"

He sighed. "Relax and let's be rational here for a second."

"Nothing about this situation is rational!" I shouted, my voice echoing off the paneled walls. "If the baby is mine, why didn't she say something over the last nine months? She knew where I lived. My apartment doesn't look like much, but she knew about Kaleidoscope. She knew I had money."

"She robbed you the last time she saw you. My guess is she thought you'd call the cops if she showed back up."

"Oh, I absolutely would have. But a simple, 'I'm pregnant and the baby is yours,' while she was being hauled away in cuffs would have gone a long fucking way in me not having a nervous breakdown right now."

He barked a laugh, but I found not the first thing funny.

"You fucking suck at this."

"We can both be flipping our shit over the possibility of you being a father." My stomach rolled at the F-word—not the four-letter kind. "Relax, Caven. Take a deep breath. No one is dead or dying. It's a baby. Not ideal. But not exactly cause for you to give yourself a heart attack."

I sucked in a deep breath and willed my heart to slow. "You're right. We don't even know if it's mine."

"There you go. What's your gut telling you?"

"Mexico. Start a new life, buy a tequila distillery, and never look back."

He chuckled.

If only he knew how serious I was.

There was a knock at the door, then a plain-clothed officer with a round face and a salt-and-pepper beard, wearing his badge on his hip, came in followed by my attorney, Doug Snell.

I rushed toward them. "What's going on? Have they found Hadley?"

Doug shook his head.

I turned to the cop. "But you're looking, right?"

Ian's hand landed on my shoulder. "Cav, stop. Let the man talk."

But I couldn't stop. I needed them to find Hadley. And I needed her to come back and tell everyone that this was some kind of joke and the baby *wasn't* mine.

More, I needed that baby to truly *not* be mine.

Everyone settled in chairs around a small conference table. Everyone but me.

My heart was beating at a marathon pace and my mind was sprinting in circles; there would be no relaxing.

"We're looking, okay?" the officer, who identified himself as Detective Wright, said as he flipped a file folder open. "According to the doctor at the hospital, the baby appears to be in good health, but given her age, they want to keep her for a few days. So this gives us a little time to get things figured out."

Her.

It was a girl.

Dear God. I really couldn't handle this.

"Her age?" I questioned. "How old is she?"

"Doc estimated she was born sometime earlier today."

Ian cursed under his breath, but I couldn't do anything but grit my teeth and shake my head. I didn't want to acknowledge the way my stomach churned at that revelation. Anger was an easier emotion for me to process. But for fuck's sake, who abandoned a newborn? The poor kid could have died in that chilly hallway or been stepped on by any number of people leaving my apartment.

Fucking Hadley. Such a waste of a beautiful woman.

"We've been searching the hospitals and birthing centers in the area, but judging by the hack job on the umbilical cord, I'm not expecting to find any answers."

"What does that mean?"

He shared a knowing look with Doug. "It means you need

to accept the possibility that we may never find her. Without a picture or a last name, we have so little to go on."

"What about the prints you lifted from my apartment after she stole my stuff?"

He sighed. "We got thirteen prints excluding yours. You'd just moved into that apartment. For all we know, those belong to the previous tenants and their family."

"Or they could match fucking Hadley," I rumbled, my already waning patience vanishing.

Doug interrupted my meltdown. "Finding her is not going to solve the problem. You need a DNA test. End this before it even gets started. I've got a lab lined up. They've agreed to rush it, so it will take about thirty-six hours to get the results."

I swallowed hard and prepared myself to ask the one question I didn't want the answer to. "And what then?"

"Well," he drawled, shifting in his chair. "If it comes back that she's not yours, we walk away. The child will be turned over to social services and the police will handle it from that point on."

"And if I am…you know…the father?" Christ, I could barely get the word out.

"As long as we have proof of paternity before the child is discharged from the hospital, it will be a breeze to have the child released to you. Because we don't even have a name to list on the birth certificate, sole custody will be yours. I can't imagine there will be any issues."

It was at that moment that I knew Ian had been wrong. With the words *sole custody,* a vise cranked down so hard on my chest that I was pretty positive I was going to die—or, at the very least, be broken in two.

Having a baby with a woman you didn't know was bad.

Having a baby with a woman who had robbed you before sneaking out of your apartment was even worse.

But having a baby with a woman who had dumped the child at your door before taking off, thus leaving you—a man who had no idea how to even hold a baby—to care for said child *alone* for the foreseeable future was by far the worst-case scenario.

And thanks to Hadley fucking no-last-name, I was only one DNA test away from living it all.

FIVE

CAVEN

My eyes were bloodshot and my body exhausted when I heard the knock on the door.

I knew.

I didn't even need to answer it.

I'd spent the last thirty-some hours counting cracks in the ceiling while considering every possible ending to this nightmare.

My favorite was the one where Doug called announcing like he was Maury Povich that I was *not* the father. I had big plans for this scenario. I was going to get a vasectomy and then buy a yacht and sail down the coast, where I'd celebrate every child-free sunrise by standing on the bow naked and yelling "Freedom!" Mel Gibson–style. Not that he was naked in that movie. But in the middle of stress-induced insomnia, I'd thought there was no better way to celebrate my eternal childless status than to be naked.

In the scenarios where I *was* the father, I spent my time mentally listing all the ways I would absolutely screw up a child in the next eighteen years. It started with your average run-of-the-mill fears. Things like maybe she would become a serial killer because I worked all the time and she was raised by evil, child-hating nannies. I'd Googled nanny agencies shortly after this and left a few sleep-deprived messages on answering machines, asking for the stats on how many of their past clients were now in jail or on the run from the law. Not surprisingly, I didn't receive any call-backs.

After that, I moved on to the selfish phase where I obsessed about all things Caven: thoughts of losing my mind while listening to a baby scream all day, juggling work and dirty diapers, toys covering my apartment, and never being able to have sex again. It was a pity party of epic proportions.

In the middle of those manic moments was a lot of moral introspection after I'd considered giving the child up for adoption. There were good parents out there who desperately wanted children. There were also shitty ones like my father who were nothing more than wolves in sheep's clothing. How would I ever be able to tell the difference?

I might not be a good father, but I wanted to at least ensure that she'd always be safe. Which was far more than I'd gotten growing up.

This thought process led to me texting Ian at four in the morning to offer him a hundred million dollars to adopt her if she ended up being my daughter.

The bastard didn't even try to negotiate before texting me back with a blunt *no*.

To say I was floundering was an understatement. Most men had nine months to come to terms with the idea of having a child. God was not an idiot. He knew we'd need every minute of that time to prepare. But, apparently, he also had a twisted sense of humor, because I was only given thirty-six hours.

During that time, I went through each of the seven stages of grief. It wasn't until a thought struck me that I landed somewhere in the realm of acceptance. I'd been adamant about not passing on any part of my father to a child, but that meant I'd never pass on any of the pure and intrinsic good that was my mother.

So, no, I didn't know how to take care of a baby. But knowing that even a tiny piece of my mother was lying in a hospital across town, living, breathing, and more than likely still crying broke me in unimaginable ways. It had been over twenty years since I'd had anything more than two pictures of her and a necklace that Hadley had stolen to remind me of my mother.

But, now, there was this little girl.

By eight that morning, the window of time from the genetics lab had expired. I knew the results when no one had called or texted. Bad news was an arrow best delivered in person.

She was mine.

My stomach twisted and the weight in my chest became suffocating as the knock at the door sounded again.

I didn't move. Not even a muscle. I was dressed, showered, and shaved. Shoes on, wallet and phone sitting on the coffee table in front of me. But I wasn't ready.

That's the thing about life though. It operates best on the element of surprise.

There were no choices left. No options. No outs.

There was just me and a baby girl who had no idea the quicksand she had been born into.

Ready or not, it was time.

Sucking in a deep breath, I rose to my feet, tucked my wallet and phone in the back pocket of my jeans, and headed to the very same door where this had all started. I didn't know the first thing about diapers, cribs, or bottles. But I knew to the core of my soul, with an absolute certainty, that I was going to be a better parent than Hadley. And that was based on nothing more than the fact that I was going to be there for that little girl.

Ian and Doug were standing outside when I opened the door, their somber faces confirming what I already knew.

"Hey," Ian started. "We need to—"

I didn't let him finish. There was only one thing I needed to know. "When can I pick her up?"

SIX

CAVEN

I was ninety-percent sure the hospital staff thought Ian and I were a gay couple adopting our first child. I was a nervous wreck, and in true Ian fashion, he was utterly unfazed. To his credit, he never left my side—not even when we were guided into a small room with four new moms in hospital gowns and forced to watch a video that boiled down to "don't shake the baby and always put it in a car seat."

Ian, and at least two of the other mothers, scrolled through their phones the whole time. I, however, had never been so engrossed in a film in my entire life. I needed all the help I could get.

After I miraculously passed the pop quiz they'd passed out after the video, we were escorted into an empty hospital room and handed a stack of papers thicker than when we'd sold Kaleidoscope. Like a good little husband, Ian whipped out a pen, settled in the only chair in the room, and got busy on the paperwork. He knew everything about me anyway, right down to my social security number and mother's maiden name.

While he made himself useful, I made myself useless, alternating between nervously sitting on the corner of the bed, crossing and uncrossing my legs before giving up and getting up to pace. I couldn't count how many times I checked the hall to see if the nurse was coming with the baby as promised.

It was the strangest feeling during those few minutes waiting for her. My stomach was in a million knots, but it wasn't close to anything I would describe as excitement. It was more like an ominous dread.

Dread for what was about to happen.

Dread that I had to wait for it to happen.

Dread that it would eventually be over and I'd be faced with eighteen-plus years *because* it had happened.

I was considering flinging myself from the room's fifth-floor window when the door suddenly opened. A nurse came in, rolling a little basket on wheels behind her.

My heart stopped and my lungs momentarily forgot how to process oxygen. I'd seen that little girl in Ian's arms when we'd first found her at my door, but that was before I'd known she was mine.

This was different. This was monumental.

This was *terrifying*.

"Here she is, Dad. Your little princess," the nurse all but sang, parking the basket directly in front of me.

My hands shook as I willed my heart to beat again. She was tiny—even smaller than I remembered—wrapped like a burrito with a pink-and-blue-striped hat pulled snug on her head. All I could see of her were eyelids, chubby cheeks, and pouting lips suckling on nothing.

She didn't look like me.

She didn't even look like Hadley for that matter.

She just looked like a baby.

"You want to hold her?" the nurse asked.

"Uhhhh...I think I'm good for now. Actually, maybe I should watch that video again."

"Oh, come on now. This one doesn't bite."

With wide eyes, I swung my puzzled gaze her way. "Do some of them bite?"

Laughing softly, she scooped the baby into her arms. Then she propped it on her shoulder before whispering in her ear, "Your daddy's funny."

Daddy. Jesus. What the hell was happening?

"Go ahead and hop up on the bed and get comfortable. I'll hand her to you. She just ate, so she should be snoozing for a while."

I flashed Ian one last pleading look, suddenly hoping he had reconsidered that hundred-million-dollar offer, but his only response was a chin jerk toward the bed.

Shit. Okay. I could do this. I was a grown-ass man. She was a tiny baby. It could be worse. She could have been one of the biters.

"Should I, uh…take off my shoes or anything?"

The nurse rolled her eyes with a smile. "Just get on the bed."

After sparing one last longing glance at the window, I climbed up.

Swear to God, my back had barely hit the upright bed before the nurse plopped that child on my chest.

Instinctively, one of my hands went to the baby's butt and the other to the back of her head, but that was literally the *only* instinct I had. "Whoa, whoa, whoa," I called as she started to walk away. "What am I supposed to do now?"

She grinned and shrugged. "Get to know your daughter." As she walked to the door, she called over her shoulder, "As soon as you get that paperwork finished, I can start on getting you guys out of here. The doctor will be in to give her one last look before you leave, but give me a buzz if you need anything."

Had it not been for the fact that I was balancing a child on my chest with both hands, I would have given her a buzz right then.

I looked to Ian. "She's just going to leave us alone with her like that?"

Ian chuckled. "Did you think she was going to come home with you too?"

"Good point. Go ask her how much she makes and tell her I'll double it."

He shook his head with a smile and walked over to the bed. With two fingers, he stroked her cheek. "You sure this one's yours? She's cute."

I looked down at her, doing my best to lean to the side to see her face without having to move her. I didn't know what I'd expected. Maybe some latent fatherly emotions to suddenly rise to the surface the moment I touched my own flesh and blood. But, to be honest, I didn't feel anything. Which was obviously the first clue that I was going to be a total failure at this parenting gig. "I feel like I'm holding someone else's kid."

He moved back to the chair and started on the paperwork again. "That'll change."

In a show of pure positivity, I shot back, "What if it doesn't? I'm pretty sure my dad never liked me. Maybe that's just the way my family is built."

His head came up and he gave me a slow blink. "Caven, I'm not even going to waste time commenting on your dad. You can't base your ability to love your daughter on that asshole. Look, I'll be honest. I can't think of a man less equipped to be a father than you are, but you'll figure it out. You're a good man with good intentions. That's, like, ninety percent of parenting right there. So stop stressing about liking her and worry about her becoming a teenager and growing boobs. That's going to be the scary part."

I barked a laugh, quickly silencing it when the baby jerked as though I'd scared her.

We both fell silent, and as he went back to filling out paperwork, I stared down at my daughter.

Holy shit. *My daughter.*

It was so surreal. In the span of a few days, my life had changed so drastically that it wasn't even recognizable anymore. And that change was going to continue in the days to come. She wouldn't stay a baby forever. One day, she'd be a grown woman, holding a baby of her own, looking back on her life. She didn't have a mother, but I could give her something worth remembering. I could give her a father she wanted to pass on parts of to her children—DNA she could be proud of.

There were going to be a lot of failures in my near future, but dammit, I could give her a good life.

"What do you want her middle name to be?" Ian asked.

My head popped up. "Her *middle name*? What's her *first name*?"

His dark brows drew together. "I assumed it was going to be Keira. That was what the note—"

"Fuck the note," I hissed. Fighting against gravity, I shifted her up my chest until her head was just below my chin. Lazily trailing my hand up and down her back, I kept my voice low. "Hadley abandoned her. She made that choice, but that is the last one she will ever get to make. She's mine now and her name is not fucking Keira."

He smiled, beaming with pride. "Okay, then. So, what's it going to be?"

I swallowed hard and nuzzled my chin against the top of her hat. There was only one woman who deserved the right to name that baby, and unfortunately, she'd died when I was ten. She would have loved that little girl—unquestioning and without judgment, welcoming her into our family with open arms and a bright smile, including a smack on the back of my head for taking so long to come around. Fresh as the day I'd lost her, grief punched me in the gut. I closed my eyes and imagined her face.

She was the only happy memories I had of my childhood.

And she was about to become my daughter's first too.

"Rosalee," I whispered. "Her name is Rosalee."

SEVEN

CAVEN

Four years later...

"I'm hanging up now," I growled into the phone. I'd been on that damn call for over an hour, negotiating the never-ending deal.

"Now, wait just a minute, boy. I'm not done here."

I bit the inside of my cheek, trying desperately to control my temper. Boy? *Seriously?* I was going to kill Ian for passing this guy off to me. Lance Goodman had been attempting to talk me in circles for days. He was arrogant and pushy, and he thought he shit gold bars, but damn if he didn't have a tech security firm that was going to be worth millions by the end of the year thanks to a new development in safeguarding cryptocurrency. It was a side of the market I knew nothing about, but private investing didn't always require expertise other than how to wire funds. This was absolutely one of those times.

"I hate to say it, Lance, but I'm an hour past done. It's clear we can't make this work."

"Who said we couldn't make it work? Three hundred million will get you twenty percent. Just say the word."

I sighed, pinching the bridge of my nose. We'd looped right back around to where this conversation had started. Money was great and all, but I was already late for a date and my patience was shot. Ian had been adamant on getting at least twenty percent, and since my best friend couldn't charm five pennies from a nickel, the schmoozing landed on my shoulders.

There was no chance in hell I was paying *three hundred million* for a company that was currently only valued at double that. Sure, there was tons of potential with the new launch and I was willing to invest in that, but for fuck's sake. This was ridiculous.

"Look, Lance. Ian and I both wish you the best of luck. But your evaluation is bullshit and you know it. *Two* hundred million for twenty percent is the best I can do. If you have another investor on the hook willing to do three for twenty, then as a businessman and friend…" God, I was full of bullshit. I rolled my eyes at myself as I buttoned the top button on my suit jacket. "I highly suggest you take it. But, unfortunately, we've both reached our bottom lines. And they don't match. It's time we stop wasting time and move on." Straightening my tie, I glanced down at my watch. She was going to be pissed I was late. This would not bode well for the party later. "I need to go. Have a good da—"

"Two fifty and twenty-one percent," he rushed out before I had the chance to hang up.

I froze, a slow grin curling my lips. The fact that he'd upped the percentage told me this deal was more than just him taking on a new investor. He needed cash—and fast. Why? I didn't know, but Ian would take a hard look at his financials before the deal was finalized, so I didn't hesitate before countering with, "Two fifty and twenty-five."

He let out a string of cuss words. "We'll discuss it over a drink this afternoon."

"Nope. My day's packed."

"Don't bullshit me. It's a Saturday."

"And yet here I am on the phone with you."

"Today, Caven. If you're going to fuck me this hard, the least you can do is buy me a drink first."

I laughed and peeked around the corner. She was already at the table, sipping on orange juice in a wine glass, a plate of untouched pastries sitting in the middle. I was right. She was *pissed*. But I really needed to seal this deal before word got out and he actually found someone to give him the three hundred million he probably deserved.

I jumped out of view when her head popped up.

This was going to be a clusterfuck. But I did have to pick up a few things before the party. Surely I could squeeze in one drink without it being considered *work*.

"One drink. And it has to be near me."

"You've lost your damn mind if you think I'm driving to Jersey today."

It was only a forty-five-minute commute to the city. If I could do it every damn day, this guy could do it once.

I was pointedly silent.

"Okay, okay. Fine. Two fifty. Twenty-five percent and I'll drive my ass to Jersey. However, I need you to bring a gun because if I catch the suburb bug and start looking at houses while I'm there, I need you to kill me immediately."

Victory sang in my veins. "Noted. I'll text you the address." I didn't give him the chance to get another word out before I hit the end button.

I typed out a quick message to Ian before shoving my cell in my pocket. Then, drawing in a deep breath, I patted down the inside of my jacket to make sure the black velvet box was still inside and prepared to face the music.

"Rosie. My baby," I purred as I exited the hallway. She was

easily the most beautiful thing I had ever and would ever see, even when her angry, green glare landed on me with the attitude of a scorned woman in her twenties.

I shot her a wink as I made my way to the table. When I got close, I reached for one of the muffins.

She slid the plate away. "You're late."

"Yeah. I know. I'm sorry." I straightened the lapels on my navy-blue suit.

While I was in the shower, she'd slipped a formal hand-written—in crayon—invitation under the door, inviting me to her royal birthday breakfast. Or at least that was what I'd thought it said. It was really just her name, a birthday cake, and a stick figure drawing of the two of us holding hands. As I was drying off, she'd yelled, "I'm hungry, so dress like a prince!" through the door before I heard her feet scurrying away on the wood floor. This was the second year of princess birthday breakfast, so I'd thankfully prepared with chocolate chip muffins and pink-sprinkle donuts. Ya know, the breakfast of royalty everywhere.

I stopped halfway to my chair and gave her a once-over. "Wow, you look incredible."

Her hair was a messy nest of red waves, a silver crown precariously perched atop her head, and her baby-blue ballgown was straight out of *Cinderella*, complete with elbow-length gloves and plastic gemstone bracelets.

She harrumphed and looked away, begrudgingly muttering, "Nice tie."

I toyed with the end of it. "Yeah? You like it?" It was the most hideous monstrosity I'd ever seen. Bright yellow with slopes of brown on the top and bottom, it was a giant silk banana. No prince would ever be caught dead in it. But she'd bought it for me when Ian had taken her shopping for Father's Day, so I wore it when I didn't have to leave the house. "Mind if I sit down, your highness?"

Her glare turned into a full-on scowl, and I had to bite my lip not to laugh.

When I got settled across from her, I made another attempt at a muffin, and this time, she let me have it. I jerked my chin toward the full platter. "I thought you said you were hungry?"

"I know you were working."

I slapped a hand to my chest. "Who, me? Working? *Today*? It's a Saturday. That would be strictly against the rules."

"It's not just Saturday," she huffed. "It's Rosie-Posie day." Her eyes narrowed into a powerful glare a four-year-old should *not* know how to possess. "I heard you on the phone."

I hooked a thumb over my shoulder. "You mean just now in the hall? Pssh. That wasn't work."

"Now, you're going to make up a story," she said before leaning back in her chair and linking her fingers like she was sitting in a boardroom rather than a breakfast nook. "Go ahead. Let's hear it."

Clearly this was not the first time she'd caught me working. She knew the drill.

And so did I. "See, when I took the trash out earlier, there was a baby seal in the middle of the road with a bunch of plastic straws stuck to his flipper." I leaned toward her. "See why we have to recycle?"

"We don't live near the water."

"Right? Which was why I was so surprised to find him there."

Her scowl became more scowly, but I'd committed, so I had to see it through.

"I was only late today because I stopped traffic, carried him to safety, and removed all the fishing net."

"You said straws."

"Yeah, but when I got closer to him, it was a bunch of straws, a fishing net, *and* a boot. Don't get me started on why there was a random boot, but in my experiences rescuing seals, there is *always* an old boot involved."

She pursed her lips, but it was only to hide a smile. With my Rosalee, that was halfway to being out of the doghouse.

"Anyway, that was the seal's dad on the phone, calling to thank me. I told him that I was in a rush for my girl's birthday breakfast, but he just wouldn't stop going on and on about sending us two hundred million fish as his way to say thanks. Apparently, that's the seal equivalent of a muffin basket. I tried to tell him that we didn't need that much fish for just the two of us, but he wasn't having it. So then we started arguing. I know it's rude not to accept a gift, but where would we even keep two hundred million fish?" I paused to tap my chin. "We could probably fit at least a million of them in your room."

"Ewwww!" she cried, adorably crinkling her freckled nose.

"Maybe another million if we cleaned out from under your bed first."

Her eyes flashed wide and she shook her head so fast that it was all I could do not to laugh. But she was smiling and not giving me the death glare anymore, so I continued to ramble faster with each sentence.

"But that would still leave us with two hundred forty-eight million. I tried to tell him that we'd take twenty five percent, but that's still, like, fifty million, and I don't think your playroom could hold more than a hundred fish max with all the junk you have in there, so the rest would fill our whole house." I popped a chocolate chip off the top of the muffin into my mouth and shrugged. "I'm not sure about you, but I don't want to smell like a salmon for the rest of my life. Unfortunately, Mr. Seal would *not* back down." I paused dramatically, lifting a finger in the air. "But then I got an idea."

"What?" she asked, damn near giddy, all her frustration with my punctuality forgotten.

I made a show of looking around the empty space before curling my finger to signal her closer. When she got as far across the table as her torso would allow, I whispered, "I gave him Uncle Ian's address."

She burst into a fit of laughter, the crown on the top of her head shaking with her shoulders as she giggled.

Smiling, I listened intently, like it was the first and not closer to the billionth time I'd heard the masterpiece that was her laugh. It was moments like that that filled my chest with more happiness than I'd known was possible four years earlier.

How had it already been four years?

In some ways, it seemed like it was just yesterday that I'd held that tiny, squishy baby on my chest in the hospital. But, in other ways, it seemed like an eternity ago. I honestly couldn't remember my life without her.

Technically, I didn't remember much of the first four months of my life *with* her, either. Bringing her home from the hospital had been a culture shock. My life of coming and going as I pleased had been over. Even going to the gym had become a scheduling nightmare, and that was assuming I'd had the energy to do anything more than climb out of bed, fix a bottle, and get right back in bed to feed it to her. Sleep deprivation was no joke.

I hired a nanny for the first week, but I never left the house because I'd convinced myself that something was going to happen to Rosalee while I was gone and it would have been all my fault because I wanted to maintain my six-pack. A six-pack that's only purpose was that of a hood ornament. It wasn't like I had the time to entertain the idea of having sex again.

Veronica had sent me exactly one text message after that night we'd found Rosalee.

She asked if she'd left her purse at my house.

She hadn't.

We never spoke again.

Whatever. I had more important things to worry about. Like counting how many dirty-versus-wet diapers I changed each day. I had no fucking idea you had to count that shit. Pun intended. The nanny had taught me a lot while I was obsessively hovering over her, questioning her every move, complete with dictating her answers into my cell phone for future reference.

According to the agency, this drove her crazy, and she ended up quitting after nine days.

After that, I entertained the idea of hiring a live-in au pair. It would have been nice to have someone to teach Rosalee about another culture and maybe even another language— fine, also someone who lived with me and was available to help twenty-four-seven.

Until I considered how easy it would be for that woman to steal my child, fly her to a different country, and sell her into human trafficking.

Then I realized how easy it would have been for *anyone* I hired to steal my child, fly her to a different country, and sell her into human trafficking.

And then I realized that I was going to have to burn Ian's house down so he was forced to move in with me because he was literally the only person in the world I trusted with her.

In the midst of my drowning in fatherhood, Ian decided we should use the Kaleidoscope profit to dabble in private investing. Given our history of growing a multimillion-dollar company—regardless of how controversial it had ended up being—from the ground up, we were quite good at recognizing a smart concept and strong work ethic when we saw them. But there were too many days I could barely keep my eyes open. It was then that Ian defined the title of "best friend." He started coming over every Saturday night and would stay up all night long walking Rosalee around my apartment, feeding her and changing her. And more than once, I'd caught him singing to her. He was great with her. But it didn't matter who had her. Rosalee was this little ball of never-ending pissed-off energy.

Around the three-month mark, I'd been convinced something was wrong with her. She'd fall asleep crying, wake up crying, cry because she wanted to go to sleep but couldn't. Colic was what the pediatrician called it—the twentieth time I'd taken her into the office in so many days. I must have looked like hell, because she'd suggested I hire someone for more than just Saturday nights. I informed her about the human trafficking thing. She blinked a lot. Then she gave me the number of her personal nanny who had never once sold her children in twelve years of knowing her.

This was how we met Alejandra, the goddess of child rearing. She was in her early sixties, had three grown children of her own, and was interested in picking up extra hours when the good doctor didn't need her to help pay for her daughter's college tuition.

She was incredible from the start. Kind and knowledgeable, and she had no qualms about reading me the Riot Act the one time I'd left Rosalee on the changing table to grab a diaper on the other side of the room. Within a few weeks, Saint Alejandra had my girl on a daytime schedule, which caused her to start sleeping in six-hour stretches at night. It was the most glorious thing that had ever happened to me. Not long after that, Alejandra started cooking me meals that didn't consist of coffee and takeout. She even left a few in the freezer every Friday for the weekend when she wasn't there.

Rosalee was young, but I could tell she loved Alejandra too. And I was coming to the realization that I couldn't live without her. The twenty hours a week she was working for me just weren't enough. It made me a horrible person. And I genuinely felt bad—for about two seconds. But when Rosalee was six months old, I offered Alejandra a full-time position that tripled what the doctor was paying her and included healthcare, a retirement plan, and college tuition for her daughter. A few months later, when I finally broke down and bought a house in Leary, New Jersey, two miles away from Ian's place, Alejandra also got a private guesthouse with paid utilities and a Lexus so she could commute back and forth to see her kids.

The peace of mind, knowing my baby was in good hands, was worth every fucking penny.

From then on, things got easier. Rosalee grew up, and as a father, I grew with her. In the blink of an eye, she went from being this little, helpless baby to a walking and talking tornado. I swear I must have purchased every baby gate in existence to keep her from sneaking into the bathrooms to play in the toilets. And then, a year later, when it was time to start potty training, I couldn't force her into the bathroom. Not even Alejandra had a magical fix for those three months filled with random puddles of pee we'd discover around the house any time we were barefoot.

What my baby lacked in bladder control, she excelled at in other areas. Rosalee was smart, loved animals as long as they had fur, and could talk her way out of trouble with a well-thought-out argument that would put a few attorneys I knew to shame. She was sassy and sweet, loved cuddles, and cried like the world was ending when she had to get shots at the doctor. (Not the same doctor we stole Alejandra from. We were asked to leave her practice immediately after that. Still…totally worth it.)

Ian had been right when we were in the hospital. My past hadn't dictated my ability to love another human being. Yes, my life had been hell, filled with more pain and chaos than others saw in a lifetime. But falling in love with Rosalee Hunt was the easiest thing I had ever done.

It was funny how life worked. I'd spent twenty-nine years without the first desire to be a dad. But with Rosalee, I couldn't look at her without thinking of all the incredible, life-altering things I would have missed.

And her laugh, as she sat across from me, dressed in a ball gown and giggling like a maniac over a silly story I'd made up to get of out trouble for working on her birthday, was at the very top of that list.

Reaching into my pocket, I took out the little, black box and slid it her way. "Happy Birthday, Rosalee."

She squealed, diving for the box. "Is it a ferret? Oh, Daddy, please let it be a ferret."

Yeah. She called me Daddy. And yeah. I loved it.

The first time she'd babbled *dada*, I'd known I was in trouble.

The first time she'd called me *daddy*, I'd nearly hit my knees.

And the first time she'd said "I love you, Daddy," I'd frozen, my chest so tight that I thought there was a solid chance I was having a heart attack. Once I'd felt comfortable that I didn't need to call an ambulance, I'd immediately gone to the bathroom, gotten in the shower, and fought back manly fucking tears in private.

Well, until she had come looking for me, thrown the shower curtain back, and asked why she didn't have a penis.

After that, I'd started locking the bathroom door.

I looked from her to the box and then back to her again. "How big do you think ferrets are?"

"I don't know."

"Exactly. Which is why you can't have one."

Her mouth fell open, ready to fire off an objection more mature than any four-year-old should be able to muster.

"Ever," I added. "You know the rule. No pets until you are old enough to take care of them yourself…and I mean in your own apartment when you're old enough to move out."

"That's not fair!"

"I know, right? Your dad is the *worst*."

She glared.

I smiled and then took a bite of my muffin.

While I was chewing, she pried the box open and, in true Rosalee fashion, let out a dramatic gasp.

She loved it. I had known it the minute I'd picked it up from the jeweler that she would, but she had no idea how much *I* was going to love seeing her wear it.

Rosalee was as girlie as little girls came. She loved dresses, purses, nail polish, and all things lip gloss. But the one thing she loved more than anything else was jewelry. She didn't have her ears pierced yet, but the child had a full assortment of clip-ons, bracelets, and necklaces. All of which were cheap costume jewelry she'd picked out herself.

But this… This was real. And for the way it made my chest tense, it was almost too real.

"It's a necklace!" she exclaimed as though I hadn't been the one to give her the gift.

I stood from my chair and walked around the table. "Do you remember me telling you how I named you after Grandma Rosalee because she was my mom and very special to me?"

She nodded eagerly.

"Well, I wanted you to have more than just her name."

She gasped again. "This is Grandma Rosalee's necklace?"

My gut wrenched, and I clenched my teeth, looking away to hide my anger.

I hadn't thought about Hadley much over the years. Not surprisingly, the cops had never found her, and if I was being honest, I didn't care if they ever did. The fiery hate I had for that woman was only tolerable because of the way I loved our daughter. No. Strike that. *My* daughter. Hadley didn't factor into any of that.

When Rosalee was three, she'd asked if Alejandra was her mommy after watching some silly cartoon on her iPad. It had broken my fucking heart, because not only did she not have a mother, I didn't even have an explanation for why.

The truth—*Your mommy was a selfish bitch who didn't care about anyone but herself so she abandoned you and never looked back*—seemed a tad harsh for a child. So I went with a slightly gentler approach and told her, "Well, there are all kind of families in the world. Some kids have two daddies, some have two mommies, and some have a mommy and a daddy, but the extra special ones? They just have a daddy who loves them double as much."

Alejandra had given me a disappointed scowl, which I'd strategically avoided by tickling Rosalee into exhaustion.

No. It wasn't my finest parenting moment. One day, she'd realize that I lied and I'd have to find a way to tell her the truth. But that day could wait. Hopefully forever.

I cleared my throat and removed the necklace from the box. "No, this isn't my mom's. That one was lost a long time ago. I had this one made just for you. It's identical to hers though." I draped it around her neck, clasping it with bumbling thumbs.

"It's so pretty," she whispered, toying with the heart.

Dodging the crown, I kissed the side of her head. "Just like my Rosie Posie." I walked back around to my seat. "Now, am I forgiven for being late?"

She aimed a bright, white smile my way. "Maybe. Did you remember to get the pony?"

I tipped my head to the side. "I was supposed to get a pony?"

Panic contorted her round face, which was more little girl than baby now. "Yes! You promised you'd get one for my party. I told Molly and everything."

I abandoned the joke when her eyes started to fill with tears. "Hey, hey, hey. Relax. Of course I got the pony. She'll be here at two, so you'll have her to yourself for a whole hour before your friends get here." I scooted my chair around to sit beside her and placed a donut on her plate. "Stop stressing. Okay? The party is going to be great. Molly, Ava, *and* Paisley are coming. Plus about fifteen other kids from your gymnastics and dance classes. We've got plenty of food and flowers on their way. And before you even ask, yes, you can decorate the door."

"Did you remember the goodie bags?"

I gave her hand a squeeze. "Your faith in me is insulting. Of course I remembered the goodie bags. I personally filled them with cigars and whiskey."

"What!"

"I'm joking. Every bag got two glow-in-the-dark bracelets, a pack of scented markers, one lip gloss, and enough candy to ensure no parent will ever allow their child to come back to our house again."

She smiled, which made my mouth stretch too. I'd do anything for that smile—this included spending my Friday night filling two-dozen glittery, pink bags with over a hundred dollars' worth of junk that would all be in the trash can by the end of the weekend.

"Did you get the unicorn cake?" she asked.

"Not yet. I'm supposed to pick it up at noon. I have a few more errands to run too, like picking up the balloons and ice. I texted uncle Ian though, and he's going to come over and help you and Ale decorate. Okay?"

"Okay, but if he tries to bring Star Wars stuff, I'm not inviting him to my next party."

I laughed. "Fair enough. I'll be sure to warn him. Now, what do you say we stop worrying about the party and just eat our breakfast? It's Rosie Posie Day. And on Rosie Posie Day—"

"We eat sweets," she finished for me.

"All day long."

She giggled, and instead of tearing into her donut, she climbed into my lap, sliding her plate over next to mine.

When she was younger, she'd insisted on sitting in my lap at every meal. Alejandra had told me that it was a bad habit to form. I didn't mind though. I loved being close to her just as much as she loved being close to me. Over the last six months, she'd been doing it less and less, opting for her own chair at the table rather than my thigh. It was bittersweet. I missed my baby girl who needed me for everything, but I was so damn proud to see her growing up and embracing her independence.

But I didn't care how old she got. If she wanted to crawl into my lap and eat her birthday donut every year for the rest of my life, I'd sit there, smiling like a maniac in an ugly banana tie, eating one with her.

EIGHT

HADLEY

E very little girl dreams of the fairytale. The white knight rushing in to save her from the clutches of evil. After that they fall in love, move to a castle, have babies, and live happily ever after.

By that definition, my life should have been a fairytale too.

When I was eight years old, Caven Hunt saved me from the worst kind of evil to walk the Earth. It didn't matter that I was a kid. I'd fallen in love with him immediately, unquestionably, and without hesitation.

But that was where my fairytale ended.

Instead of the castle, I moved into a small three-bedroom ranch-style home with a grandfather who could barely remember my name most days. I struggled for years with severe PTSD and depression, and eventually, I convinced myself that some lives just weren't worth living.

Years later, there was a baby, conceived on accident during one of the darkest moments imaginable. But that darkness was a summer's day compared to the pitch black that was the day she was born. Now, that innocent child was only mine in the sense that my DNA ran through her veins. She belonged to Caven in every way that truly mattered.

At the end of every fairytale, the one thing that always remains consistent is the happily-ever-after. It wasn't going to be mine, but there hadn't been a night that passed where I didn't pray that it would be hers.

The only way I'd slept at night was knowing that Caven had her. She'd be safe with him. The same way I had once been.

To some, it would seem like I was the villain of the fairytale. The evil mother come back to wreak havoc on the white knight and his little princess.

But hurting him was never part of the plan. After everything he'd given me, I owed that man my life.

It was just… I owed that innocent child more.

"What the hell are you doing?" I whispered to myself, my heart in my throat as I drove through the iron gates in front of a towering gray-stone mansion. The sprawling green lawn was manicured to perfection, and the rich bed of newly blossoming spring flowers bore the touch of a professional. It was the start of a warm spring in Jersey. We didn't usually see flowers until May. Though, judging by this place, those flowers had been planted specifically for the party.

Her party.

Her *birthday* party.

I couldn't believe she was turning four. She wasn't a baby. Not even a toddler. At four years old, I'd already started taking pictures. I had memories of making mud pies in the backyard with my sister and arguing with my mother over a hideous dress she'd sewn for me.

Keira was four and had no idea who I was.

Guilt slashed through me as I imagined her growing up without a mother. Regardless of how deeply it gutted me, I knew with my whole heart that it was the best thing that had ever happened to her.

The Hadley from four years earlier had had no business raising a child. That woman was nothing more than a shadow of the eight-year-old who'd lost her innocence in the midst of a bloody, heartbreaking tragedy. The gunshots and screams still haunted her even though it had been over a decade. Her demons were unshakable, their claws anchored so deep into her soul that they seemed impossible to escape. Therapy hadn't helped. Medicine only took the edge off. Self-harm, self-loathing, and self-sabotage had become a way of life. Sure, that Hadley could have kept the baby. She could have tried to be a good mother, but she never would have been able to forgive herself if—and ultimately *when*—she'd failed.

Not everything was black and white. It was often in the gray areas where the hardest decisions were made. And four years ago, in the darkest gray imaginable, dropping Keira off to Caven had been the only option.

But that was a different time.

A different place.

A different world.

And a different life.

The Hadley of now was a different person.

When the monstrous task of living had begun to suffocate me, I'd considered ending it all. Thankfully, my mother's green eyes, frantically trying to figure out how to keep me alive even as she took her dying breath, flashed on the backs of my lids, convincing me to give therapy one last try.

And, this time, it changed my life.

I explained to my doctor that I was in the prime of my life, as some would call it, but most days, it was all I could do to pry my lids open. It felt like I was walking through life, dragging two cement boulders tied around my ankles and a semi-truck strapped to my chest. How was I ever going to survive the rest of my life if I couldn't even climb out of my bed?

He looked me straight in the eye and said, "If you objectively look at life as a whole, it's a daunting and impossible process. There are just far too many obstacles for one person alone to conquer. The world sucks. People are judged rather than accepted. Hate spreads far more easily than love. Power and money are valued more than morality. Insecurities are preyed upon rather than quelled." His intense gaze never left mine when he asked, "Why would any of us want to live like that?"

I didn't have an answer for him because I sure as hell didn't.

And then he set his folder aside, leaned back in his chair, crossed his legs, and saved my life. "Because life isn't lived as a whole. You aren't given a hundred years all at once. Time is doled out one very manageable second at a time. Stop looking at the big picture and find happiness in the seconds."

I'd always loved photography—before and especially after I'd lost my parents. It was my escape. But it wasn't until that moment that I realized why.

A camera could capture a million different emotions.

But only one at a time.

One second.

One snap.

One memory forever frozen in time.

When I looked back on the picture of my parents taken exactly one second before my father was killed, they were genuinely happy.

There was no pain.

No terror.

As a family, it was our final second untouched by such brutal violence and staggering fear.

And it was beautiful.

My parents hadn't lived their lives trembling because of what *could* have happened to them.

They'd lived their lives for moments like that picture.

And from that day forward, with my camera at my side, one second at a time, I started my uphill battle to do the same. To live my life the way my parents had. The way they would have wanted me to as well.

It had taken a while, far longer than I would have liked, but I could finally breathe again without pain. I was able to find warmth in the sun again and stare up at the night sky without wishing it would devour me.

For the first time since I had taken back control of my life, I wasn't living in the gray anymore.

But I feared that was where Keira would always be.

I should have called. I should have turned myself in to the police. Caven would have been notified that I'd been arrested and he'd have had time to process my return. But that would have given him time to plan for it.

There was a good chance he was never going to let me see Keira. And rightly so. After everything that had happened, I couldn't fault him for that.

But if I was about to wage war with the likes of Caven Hunt, I wanted to at least have a mental snapshot of what I was fighting for.

I had to see her.

Just once.

My palms were sweaty as I white-knuckled the steering

wheel. I'd spent most of my drive over wondering what she'd look like. My mother? My father? My sister?

Me?

A tear rolled down my cheek and I quickly swiped it away. This was going to hurt. Seeing Keira walking, talking, laughing—knowing everything I'd missed out on was going to break me.

And seeing Caven again? Well, that was a different kind of sword through the heart.

After the shooting, I'd reached out to him no less than twenty-five times. Asking around Watersedge, I'd found his address and mailed him letters, begging him for help. I didn't know what I'd thought a fifteen-year-old boy could do. I was just so lost in my own emotions, and he'd saved me once. I believed he could do it again.

He never answered.

On my tenth birthday, I rode my bike to his house, four hours each way. It was an old, dilapidated trailer without the first sign of life inside. I cried the whole way home. But that probably had less to do with the fact that he wasn't there and more to do with the fact that, back then, all I ever did was cry.

Logic told me that he was gone and I should let him go.

But he was my hero.

As I woke up every morning feeling as though the sky had fallen down on top of me, I *really* needed a hero.

My last-ditch effort came when I was thirteen and at rock bottom. I'd managed to find out where he had moved and used the computers at the library to track down a phone number for his brother, Trent. Let's just say that conversation had *not* gone as planned. Trent told me that Caven wanted nothing to do with me and he had moved on from the shooting. This was said just seconds before cussing me out and hanging up on me. His number was disconnected by the next day.

My heart was broken, but Trent had a point. I relived that day of terror every time I closed my eyes. If Caven had managed to move past it, who was I to drag him back?

Yet there I was, eighteen years after the first shot was fired, preparing to do just that.

My leg bobbed nervously as I pulled into the last spot of the horseshoe driveway. There was another area for parking off to the side, but this would be the quickest way to leave when he inevitably had me escorted out—that is if I even made it inside at all.

Pushing my sunglasses up to the top of my head, I stared up at the front door decorated in uneven pink streamers, jagged unicorn cut-outs, and a crayon-scribbled *Happy Birthday* sign placed completely off-center. It was homemade chic at its finest. However, that was where *homemade* ended. Pink and purple flower garlands were draped from the tall trees, and little paper lanterns of all shapes and sizes hung from the branches. A large wooden arrow with intricate purple swirls etched in the wood pointed around the side of the house to a path created by what had to be thousands of dollars' worth of pink rose petals.

As I sat in my car, nerves violently buzzing inside me, a few guests passed by, holding gifts and laughing. My chest ached with hollowness as I thought about how each and every one of them knew Keira in some way, yet I wouldn't have been able to pick her out of a lineup.

It was four years overdue, and I would have to live with that for the rest of my life, but it was time to right the wrongs.

Starting with her.

For that reason alone, I grabbed the gift bag off the

passenger seat, pushed my car door open, forced one foot in front of the other, and followed the pink-petal path.

My heart pounded harder with each step as my heels sank into the grass. I'd tried on everything from cocktail attire to jeans before landing somewhere in the middle with a simple emerald-green shift dress and brown heeled booties. I knew that it didn't matter what I wore, but somehow, it still seemed important. First impressions and all.

My breath caught in my throat when I made it around the corner. The decorations in the front were a sham job compared to the back. With two large, open tents, a dozen or more tables, and roses upon roses everywhere, it looked more like a wedding than it did a child's birthday. Had it not been for the line of children and two brown ponies making laps around the yard, I would have been positive I was in the wrong place.

Adults were scattered, chatting in small groups, and the few children who weren't waiting at the pony ride were dancing through a continuous stream of bubbles.

And that's when I saw her.

My heart stopped and my lungs seized, refusing oxygen in or out.

I'd been wrong about not being able to pick her out of a lineup. I would have recognized that little girl even if the entire world was standing in one room.

She looked like every single person I'd ever loved.

Tears pricked at the backs of my eyes as I stood frozen, watching her jump to pop a particularly big bubble. Her hot-pink dress, complete with a tutu and the number four outlined in sequins on her chest, bounced with her, revealing the top of her jeans, which she'd paired with cowboy boots. It was ridiculous but so freaking cute that I couldn't help but smile and allow a tear to escape the corner of my eye. But it was her laugh when she caught a bubble in her mouth that hit me like a freight train. I stumbled back, bumping into someone before righting myself.

"Sorry," I whispered.

"It's okay," a man with a deep, masculine voice replied.

I kept my gaze locked on her as she twirled with another little girl, an infectious smile splitting her face.

"Can you believe she's four already?" the same man said, only this time he was no longer behind me. He was standing directly beside me, a glass of what appeared to be punch in his hand.

He was tall, so I kept my head low, only glancing at him from the corner of my eye. It had felt like a lifetime since I'd last seen Caven, so I couldn't recognize him on torso and voice alone, but if this was him and I looked up, there was no doubt he'd recognize me.

Well, he'd recognize me from the night Keira was conceived anyway.

He was clueless to our past together.

And knowing that had only hurt slightly less than the idea of facing him again.

"Yeah. Four. That's almost college age, right?" I halfheartedly joked.

He chuckled. "Here. Let me get that." He took the present then handed it off to someone passing by. "So, which one of these rugrats is yours?"

I swallowed hard, unsure how to answer. I stole one more glance at Keira in case it was my last and asked, "Any chance you can tell me where the restroom is?"

"Oh, yeah. Sure. Just inside. First door on the left. There's also one at the top of the stairs."

"Thanks," I mumbled, starting away.

"I'm Ian by the way," he called after me.

I blew out an audible sigh of relief. Ian Villa. Caven's best friend and business partner. Not ideal. But also not Caven.

I offered him a finger-wave over my shoulder as I tiptoed to keep my heels in the grass from tripping me up.

That was the moment I should have left. I'd gotten what I'd come for. I'd seen her. I'd memorized her. And even if this didn't work out and I spent the next five to ten in jail, I'd always have that picture of her smiling and laughing in my head. But when I reached the steps to the huge wooden deck, I couldn't force my feet to take the first one. She was right there.

After all this time, she was so damn close.

I'd promised myself I wouldn't approach her. The last thing I wanted was to hurt her in any way. But she didn't have to know who I was. A quick happy birthday from a stranger never hurt anyone.

At least that's what I told myself as I steeled my emotions, turned on a toe, and headed in her direction.

NINE

CAVEN

How was it possible to confuse a fucking frog with a unicorn? I mean, seriously What. The. Fuck.

My drink with Lance Goodman had gone surprisingly easy.

He'd downed a beer.

I'd had a cup of coffee.

He'd rambled about percentages and cash flow.

I'd put my foot down on two hundred fifty million for twenty-five percent.

He'd bitched loudly but eventually relented.

I'd been out of there in less than a half hour.

But that was where the ease of my day had ended. First, I'd stopped to pick up Rosalee's special balloon. The party planner had offered to handle it, but it was something of a family tradition for me to get it myself. When my mom was alive, she'd always buy Trent and me one of those balloons with some kind of stuffed animal inside for our birthday. She didn't care that she had two sons who didn't give a damn about teddy bears. She just like getting them for us. When Rosalee turned one, it was the first thing I'd thought to buy her. Alejandra had informed me that the balloon was a choking hazard, so I'd had to pop it and give her the bear. But every year, I bought her another one.

This year, it'd popped before I even got it to the car.

I'd gone back inside to ask for another, but lo and behold, the woman who made them was off that day. Seriously, I had no idea shoving a bear into a balloon was such a niche trait that there was only *one* woman who could do it.

There was no way I was going home without that balloon, so I threw a wad of cash at the florist and told him to call her in for an hour.

I was running out of time, so while I waited for the balloon sorceress to make my replacement, I drove across town to get the cake—the three-tier unicorn cake I'd custom-ordered months earlier. Only when I got there to pick it up, the cake they gave me was a frog, sitting on a lily pad, complete with little black fondant flies floating on wires around it.

I was a huge proponent of Alejandra's "you get what you get, and don't pitch a fit" style of parenting. But if I brought home a cake with *insects* on it, my daughter was going to lose her damn mind.

Another wad of cash later, the baker took a sheet cake out of the display case and decorated it so that it loosely resembled a unicorn theme. It was going to have to do. I didn't have time for anything else.

After swinging back to pick up the balloon and getting stuck in traffic on the way home, I was ten minutes late to my own daughter's birthday party.

Ian had been sending me pictures of her riding the pony before the guests had started arriving, but I was pissed I'd missed it. That damn pony was all she'd been talking about for months.

Despite my financial situation, I tried my best not to spoil her. Christmas was kept to a six-gift maximum, which included new shoes and at least one book. It was another of my mother's traditions I was carrying on. Unlike my mother though, I could get Rosalee damn near anything she could ever want. But that wasn't how I wanted her to grow up. We had a nice house, I drove a nice car, and she had plenty of clothes, but that was where our spoils stopped.

Recently, I'd started paying her an allowance for doing chores around the house. Mainly, it was stuff like picking up her toys and keeping her bathroom tidy, but it was her responsibility—one she'd taken very seriously from the start. She loved counting her dollars, and I was proud of how rarely she wanted to spend them. She was a saver—as long as I didn't take her to the jewelry section at her favorite store. Then all bets were off.

She was still young, but I'd done my best to make sure she appreciated the small things in life.

The one exception to this rule was her birthday.

Because, to me, it wasn't just her birthday. It was the day we became a family.

I didn't have a lot of fond memories of those first few days after I'd found her outside my door. The uncertainty. The indecision. The fear. But the family I'd been given that day meant more to me than I ever could have fathomed.

That little girl was my life. And while her very first birthday had been celebrated wrapped in a blanket, abandoned by her mother, and rejected by her father, I swore to myself, every year on her birthday, I'd make damn sure she knew exactly how loved and wanted she truly was.

So, for birthdays, my baby got the party of her dreams.

And I'd missed the first ten minutes, thanks to a popped balloon and a fucking frog.

"Could you have taken any longer?" Ian asked.

"Probably not," I clipped, setting the cake on the table. "Did she notice?"

"Nah. She's been in heaven since they set up the bubbles. She wasn't too happy about getting off the pony. But then she saw Molly and it's been smooth sailing ever since."

"I can't believe I missed that. Will you talk to the horse lady and see if I can pay her to stay an extra hour after the party ends?"

"Way ahead of you. You're golden until six." He lifted the top of the baker's box. "Shit. Is that enough cake to feed everyone?"

"Don't know. Don't care. It was the best they could do. Just make sure Rosie gets a piece."

"Why you don't hire people to handle this, I will never understand."

I unwrapped the trick candles that always made her giggle and started strategically arranging them on the saddest unicorn cake to have ever been made. "Because I'm her father. I can't do the flowery fru-fru crap she likes, so I hired a party planner, but the cake and the balloon are always my responsibility."

"Right. And you do it *so* well."

I lifted my head to scowl. "Shut it. Part of the reason I'm late is because I had to spend my daughter's birthday listening to Lance Goodman moan and groan about numbers. Any chance you're going to be growing a set of balls anytime soon that will allow you to have conversations with people other than me?"

"I wouldn't count on it. I just got shot down by a woman before she even looked at me. Besides, we all know I'm the brains of this operation. The negotiating and swindling are your roles. And, for the record, you are way better at them than you are balloon-and-cake duty."

"Please tell me you're not trying to pick up women at my kid's party?"

"Oh, how the tables have turned, Caven."

I laughed, finishing with the candles and finally having a second to look around. The back yard looked amazing, but Ian was right. That cake was not going to be big enough. "Shit. I don't think I invited all these people."

"Yeah, I was surprised too. I didn't think this many people liked you."

I chuckled. "Where's my girl? I need to do some groveling."

"She's with Molly at the bubbles."

I turned in search of my daughter, but what I found was a portal to some fucked-up alternate dimension.

Time stopped, the world tilted, and it was all I could do to keep from sliding off the edge.

Because right in front of my eyes—in my own goddamn backyard—was Hadley, squatting in front of *my daughter*, laughing like she'd been there every day and not a fucking ghost for the last four years.

My vision flashed red, all the anger I'd ever felt toward her bubbling back to the surface. But it was the sheer panic that she was standing next to Rosalee that caused my body to fire off enough adrenaline to fuel an inferno.

I didn't know that woman. But with an absolute certainty, I knew that she had never once had my daughter's best interest at heart.

"That's Hadley. Call the police," I snapped at Ian before taking off.

I dodged children and raced around the gift table, my eyes never leaving the two of them. The muscles in my neck and arms strained in objection, but I forced myself to slow to a walk. I'd already caught the attention of a few guests, so I slapped on a smile and did my best to play it cool as I made my approach. I'd taken a route so that Hadley's back was to me. I did *not* want her to see me before I got my hands on Rosalee in case she tried anything stupid.

I didn't have the first clue what she was doing there, but I wasn't taking any chances.

"Ferrets, huh?" Hadley asked. Just the sound of her voice raked down my spine like the point of a rusty dagger.

I was only a few steps away when Rosalee's head snapped up, a huge smile splitting her mouth.

"Daddy!"

"Hey, pretty girl." I darted toward her, scooping her into my arms and securing her on my hip before I even bothered to look at Hadley.

She didn't say a word as she rose to her full height, which wasn't much compared to my six-four. The true story was told in her pale face and wide eyes, but I had to give her credit. She squared her shoulders before meeting my gaze.

I'd shared one night with that woman. Mere hours. Most of which had been spent in the dark. But I'd never forget what she looked like. However, seeing her then felt like the biggest slap in the face.

Because she was fucking beautiful.

Long, red hair. Creamy, white skin. Bright, green eyes. Subtle freckles across her nose.

She looked just like Rosalee.

And I fucking hated her that much more because of it.

If all was fair in the universe, Rosalee would have had my dark hair, my blue eyes, my olive complexion. But no. Hadley had not done one goddamn thing for that child and still managed to give birth to her perfect clone.

I kept my gaze locked on her as I whispered in Rosalee's ear, "Go tell Uncle Ian to gather everyone inside so that you can open presents."

She sucked in a sharp breath, thoroughly thrilled with this turn of events. "Now?"

"Yep."

She let out a squeal and started wiggling to get down. "I hope I get a ferret!"

I turned, blocking her from Hadley's reach before setting her down. And even still, I kept a close watch on the woman out of the corner of my eye. "Go, baby. Tell Ian it's okay if you start without me."

"It's present time!" she yelled.

I caught sight of Ian standing only a few feet away, the same confusion and anger ricocheting in my chest showing on his face. He had his phone held to his ear, one arm outstretched to Rosalee, grabbing her only steps after I'd put her down. I didn't have to say a word before he took off with her toward the house.

Only then did I give that fucking woman my full attention.

Rage brewed inside me, my whole body igniting in fury now that my child was safely out of the mix. With two heavy strides, I closed the distance between us to keep her within arm's reach. She wasn't escaping again. I didn't give the first damn if I had to tackle her to the ground until the cops got there.

I had a million questions for her, starting with, but not limited to, what the fuck she was doing at my house. That could wait though. I didn't want her in my life, but knowing who she truly was would go a long way in figuring out how to keep her *out*.

"What's your name? And don't fucking lie to me."

"Caven," she whispered, giving a slow, awe-filled shake of her head as her eyes filled with tears like I was the phantom, rather than her.

"Answer me!" I boomed. "What is your name?"

Her lashes fluttered shut, not opening for several beats.

Fuck it. If she wasn't going to answer me, I'd figure it out myself. Kaleidoscope had long since been disabled after a judgment by the Supreme Court. But I didn't give the first damn if I had to paint her face on every billboard in North America. I was going to figure out who the hell this woman was, and then I was going to make sure she never came near my daughter again.

Bringing my phone up, I snapped a picture of her, the flash sparking only inches from her face.

Her eyes flew open, and she brought a hand up to cover her face. "What the—"

"Your name," I ordered while continuing to take pictures.

She turned to the side, curtaining off her face with her hair. "Would you stop? You're going to blind me with that thing."

I finally put my phone down and leaned in close. "You think I give one single fuck what happens to you? Four years ago, after you'd already robbed me, you handed *my daughter* off to a prostitute who left her on my doorstep. You left a newborn baby cold, hungry, and alone where any-fucking-thing could have happened to her. You never even looked back. You never tried to contact me. You just fucking disappeared. Then you show up here today, talking to her like you have any right to share her oxygen? *Fuck you.*" I spat, my chest heaving as I let four years of pent-up rage fly. "Go blind. Go deaf. Fall off a damn cliff. I do not care. But don't you dare think you are going to drag my daughter into your latest play. She does not exist for you. She will *never* exist for you. Do you understand?" I was panting by the time I was done, the anger stealing my breath more than my words.

She just stood there. Her shoulders had rounded forward, but I couldn't see her face because of her hair. Her fucking *red* hair.

"Say you understand me," I seethed.

"I understand you," she replied softly, but not gently. "But I don't think you understand *me*." She lifted her head, her hair falling away, and stared me right in the eyes. "I do exist. And one day, I *will* exist to her whether you want me to or not. At some point in the not-so-distant future, Keira's going to want to know who her mother is. And I'm here today because I want to be the one to tell her."

Keira?

Jesus Christ. Keira.

That little blast from the past lit me on fire.

"Her name is Rosalee, not fucking Keira. You don't even know your own daughter's name and you think you deserve a role in her life? You're delusional."

Her head snapped back. It may have made me a dick, but I enjoyed every second of her pained expression.

She blinked, devastation crumbling her bravado. "You... you changed her name?"

"I didn't have to change it. She was never yours to name."

Her mouth fell open, but she didn't have time to get a word out before the cops rounded the side of my house.

Taking a step away, I shot her a smile. "Perfect timing. Maybe these guys can get you to talk."

She flicked her gaze to the approaching officers, not appearing the least bit surprised that they'd been called.

"Talk? Is that what you want?" She took a step toward me. "Because short of demanding that I give you my name, you've been too busy running your mouth for me to *talk* at all." She took another step toward me. "My name is Hadley Banks. And I know you hate me for what you *think* I did to *our* daughter. But the fact that you love her enough to be this angry proves that I did something right. So, before this goes any further, let me be very clear. I'm *not* here to take her from you."

I should have laughed. It was such an absurd statement. The woman was about to be arrested for theft and child abandonment. She was in no position to be taking anything from anyone. But to my ears and to my heart, it was a threat all the same.

"*You will never take her from me!*" I roared.

"I just want to know her!" she roared right back, her wild greens locked with my feral blues.

The cops jogged over, stepping between us, one shoving at my chest as the other guided her back a few steps.

I had so much I wanted to say to that woman. What I thought of her. Where she could shove her bullshit. The fact that I would bury her before ever letting her take my daughter. But as badly as I wanted to unload the years of hatred, rational thinking hit. I needed her as far away from Rosalee as I could get her.

"I want her off my property. Now," I snarled.

"Okay. Let's calm down for a minute," the cop urged, but I was way past that.

"No. I'll follow you to the station. Whatever you need me to do. But that woman is wanted on multiple charges and I'd like to add trespassing and attempted kidnapping to the list."

"Kidnapping?" Hadley gasped, leaning around the cop. "I didn't try to kidnap her. Officer, I simply asked her what she wanted for her birthday. I never even touched her."

There were other words spoken.

By the officer in front of me.

By the officer in front of her.

By Hadley.

But I said nothing else.

Because when I tore my gaze from the green eyes I hated more than anything in the world, I saw an identical pair staring back at me as Rosalee fought like hell against Ian's attempts to drag her away from the window.

TEN

CAVEN

Thirty minutes after the party had started, the last of the guests were trickling out the front door while Rosalee cried in my arms. I'd tried to get people to stay, all but begging a few of the parents, but three cop cars, six officers, and a screaming match in my backyard had really killed the vibe.

The cops had been ecstatic when I'd stomped away, leaving them alone outside with Hadley. One of them had followed me inside, but I'd only had eyes for my daughter.

The good news was, when she'd seen the police outside, she'd thought one of them was my brother, Trent. Just the year before during a visit to Pennsylvania, where he was the chief of police, he'd taken her for a ride in a cruiser, letting her play with the lights and siren.

The bad news was that she'd seen enough out the window to know that Trent wasn't there and that Daddy was *really* mad.

By the time I'd reached her, peeling her out of Ian's arms, she was scared and had a dozen questions, including wanting to know what the "nice lady" had done wrong.

I'd lied—because it seemed that was all I ever did—and told her that the police needed the *nice lady's* help with something as they escorted Hadley to their car. Covering for that woman felt like a gut shot, but I made peace with it because I'd lied for Rosalee's sake, not Hadley's. There was no way I was explaining what she had done wrong until I had some solid answers of my own. Hopefully, all of which would lead to her skipping town again and me never having to tell Rosalee anything about her at all.

After calling the cops, Ian had phoned my attorney. God bless Doug. He was there in thirty minutes and spoke to the police on my behalf, explaining our situation, while I split time between losing my shit in my bedroom and consoling Rosalee with the promise of another party.

From the moment I saw Hadley until the moment I had her car towed from my driveway, the entire ordeal lasted under two hours. But the hell of Hadley's return was just getting started.

"Four hours," Doug said, swirling a glass of scotch.

It was now past nine. Alejandra had cooked us all a dinner we didn't touch and bathed Rosalee before leaving. She'd offered to let my girl spend the night with her in the guesthouse, but after the day we'd had, I felt better keeping her close.

This turned out to be the best decision, because only four hours after her surprise return, Hadley Banks was released from police custody.

"How is that possible?" I asked as I paced my kitchen. "They just fucking let her go?"

Ian walked past me to the fridge and pulled out two beers. He handed one to me then resumed his position on the barstool next to Doug. "Keep it down. Rosie's still awake."

I tipped the beer up for a long pull, but it was going to take a tranquilizer dart to get me to calm down.

"They were ready," Doug replied. "From what I've heard, her attorney was waiting for her at the station with a whole pile of paperwork. They spent an hour in questioning, rushed her through processing, and released her on a fifty-thousand-dollar bond."

I raked a hand through the top of my hair. "You have got to be shitting me."

"She has no record, Caven. They couldn't charge her with theft of your property because, as we expected, none of the prints lifted at your old apartment matched. A date has been set before a judge on Monday for the child abandonment charges, but I'm warning you: Her attorney is *good*. I'm not sure the prosecution is going to be able to keep up."

The blood thundering in my ears reached new decibels. "What the fuck does that mean?"

"It means, I don't know that she'll be convicted of anything. If I were her attorney, I'd argue that she didn't abandon the child, but that she was unable to care for it and simply asked a friend to deliver her baby to the father. The endangerment that happened after that wasn't her fault. Personally, I think the prosecution's best bet would be a neglect charge. And I don't doubt that they will see that too. But with it being her first offense and since a judge would probably agree that Hadley did what was best for Rosalee by leaving her with you, I can't imagine she'd get slapped with anything more than a misdemeanor and some community service. Though, if that happens, we could definitely hit her hard with a child support case."

I loved Doug. He'd been my attorney for a lot of years, and despite the fact that he was creeping up on seventy, I even considered him a friend. He'd been there for me every step of the way when we'd first found Rosalee, and he'd gone so far as to invite us over to his family's house for Christmas dinner a few times. But never, not once, in all the years I'd known him had I considered ripping his head off his body like I did in that moment.

"Child support," I hissed. "You want me to sue that woman for fucking *child support*."

"Caven, listen."

"No, you listen. I don't need whatever measly check a judge orders her to write. What I *need* is for that woman to scurry back into the pits of Hell where she belongs. She told me today that she wants to be there for Rosalee. To be a part of her life. And please, Doug, tell me you hear me when I say that is *not* going to fucking happen."

"I hear you, and that's exactly what I'm trying to prevent. Look, my specialty isn't family law, but if we get the neglect on her record, then she gets dinged on the child support because she can't afford to pay four years all at once, the chance of her getting any kind of custody is—"

With a hurricane brewing inside me, I slammed my fist on the granite counter. "None! The chance of her getting any kind of custody is *none*. It's not happening. Not today. Not four years from now. Not fucking forty years from now. I don't give a damn what it costs. Hire the best family attorney the country has to offer and get a team going. This—"

"I can't."

"What the fuck do you mean you can't?"

Doug rose to his feet, his stool scraping the hardwood. "Beth Watts is already working for Hadley."

My head snapped back and I stared at him. The best was expensive. This was true in pretty much every facet of life, but especially when it came to lawyers. I didn't know shit about Hadley; the one night I'd spent with her, we hadn't done a lot of talking. But the fact that she'd robbed me on her way out of my apartment told me she wasn't loaded.

"How is she affording this? Fifty-thousand-dollar bond

and a bigwig attorney? That Prius we had towed did not scream cash."

Doug sank down on the stool. "That I don't know. Beth is known to take pro-bono work as long as it makes her look good. I can definitely see her taking on Hadley's case knowing that she might get some press for going head-to-head with you."

My stomach wrenched. *The press.* Fuck.

I was far from famous. Paparazzi didn't stalk me in the streets or camp outside my house, but thanks to Kaleidoscope, my name was well known enough to hit the gossip news if anything juicy happened to me. Like, say, the mother of my child coming back and causing an uproar.

No one batted an eye when they found out I had a child. Reproduction by a one-time tech owner wasn't interesting enough to warrant a ping on anyone's radar. However, if the facts about Rosalee's birth and how she'd been delivered to me were revealed in a messy court battle, it was going to ping on *everyone's* radar.

"Son of a bitch," I snarled, resuming my pace.

"What about a payoff?" Ian suggested. "Give her some cash and tell her to take a hike."

"I'm not giving that bitch a fucking penny."

He rose to his feet, his anxiety finally making an appearance. "Not even if it got her to leave? For fuck's sake, Caven, this is not the goddamn time to hold a vendetta. We're talking about Rosalee."

I planted my hands on my hips. "I know what the fuck we're talking about. She's my daughter. But I'm not doing this every fucking four years. So what if I pay her off this time? Maybe we'll get lucky and she won't come back for another four years? I am *not* the Bank of Hadley. She does not get to use my daughter as collateral to blackmail me any time she's short on cash. For all we know, that's what she's been planning from the start. Who the hell knows how many other men she has on the hook with this bullshit. But I'm not playing into it. I want this over. Once and for all."

"Caven," Ian growled, I assumed to scold me for my outburst.

That is until I heard, "Daddy?"

Clearing my throat and tamping down my anger, I walked toward the mouth of the stairway, calling up, "Yeah, baby?"

Her little feet appeared first. Then her favorite polka-dot Minnie Mouse nightgown brushed her shins as she made her way down. She had a plush baby doll in one hand, the other firmly anchored to the rail like I'd taught her the day I'd taken the baby gate off the top stair.

I had no idea what my blood pressure was, but based on the throbbing of my head, I'd definitely say it was in the red zone. Despite feeling like my head was in a vise that wasn't planning to let up anytime soon, I plastered on a mega-watt smile and asked, "Is everything okay?"

She pouted her bottom lip. "Nobody gave me a ferret for my birthday."

I chuckled, the tiniest bit of tension leaving my chest. "This is probably for the best. I'd hate for you to have to move into your own apartment now. You haven't even started kindergarten yet."

She yawned, taking the last few steps down, and lifted her arms for me to pick her up. It was an offer I never refused. "At my new birthday party, can we ride ferrets instead of ponies?"

"You have no clue what a ferret looks like, do you?"

"I do too," she argued and then yawned again. "Can I sleep in your bed tonight? It's still Rosie Posie Day."

A pang of guilt struck me. This was the first year she really understood all the traditions we did on her birthday. Up until then, they were all just silly things I'd done to feel like a decent parent. Now, she expected them, and because of Hadley, I'd failed on nearly all of them.

I wasn't going to sleep a wink that night; my swirling mind would never allow it. But the least I could do was lie down with my daughter to ensure she could.

"Yeah, babe. Uncle Ian and Doug were just leaving. Go ahead and get in bed. I'll be up in a minute."

As I was setting her back on her feet, she dropped her doll. I picked it up and started to hand it back only to freeze when I got a good look at it.

The name *Keira* was embroidered in pink script letters across the front of the doll's dress.

"Where did you get this?" I asked entirely too roughly.

"For my birthday." She extended a hand up to take it back, but I moved it out of her reach.

What the fucking hell? Hadley had brought a gift. Nothing said "sorry for handing you off to a prostitute when you were less than a day old" like a twenty-five-dollar doll she'd had personalized with a meaningless name.

Fucking, fucking Hadley.

"Hey, I think this needs to go in the washer," I told her. Even if it was for a completely and utterly selfish reason, I needed to get that damn thing away from her.

"Why?" Rosalee complained.

"You dropped her and she's all dirty now."

"No, she's not. Let me see?" She jumped, but I tossed it to Ian.

His eyes flashed wide as he looked at the doll, but in the very next beat, he faked a smile. "Yeah. She definitely needs a wash. Why don't you sleep with the ferret stuffed animal I got you instead?"

"Ew, no! That was a long mouse, not a ferret."

Jesus, I needed to buy the kid some books about animals.

Ian kept on grinning, tucking the doll behind his back. "Right. My mistake. What about that unicorn Molly got you then?"

"Oh, yeah!" she breathed, turning on a toe and racing up the stairs.

"Hold on to the rail," I called after her.

She groaned, reluctantly taking the wooden bar before disappearing again.

The minute she was out of sight, my smile fell away and the shit storm that was my life rained down all over again.

I went straight to Ian, snatching the piece-of-shit doll from his hands before throwing it into the garbage.

"This has to end," I barked. "Doug, gather a team. Fuck that Beth woman. Figure out who has beaten her in the past and hire them. All of them. I don't know what Hadley was hoping to gain by showing up here today, but I can promise you it's not going to be my daughter."

ELEVEN

HADLEY

"Y ou want to stop and get something to eat? My fridge
is pretty bare," Beth asked, never taking her eyes off
the road.

I stared out the window, the world passing me in a blur,
but all I could see was the disgust on Caven's face when he'd
seen me at the party. He was still as ridiculously gorgeous as
I'd remembered—the definition of tall, dark, and handsome.
Though it was his blue eyes that I'd never forget. I'd felt him
the minute he'd gotten close to me at the party. The hum in
my veins was followed by the calm I'd never felt outside of his
arms.

But she was bigger than any history he and I may have had
together.

Even the one where he'd saved my life.

"I'm not going back to your place. I want to go home."

Beth sighed. "I don't think it's a good idea for you to be
alone tonight."

"I'll be fine. I just…need some space."

I was exhausted both mentally and physically. I hadn't run
a marathon or anything, but between the peaks and valleys of
adrenaline and the near-constant pounding of my heart, I was
spent. It was all I could do to stay awake. Though, with his eyes
and her bright smile on the backs of my lids each and every

time I blinked, it was for the best that I kept them open a while longer.

I hadn't said much at the police station. I hadn't needed to. Beth had effortlessly handled it all. She'd come a long way from the mousy girl who'd once lived next door. She was a few years older than I was, but we'd been inseparable since I'd caught her peeking over the fence shortly after we'd moved into my grandfather's house. The day she'd told me she was going to apply to law school, I'd laughed myself sick. Back then, she could barely speak to a stranger without squeaking. I had to give it to her though. Beth had turned into a beast. And after seeing the look on Caven's face at the party, a beast was exactly what I needed if I ever wanted to have anything to do with…

I closed my eyes, the first tears of the day escaping. "He named her Rosalee."

She reached over and took my hand. "I know. But it doesn't change who she is."

In theory, she was right. Keira or Rosalee—it didn't matter. Though the idea of someone erasing my mother's name did make my heart feel like it was being crushed.

"Maybe this was a bad idea," I croaked.

She gave my hand a squeeze. "Bad? Absolutely. But it's also the *right* thing to do."

"I don't know how I'm going to do this. Seeing him again…" I shook my head. "He was so mad."

"He just doesn't understand. He loves that little girl. We *all* love that little girl. But Caven is assuming the worst."

"Maybe I *am* the worst when it comes to him," I whispered.

"Oh, come on. Now, you're just wallowing in pity. You aren't the worst. Unless we are talking about singing, in which case you are absolutely the worst."

She'd been cracking jokes all afternoon, but I didn't have it in me to laugh.

"I don't know. I want this to be a good thing for her, ya know? I didn't have a mom growing up, and she's already missed out on so much. But today, when I saw her looking out that window… She was so scared, Beth."

"She was scared because Caven was scared. Kids can sense that kind of stuff."

"Oh, he wasn't scared. He was *pissed*."

"He told the police you were trying to kidnap his daughter. Pissed or not, trust me, the man was *scared*."

I scrubbed my hand over my face. It was late, but she was right. I probably didn't need to be alone that night. "Any chance you can drop me off at the cemetery?"

"Now? Are you crazy?"

"Please. I need to feel her. I need to feel all of them."

She tore her eyes off the road long enough to give me an appraising glance. "I really, really, *really* don't think that's a good idea."

"I'm not asking, Beth. I'm going whether you drop me off there or at home."

She groaned. "Fine. But I'll wait in the car. I don't want you to be out there all alone at night."

I nodded. There were no more words left to say. At least not to her.

We drove in silence for over an hour to the Watersedge Cemetery.

When we arrived, the main gate was locked, but the walk-through beside it was always open.

"I'll be right here," Beth called as I climbed out of her car.

"Thanks," I murmured.

84

It wasn't far to my family's plot. My grandpa had bought it when my grandmother died. I was six at the time, and he'd told my father that he wanted his whole family to be together. So, morbid as it was, he'd bought one large enough for all of us.

Little did he know how quickly it would fill up.

I'd been to that cemetery no fewer than a thousand times throughout the years. First with my father to deliver flowers to my grandma's grave. Then, only a few years later, I went with my grandfather to deliver flowers to my parents final resting spot.

But that night, as I forged through the darkness, I went to visit them as the only surviving member of the Banks family.

That is if I didn't count...*Rosalee.*

There was a white-speckled headstone with all of their names listed. The newest addition being added only four months prior.

The inscription was simple, much like my parents'. But seeing it there nearly brought me to my knees every time.

Willow Anne Banks.

Loving daughter and sister.

I went to her first.

It was still so fresh that the tears were already pouring from my eyes by the time I reached the dirt rectangle. Due to the winter, the grass hadn't grown back yet.

But she was there.

They were *all* there.

"Hey," I said, dusting a few leaves off the headstone.

Not surprisingly, she didn't answer.

I had so many things to tell her. Things like: It was going to be okay. And to just keep fighting. I wanted to tell her about living for the seconds and savoring the good times. But none of that mattered anymore.

She was gone.

They were *all* gone.

Unable to choke out anything else for my sister, I moved on to my mother.

Keira Hollis Banks

Loving mother and wife.

"I saw her today," I whispered as if it were a secret rather than a fact. "Little Keira. I saw her." I didn't have the heart to tell her that he'd changed her name. My mother was dead and I still wanted to make her happy. "She's so pretty, Mama." I sniffled, wiping the tears away as I looked to my father's spot beside her. "Sorry, Dad, but she looks like Mom's side of the family. She has gorgeous red hair and green eyes. I swear those Hollis genes must be pretty potent, because her father…" My voice gave out. I couldn't even say his name without it feeling like I was being hit by a truck.

I cleared my throat and continued. "Anyway. I'm trying not to get my hopes up because I know it's going to be a *long* road. But, God, I want to be a part of her life. There's so much I want to give her, so much I want to *teach* her." Emotion once again clogged my throat. "But most of all, I just want her to have a mom. It was so hard growing up without you. No offense, Grandpa," I half laughed as I looked down the line of graves. "I don't want her to struggle any more than she already has. I think that's what I'm most worried about. What if I'm only hurting her more? She seems to have a good life with him. What if she doesn't need me?"

Clear as the night sky, I heard my mother's voice in my head replying, "But what if she does?"

I didn't believe in ghosts or messages from beyond the grave. I knew exactly where that message had come from and why I'd heard it so clearly. It was the same advice she'd given me when I was six after I'd told her I wanted to ask Shelby Wright to be my best friend. My father had recorded the conversation on his new camcorder. It was one of the few exceptions he'd made for technology in our home. After they died, I'd watched that video every night for years, torturing myself with the memories. And in it, as a scared little six-year-old peered up at her mother, asking what if Shelby didn't want to be her best friend, my mother tucked a stray hair behind my ear and then simply replied, "But what if she does?"

And that was it. At six and again now at twenty-six, it was still the right advice.

If Rosalee needed me, nothing was going to stop me from being there for her.

"I'm going to make this right," I told them—all of them—before repeating it to myself. "I can make this right."

I kissed my fingers, touching them to each of their names, allowing it to linger on Willow for several seconds longer than the others. Our relationship had deteriorated so rapidly over the last few years that it felt like it had been ages since we'd last spoken without yelling. But knowing that someone was gone forever—not just an apology and a phone call away—made the longing unbearable.

I missed her.

I would *always* miss her.

"I love you," I whispered before heading back to Beth.

I knew what I had to do, and it wasn't going to be easy.

I just had to take it one very manageable second at a time.

And those seconds all started with Caven Hunt.

My heart was in my throat as I slid into Beth's car, but resolution now ran through my veins. "I need a favor."

TWELVE

CAVEN

The lights were dim, only a single lamp on my side of the bed illuminating my bedroom. I'd been sitting there for over an hour while Rosalee slept beside me. My bed was a king, but for as close as she slept tucked into my side, we could have shared a twin. I'd alternated between staring off into space, mentally replaying the day, and scrolling to the point of obsession through the pictures I'd taken of Hadley on my phone.

It was crazy.

After all those years of wondering where she'd gone.

All those years of trying to forget her completely.

All those years of pretending she'd never existed.

There she was, Hadley *Banks*, in photos on my phone. I'd zoomed in and out over and over like I was a detective searching for clues. Only the mystery of where Hadley had been and why she had come back couldn't be solved in a few blurry snapshots.

Doug had promised me before he'd left that he'd do everything he could to prevent Hadley from getting to Rosalee. But deep down, I knew if she fought the issue of being involved in my daughter's life, there was nothing I could do to stop her. The idea was eating away at my soul.

Sure, I could fight her. No judge worth his salt was going to turn Rosalee over to a woman she didn't know. After all, I was the one who had raised her.

The one who had kissed every boo-boo.

The one who had held her for two days straight, never putting her down, when she got the stomach flu.

The one she called out for when she was scared. Or happy. Or sad.

I was her parent—her *only* parent.

But I didn't need a law degree to know that the courts always favored the mothers.

If Hadley stuck around long enough, there would be a judge who viewed me as just her dad—a second-rate citizen in parenthood.

Hadley had never contributed anything other than a womb to my daughter's life and she already had the upper hand because she was her mother—a position that should be earned and not appointed.

Unless I could stop Hadley before she ever got started, one day in the not-so-distant future, I was going to lose my little girl. I could feel it in my gut and it fucking scared the hell out of me.

In my thirty-three years, I'd survived a hell most couldn't dream about. But losing her? I wouldn't survive that.

I was in the process of zooming in on another picture when a text banner dropped from the top of my screen.

Unknown: Hey, it's Hadley. Is there any chance I could convince you to have a conversation with me without all the cops and lawyers?

My jaw slacked open as a surge of adrenaline ignited my tired body. For four fucking years, she'd been a ghost and then, out of the blue, she showed up at my house and now she was texting me like we were old friends? How the hell did she even get my number?

Me: Are you fucking kidding me right now?
Hadley: No. We need to talk. I can come to you if it's easier.

I blinked at my phone. What mental institution had this whack job escaped from? I'd had her escorted off my property by the police only hours earlier and now she could *come to me* if it was easier? Seriously? First thing in the morning, I was asking Doug to file an emergency restraining order. This woman was certifiable.

But it was funny, because even knowing that, I couldn't stop my curiosity.

Me: And what in the hell do you think we have to talk about?
Hadley: We have a four-year-old to discuss.
Me: Fuck that. I have a four-year old. You have nothing.
Hadley: Fair enough. But we still need to talk about her.

Me: Then contact my attorneys. You had nine months while you were pregnant to talk to me. Then another four years after you handed my daughter off to a prostitute. Your time to talk has passed. Delete my number and do us all a favor and disappear again.

I waited, holding my breath until my lungs burned as the text bubble danced at the bottom of the screen. I was expecting a dissertation for as long as it took her to reply.

Hadley: You're right. I messed up.

She'd messed up?

She'd fucking messed up?

Messing up would be showing up to dinner late or locking your keys in your car. What she had done was not even remotely in the same category as messed up.

Me: I think you need a mental evaluation.

Hadley: I've had one. My attorney should be mailing it over to your legal team first thing in the morning. I also submitted to a DNA test, full health panel, and background check. I have nothing to hide, Caven. I just want to explain.

Me: Sorry. But I don't have four years to spend on that wasted trip down memory lane.

Hadley: I get it. You hate me. I can't even blame you for it. I have no right to ask you for anything. But if you give me a few minutes of your time, I'll explain what happened the night I snuck out of your apartment. And while I was pregnant. And when I made the decision to leave her with you. And most of all, why I've stayed gone as long as I have. It's one conversation. If it changes nothing, then you've wasted nothing but time. But at least then you'll have all the answers to why you hate me.

I must have read that message a dozen times. I shouldn't have done it. I should have turned my phone off, put it on the nightstand, woken up the next morning, changed my number, and filed a restraining order. But there was a part of me that desperately wanted to hear her out.

There was nothing she could say that would change my mind about her. But it wasn't my opinion that mattered. If she wanted to give me some bullshit explanation, tell me why she'd stolen my stuff and dumped my kid, I'd be happy to listen.

And after I recorded the entire conversation…so would a judge.

Me: American Diner on the corner of Broad and Park. I'll meet you there in thirty.
Hadley: Thank you.

Tomorrow morning when the cops showed up at her door, she wouldn't be thanking me.

But I would celebrate that victory all the same.

After typing out a message asking Alejandra to come to the main house, I inched my way out from under Rosalee's arm and prepared for war.

I saw her the minute I opened the door to the diner. She was discreetly tucked away in a back corner, but like a moth to a flame, my eyes were instantly drawn to her. It was hard not to notice a woman like Hadley. Every man who had walked through the doors in the thirty minutes I'd purposely kept her waiting had no doubt noticed her too. She was absolutely stunning.

Unfortunately, Hadley had never been anything but a black widow waiting to inject her poison into my life.

I pressed record on my cell phone as I got closer, her emerald-green eyes tracking my movement.

I fucking hated the way relief colored her face as if she'd been expecting me not to come.

She didn't deserve even a second of relief, and it made me want to turn around and leave to spite her. But I hadn't left my daughter alone in bed on her birthday to pick up a slice of pie from the local diner.

I wanted answers, and as much as I lied to myself and said I was only there to record her, I secretly wanted to know what the fuck was so damn important that she'd been able to walk away from her own daughter and never look back.

"Thanks for coming," she said as I slid into the booth, taking a seat across from her.

She had an empty coffee mug in front of her, surrounded by a dozen little balls of rolled-up napkin. If I had to take a guess, I'd venture to say half the population did that when they were bored or nervous. But seeing those balls in front of Hadley pissed me off to no end.

Because Rosalee did it too.

She smiled weakly. "Do you want some coffee or something? I can grab the waitress."

"Talk," I rumbled. "Just fucking talk. Say whatever the hell you dragged me out here tonight to say."

She closed her eyes, her long lashes nearly brushing her cheek. "I never meant for any of this to happen. But I do realize that the majority of it is my fault."

"Majority." I laughed, propping my elbows on the table and intertwining my hands. "I'd highly suggest you recalibrate your culpability if you want me to hear you out."

Her eyes suddenly opened, the tangible weight of her gaze forcing me back in my seat.

Hadley's eyes were bright, even more so than I remembered. From this close, I could see the unique green that had flecks of both gold and blue, but what really took me aback was the storm brewing inside them.

When I was ten, the death of my mother had changed my life.

A few years later when I was fifteen, a single bullet had changed my life again.

At twenty-nine, a shrill cry from an abandoned newborn had flipped my life on end.

But at thirty-three years old, in the middle of a quiet diner, Hadley Banks changed my life all over again.

"I think we both know exactly who is culpable, Caven *Lowe*."

The hairs on the back of my neck stood on end as I sucked in a breath so deep that my lungs screamed in protest.

No one had called me Caven Lowe in eighteen years. Not since the day my brother had petitioned the court to allow us to use our mother's maiden name.

I should have known though.

That cloud of chaos was bound to find me again.

THIRTEEN

CAVEN

Eighteen years earlier...

"One, two, three... Go." The final syllable hadn't cleared my lips before we both lurched to our feet.

I'd been worried about the little girl falling behind, but with her shoulders rounded forward, her body low, and her hand locked in mine, she took off toward the pizza place, dragging me behind her.

We'd only made it a few steps when I heard his yell echo through the food court. It was immediately followed by the pounding of his footsteps and a spray of gunfire.

Ducking low, we ran faster, dodging the sea of dead bodies, my sock soaking up blood as we ran through it.

We were too far away.

Why were we so fucking far away?

It had appeared much closer when the hope was still thrumming in my veins.

I chanced a glance over my shoulder, praying like hell that he wasn't as close as he sounded.

But he was right there, charging after us, his gun held high, aiming directly at my head.

Panic hit me like a tsunami, stealing my breath and momentarily my coordination, because I tripped over something—or, more than likely, some*one*—nearly falling until that little redheaded girl I was saving saved me.

"Hurry!" she yelled, pulling my arm so hard that she kept me on my feet.

The fear was blistering me from the inside out, but slowing down was not an option.

My heart pounded as I pushed harder. Ran faster. My legs swallowed the distance to the Pizza Crust. I had no idea how she was keeping up, but she was with me stride for stride.

A blast of relief struck me when we reached the counter. I'd been working at the Pizza Crust for six weeks, so I knew exactly where to go. The double doors in the back were a direct path through the kitchen once you got around the counter.

If he didn't catch us by then, we would be home free.

"Come on!" I yelled, turning fast around the edge of the counter, her wet socks sending her slingshotting behind me.

She grabbed the back of my shirt for balance and continued to hold on as we ran together.

We were so close. Victory was already singing inside me. We'd done it. We'd made it—both of us in one piece.

Or so I'd thought.

When those doors I'd been dreaming of since the first shot had rung out while I was on break came into sight, I realized they were going to be my death sentence.

A chain was wrapped through the handles, joining them together. A padlock dangled off the end, making it impossible to open them.

I froze, the crushing disappointment so palpable that it was as if I'd been hit with a sledgehammer.

Not only had I given away our location by running; I'd trapped us in the small kitchen with no way out.

Maybe he'd been right all those years. Maybe I was worthless.

"Open it!" she screamed. "Please just open it."

But there was nothing else I could do.

He'd won.

He'd finally won.

"You stupid son of a bitch," he snarled.

Any remaining hope I had left vanished at the sound of his voice.

I turned, guiding the girl behind me.

She pressed her trembling front against me, her hands fisting at the back of my shirt. He was going to kill her no matter what, but maybe if he took us both out with one bullet, he wouldn't have the opportunity to torture her.

I lifted my shaking hands in surrender, nervously flashing my eyes around the kitchen. All hope had been lost, but my racing mind and will to live were still desperate to find a way out. "Just wait. Please. Listen. You don't have to do this."

He grinned, his blue eyes that matched my own crinkling with pure joy at the corners. "You know I do."

I was only able to get two more words out before he pulled the trigger. "Dad, no!"

FOURTEEN

HADLEY

My heart broke as the color drained from his face. I hated hurting him. But I knew he, of all people, would understand if I could just make him *listen*. My involvement in Rosalee's life hung in the balance of this one conversation.

Beth had lost her mind when I'd asked for his phone number. I'd listened to her bitch for over an hour about why reaching out to him was the worst possible thing I could do before a custody battle. It would only give him fuel to use against me. And maybe she was right.

But I didn't want a custody battle.

So I had to at least try.

There was no way he hadn't been ruined after that day at the mall. Forty-eight people had lost their lives at the hands of his father. If I could convince him to put his anger aside and step into my shoes—even if for only one conversation—he'd get it.

He needed the facts about Hadley Banks. Not the woman he'd created as the villain in his head.

"Don't fucking call me that." He glanced around the diner before putting his elbows on the table and leaning in close. "How do you know about that?"

I swallowed hard. "Because your father killed my parents."

His lips got tight and his dark brows drew together, absolute horror slashing through his handsome face.

Caven oozed pure masculinity. He had this weird aura about him that straddled the gap between guy-next-door and GQ. He was wearing a faded gray long-sleeved T-shirt and a pair of tattered jeans—not the kind that cost five hundred dollars to look tattered. They looked like a normal guy's clothes.

But with his chiseled jaw, the scruff trimmed to perfection, and his short, brown hair meticulously styled, he appeared every bit the millionaire I knew he was.

Except right then, as he flashed his gaze around the diner, looking anywhere but at me, he looked like a guilty little boy.

His nostrils flared, and the hinges of his jaw ticked. Maybe with unshed emotion. Maybe with mounting anger. I couldn't be sure.

His voice gave nothing away as he asked, "And you think I'm responsible for that? Is that what you brought me here to say?"

"No," I said firmly, sliding my hand across the table to cover his. I didn't think before I did it. I didn't consider how he might interpret it or how it might make him feel.

I was just trying to offer comfort to a man in pain. Unfortunately, it only seemed to snap him out of his guilt-driven trance and slam him back into the reality where Caven Hunt was sitting across from Hadley the Terrible.

He snatched his hand away as if I'd set it on fire. Leaning back in his seat, he held my gaze. "Don't fucking touch me. Don't you *ever* fucking touch me again."

The ache in my chest grew. "I'm sorry. I'm just trying to—"

"You were just trying to what? Please. Fucking enlighten me here. Is this the part where you ask for money? Try to blackmail me to keep quiet? Because I really hate to break it to you, but this little payday secret you think you know about me is public fucking knowledge if you dig deep enough."

My whole body turned to stone. "I would never—"

"Okay, then. Fine." He leaned to the side, fishing the phone out of his pocket before pressing at the screen and resting it on the table between us. "How much will it cost me for you to disappear? A million? Ten? Name your price and I'll have it wired over first thing in the morning."

The light on his phone caught my attention, and when I looked down at it, there was a red, circular record button showing on it. It was off. Probably to cover his attempted bribe.

"Were you recording me?"

"What's it going to cost me?" he growled, rising to his feet.

I was losing him. If he left, there would be no getting him back. Frantic, I stood up with him. "Look, I don't want your money. What I want is to make you *understand.* The only person responsible for that shooting is Malcom Lowe. I do *not* blame you in *any way.* I'm simply trying to make you see that we have way more in common than just a daughter."

His chest was heaving and the smoldering anger rolling off him was suffocating. But he didn't move.

That was a win in my book.

"Please," I begged. "Just sit down and listen to me. I did some really terrible things in the past, but I am not an evil person. I swear I'm not here to hurt you. Or steal your money. Or steal your daughter. We didn't meet in that bar by chance, Caven. There is a whole other dimension to our story that you have no idea about. All I'm asking is that you let me explain."

He stared at me for a long second with a scrutinizing intensity. I had no idea what he was thinking. For all I knew, he was about to tell me to fuck off.

When he finally spoke, his voice was filled with gravel. "Were you there?"

The *there* he was referring to didn't need to be elaborated on.

Neither did my answer. "Yes."

His whole body sagged, and his lids fell shut. "Jesus Christ."

"Sit down. Please."

His chest expanded as he drew in a shaky breath. There were a lot of things I'd expected Caven Hunt to say to me that night. But never once had I considered his next statement.

His eyes opened, blazing with grief and filled with desolation. "I'm so sorry. God, I'm so fucking sorry."

FIFTEEN

CAVEN

After the mall shooting, Trent and I had done our best to escape the filthy wasteland that was my father's shadow. For the most part, we'd been successful. Trent had been nineteen at the time, so he was able to gain custody of me, and after changing our last names, we ran as far away from Watersedge, New Jersey, as we could get. Which turned out to be two and a half hours away in Standal, Pennsylvania.

The guilt I carried with me was so devastating that it crippled me for years. Trent did his best to help me recover, but he wasn't there the day of the shooting.

Nor was he the reason my father had gone to the mall with an arsenal of guns and what seemed like an endless supply of ammunition.

Those boulders of contrition were mine alone to bear.

Trent, Ian, and more therapists than I could count spent years trying to convince me that I was allowed to have a life.

But it wasn't until Rosalee had come along that I'd finally believed I was allowed to be happy.

"You have nothing to apologize for," Hadley said, reaching for my forearm before deciding against it.

She was wrong. So fucking wrong.

I'd never spoken to a survivor of the shooting. I didn't have the courage to face them, knowing what I'd done. As I blankly stared at Hadley's face, regret and agony thrumming inside my chest, my body ached to flee.

But there would be no escaping this.

The tragedy of that shooting had now come full circle—my little girl, the one person I would die to protect, was surrounded by devastation on all sides of her lineage.

I felt like I was speaking through a barrel of rocks as I replied, "I… I'm not sure what else to say, then."

"Then don't talk. Just listen."

I nodded, sinking back down to the booth, still in shock—but not nearly numb enough for this conversation.

Hadley flagged over the waitress, who brought an extra mug and a pot of coffee. While Hadley got busy with the cream and sugar routine, I just stirred the black liquid, waiting and hoping for it to become a vortex strong enough to devour me.

"I wanted Kaleidoscope," she said, breaking the awkward silence.

My head snapped up. "What?"

"It was about the time Kaleidoscope was making national news after the false arrest." She smiled and lifted her cup of coffee for a quick sip. "I'd read that your search engines could find every image of a person that existed on the internet. And I needed that. I was in a really dark place back then and I was hoping that, somewhere out there, I could find a photo or video or something I hadn't seen of my parents before. I thought that maybe, if I could see them again, that it would make the hollowness go away—even temporarily. I was desperate."

My chin jerked to the side, trying to dodge the blow of her confession. "Hadley…"

"Please don't apologize again."

Sighing, I cut my eyes over her shoulder. "How'd you find me?"

"You were a single man living in the city. I hired a PI to get your address. Then I picked the bar closest to your apartment and waited." She tipped her head to the side. "It took about an hour for you to show up."

I chuffed, the tension in my shoulders momentarily easing. "That simple, huh?"

"Well, I took a gamble that you couldn't resist a redhead. But yeah. Basically."

I did have a thing for redheads. But not in the way she assumed. "So that's why you stole my computer for Kaleidoscope?"

Her eyes lit in a way that struck me deep, even if I didn't understand why. "I don't know. Are you recording me again?"

"Should I be?" I took a sip of my coffee.

She shrugged. "Probably."

And I probably should have, but we were way past anything I'd ever want to show to a judge.

I made sure she was watching as I powered off my phone.

She nabbed another sugar, tearing it open before pouring it into her mug. "So anyway. Yes. That's why I stole your computer. And iPad. And phone."

"And the wallet?" I clipped, nearly five years of resentment getting the best of me.

Her forehead crinkled. "I'm sorry. I can't say that enough."

God, I was a dick. The truth was: If I'd known she was a survivor back then, I would have willingly handed her my wallet, my mother's necklace included, along with the contents of my bank account just to feel a miniscule of undeserved relief.

"You could have asked me. I'd have looked up your parents for you. It was the least I could have done."

She shrugged. "Maybe, but if I'd asked and you slammed the door in my face, I'd have lost the element of surprise."

"And your element of surprise was fucking me into exhaustion instead?"

Shit. I had to get a hold of my emotions.

She leaned against the back of the booth, her body shifting from one side to the other as though she were uncomfortably crossing and uncrossing her legs. "No. That was… I don't know. I think…" She plucked a napkin from the tabletop dispenser and started shredding it. She rolled four tiny balls before finishing the thought. "I think I just needed a few hours of not feeling miserable anymore. You have to understand, I spent most of my life trying to forget the fear I'd felt that day. It had been years, but it was always on my mind, demanding my attention. I hated it. I wanted to escape it. But it almost became an obsession. So, for a few hours, I used you as a distraction. I'm sorry."

I couldn't even be mad at her. A distraction. That was exactly what she had been to me. A way to forget. A way to focus on someone else. A way to avoid the mirror.

"Was it your plan to get pregnant? Some fucked-up version of revenge?"

Her eyes flashed wide. "*No.* Not at all. I swear to you. Trust me, nobody was more surprised than I was. I had the implant birth control. I didn't even think it was a possibility. I found out when I was four months along, and even then, I didn't want to believe it." She threaded her fingers in the top of her hair, shoving it all to one side. "I thought maybe you'd call the cops after I'd stolen your stuff if I told you."

"I would have. I absolutely would have."

She bit her bottom lip and looked off to the side. "And you'd have been right to do that."

It didn't feel right anymore. It felt like I'd poached a broken woman to get my fucking cock off. Just what I needed: more guilt.

"You weren't able to get into my computer, were you?" I asked.

"Nope. I hired a guy and everything. The only thing he was able to figure out was that you had a twenty-two-character password. He was still working on getting into the computer when suddenly it shut down and wouldn't restart. He couldn't even pull anything off the hard drive or whatever it's called."

I smirked. "You don't create a technology company without learning how to secure a laptop first."

"Touché." She smiled, and as much as I fought it, it made me smile too.

This was a conversation with a woman I was supposed to hate. No one—especially me—should have been smiling.

She must have felt the awkwardness at the same time I did, because she once again leveled her gaze on the table. A tendril of her long hair escaped from behind her ear, and with the grace of a dream, she tucked it back, revealing that smile all over again.

And that was when mine disappeared.

She could explain away stalking me down at that bar.

She could explain away stealing my computer.

She could even explain away fucking me as a distraction.

But there was one thing she'd never be able to make me understand.

"How could you leave her like that?"

Her head snapped up, her eyes wide and filled with sorrow. "Caven…"

"You don't deserve her."

She flinched, quickly closing her mouth.

"We all lived shitty lives, Hadley. You don't think I'm not still fucked up from the shooting? You don't think I have my dark days? Hell, I've had *years* of darkness. But Rosalee, she didn't do anything wrong." The bitterness and resentment came rushing back like a flash flood to my system. "She didn't deserve to be abandoned by her own mother."

Sitting up taller, she squared her shoulders. "Yes. She did. Because *she* deserved better than I could have ever given her. You have no idea what it was like for me after that shooting. I was just a kid. I knew what had happened. I'd been there. I'd seen it. But I couldn't make sense of it. I had all of these new emotions that were warring inside me, but they wouldn't come out. My grandfather put me in counseling and therapy, but it was easier to pretend that I was okay than to explain the carnage happening inside me. By the time you met me, I'd been ravaged by the shrapnel of those emotions until there was nothing left of me." A muffled sob ripped through her before I felt it slashing through me as well.

"Hadley, I…" I didn't finish the thought. I had the urgent need to apologize to her again. For what *he'd* done. For what *I'd* done. But I couldn't get the words out. I couldn't apologize. Not when it came to Rosalee.

Her blazing, green eyes came back to mine. "You have to believe me. I loved that little girl, Caven. I swear to you I did. I told myself I was going to be a good mom. I *vowed* it. But the night I went into labor… All the pain and fear. I was in that mall again, waiting to die. I delivered her alone in my apartment because I was too paralyzed by fear to even walk outside. In that moment, blood covering the bed, that tiny little girl crying, those feelings and emotions that I'd never fully dealt with, they broke me. The only clear thought I had was that if I kept her, they would break her too. I hated giving her to that prostitute, and I followed her all the way to your building just to be sure Keira—uh, Rosalee was safe. But I couldn't face you. I couldn't explain all of this to you back then. However, the one thing I will never forget was the feeling deep inside my soul that I'd done the right thing for that little girl. I know you're mad because of what I did but—"

I had to stop her. My gut was sour after listening to her talking about delivering our child alone and scared. But clearly she did not know as much about me as she thought she did.

"I'm not mad because of what you did. I'm mad because you came back."

"What?" she gasped.

"Jesus, Hadley. I've been scared my entire life because a part of my father still lives inside me." I stabbed a finger at my wrist. "His blood still runs through my veins, and short of bleeding myself dry, there is not one damn thing I can do to change that. There is still a very big, very real part of me that feels like I'm responsible for every life that was affected or lost that day." I leaned in close, the intensity increasing even as I lowered my voice. "He came to that mall to kill *me*."

It wasn't a secret. My father's motives had been flashed across the screen of every national news source that day. Luckily, I was a juvenile, so they weren't allowed to use my name or picture.

But people in Watersedge still knew.

Worst of all, I still knew.

"But you didn't kill anyone, Caven."

I shook my head. "No. I didn't. But there will never be a day that I don't struggle with feeling like maybe I did. Before Rosalee, I was addicted to work and women, anything to keep my mind off who I was and what I'd caused. But that little girl saved my life. No question about it. Because, despite the fact that she looks just fucking like *you*, when I look at her, I see pieces of myself. Good pieces. Untainted pieces. *Whole* pieces. It's impossible to hate myself when I can see those pieces inside someone as perfect as her. So no, Hadley. I'm not mad anymore because of what you did. I get it. I'm sorry. I'm *eternally grateful* to you for leaving her with me. But if you've come here with the idea of getting her back, I can assure you, that is not a war you can win."

"I'm not trying to take her back," she hissed. "That is one of the first things I said to you because I knew that was what you'd assume. Yes, I had a DNA test done so that I can be added to her birth certificate. But that tiny line on a piece of paper is all I'm trying to take from you. She adores you. I've heard her speak less than ten sentences and almost all of them were about *you*." She bobbed her head from side to side and used a baby voice that was eerily and uncomfortably similar to Rosalee's. "'My daddy got me a unicorn cake. My daddy won't let me have a ferret. My daddy pees standing up but he said I shouldn't.'"

Christ. Yeah. That was my baby girl.

"I'm not trying to change that. I'm not even trying to get in the middle. All I want is to *know* her."

"And what the hell made you think you can handle that responsibility now? What happens when the past comes back or when life gets hard again? You can't come into her life just to disappear again."

"I have no intention of disappearing. I bought a house and have a construction company coming to set up a place for my studio in the back. I never thought I'd come back to Jersey. But if this is where Rosalee is, then this is where I want to be."

I'd never thought I'd go back to Jersey, either. But Ian had lived nearby and I'd desperately wanted to get Rosalee out of the city. Those ninety miles between my house in Leary and Watersedge were just enough so that I didn't have a nervous breakdown every time I hit the Lincoln Tunnel.

I'd spent a lot of years avoiding all things Watersedge. I'd anonymously donated millions to a charity that helped families who were affected by the tragedy as soon as I had been financially able. It was a cowardly way out, but it was all I could do at that point. The mall was only a ninety-minute drive from my house in Leary, but I hadn't stepped foot in that town since the day I'd left.

Now, with Hadley though, Watersedge had come to me.

"How am I supposed to believe you?" I asked.

"I'm not perfect, Caven. I have my moments. PTSD and depression don't ever disappear. But I've been working so damn hard for the last four years to get my life to a place where it doesn't own me. If anyone can understand that, I know it's you."

I cut my gaze away, not wanting to acknowledge just how accurate she was.

"Look," she said. "Bottom line. Given our unusual history with each other, a custody battle between the two of us is going to be the gossip story of the decade. I'd like to avoid that as much as possible. I don't want my past dragged into the present any more than I'm guessing you do. So let me be clear with you. I haven't filed and have no plans to file for any kind of custody.

I'm coming to you as a person. I'm asking you to give *me* a chance. Let me show you who I am. Let me gain your trust. Get to know *me* and then and only then, if you feel comfortable, let me get to know my daughter."

I stared at her. I had beyond zero interest in getting to know Hadley Banks. But she was right about the media. They would have been enthralled with our shit-show. I'd worked too hard to escape the shackles of my DNA to ever go back to living in my father's shadow. And that was exactly what would happen if I, son of mass murderer Malcom Lowe, had a custody battle with Hadley Banks, survivor of said mass murder. It didn't matter what she'd done in the past.

I would be all but crucified in the public eye for keeping Rosalee from her.

"I need to go," I said, sliding out of the booth.

Her face crumbled. "Caven, please. I'm not here to hurt either one of you. I just want—"

"I heard you," I snapped, digging my wallet out of my back pocket. I tossed a twenty on the table before lifting my gaze back to hers. "You file nothing. Not even to have your name added to her birth certificate. You stay away from my house. You stay away from my daughter. You stay away from *me.* Forget my phone number. I don't want any more texts or late-night pleas. I've heard everything you have to say."

She rose to her feet, stepping into my space, and craned her neck back to look up at me. "Please don't do th—"

"And I'm going to think about it."

She slapped a hand over her mouth and her eyes filled with tears, making my gut wrench. I didn't know what it was about this woman, but in the span of one conversation, I'd gone from wanting to have her thrown under the jail to having the most ridiculous desire to promise her that it was going to be okay. But it wasn't okay.

It would probably never be okay. For either of us.

"I don't know what the hell is happening right now, Hadley. I don't know whether to believe you. Assume you're lying. Apologize. Cuss you out. In some ways, none of this makes sense. In others, it explains a lot. But I need time to think. This is my daughter we're talking about."

"I know," she mumbled from behind her hand before remembering to remove it. "I appreciate you even considering this after everything that's happened."

"I mean it. No contact. No legal action. Nothing. You push this and I promise I'll push back so hard you'll be out of the picture completely."

And then it happened. On a day dictated by a pendulum of emotions, Hadley proved she had one more up her sleeve.

She grinned, sweet and stunning. And that grin showed from the curve of her crescent lips all the way to the twinkle in her red-rimmed eyes.

I stared, confused by the way her happiness didn't piss me off. It actually made me feel… Shit. Happy too.

"That's funny," she said.

"What?"

"You said out of the picture." She kept smiling.

I kept staring and ignored the fact that the longer I stood there, the more the ice in my veins thawed. "And?" I drawled gruffly.

"Oh. It's just… I'm a photographer. So it was a good kind of…um…punny joke."

Punny joke.

Jesus. Christ.

"Right."

She bit her lips between her teeth and looked away, but that damn smile still showed. And I still fucking felt it.

Time for me to leave. "I'm gonna take off now. It might be a little while, but when I come to a decision, I'll reach out."

"Okay."

"Okay," I replied without moving. Just standing there like a damn idiot.

Thankfully, she had more sense than I did. "I guess maybe I'll go too." Leaning into the booth, she nabbed her purse and hooked it over her shoulder.

I followed her out of the diner, rolling my eyes when she stopped to gush her thanks to the waitress.

When we got to the parking lot, we both awkwardly turned in the same direction.

I followed.

And followed.

And followed.

Feeling more like a stalker with every step until I finally felt the need to ask, "Where'd you park?"

"Right there." She pointed to the red Porsche Cayenne parked directly next to my Lexus LX.

My brows shot up. I knew cars. Mine had cost a mint. But I found it very interesting that hers had too.

"Is that *yours*?"

"Oh, God, no. It's a smidge pretentious for my tastes. It's my best friend's. I couldn't get my Prius out of impound tonight. Hopefully the environment will forgive me."

I nodded, feeling the tiniest flicker of guilt for having her car towed.

And then I just stood there.

Like.

A.

Fucking.

Idiot.

"Well, uh… Thanks for walking me to my car. That was really sweet of you."

"Actually…" I jerked my chin toward my SUV. "That's me in the pretentious gas guzzler."

She laughed. "Of course it is. Don't worry. Since I dragged us both out here tonight, I'll raid the neighbor's trash and do some extra recycling in the morning. It'll balance out our carbon footprint."

"How ecologically conscious of you," I smarted.

She walked to the door of her car, a quiet chirp sounding before she opened it. "I try."

That was my moment to leave. She was about to get in her car; surely my brain would figure out how to make my legs start working again.

But there was one thing that, even though I had no right to ask, I was dying to know. "How'd you survive?"

"Huh?"

"The mall. You couldn't have been very old and you said your parents died. How'd you make it through?"

Her smile vanished, and her already creamy white skin paled. "I was eight when it happened." She aimed her gaze over my shoulder to the door of the diner, the streetlights casting a shadow over her face. "I, uh…hid under the counter at the Chinese restaurant. Alone." Her eyes came back to mine, nervous and guarded.

Squinting, I tried to get a better read on her, but just as quickly as it had disappeared, the color returned to her face.

"I don't like to talk about it," she said.

I nodded. I couldn't blame her there. "Right. Sorry I asked."

"You should learn to stop apologizing, Caven." And with that, she climbed into her car and shut the door. She offered me a finger wave and a smile before backing out and driving away.

I stood there long after her taillights had disappeared, my mind spinning in a million different directions.

Something big had happened. I could feel it in my bones.

I didn't know if that something was good or bad.

Right or wrong.

Dreaded or long awaited.

But then again, the same could be said about Hadley's return.

After pulling my phone from my pocket, I dialed Doug's number. It was late, but I paid him to answer on the first ring. He didn't let me down.

"Are you in jail?" he asked.

After folding into my SUV, I hit the button to start it but made no move to back out. "No. Though I did just have a very enlightening conversation with Hadley."

"What the hell? Did she come back to your place?"

"No, she sent me a text. I met her for coffee. Listen, do you have that preliminary background report handy?"

He groaned. "You're lucky my wife loves Rosalee. You? She could live without. Hang on. Let me get out of bed and find it."

"I just need to know the name of her parents."

"Her parents?"

"She claims they were killed at the mall."

"Fuck," he hissed. "You believe her?"

"I don't know. That's why I'm calling you."

The sound of his computer starting up played in my ear

before several seconds of silence. "All right. Their names are Robert and Keira Banks."

Keira.

Jesus, *Keira.*

She'd named our daughter after her dead mother.

The woman my father had killed.

Dammit.

"Can you check that against the list of victims?"

"Already on it."

I dropped my head back against the headrest, closing my eyes. I wasn't positive if I wanted their names to be on that list or not. On one hand, if she'd lied to me, made up an elaborate ploy to play on my guilt, it would do wonders to uncomplicate the entire fucked-up situation. But if she'd been telling the truth, then her explanation of why she'd given up Rosalee was genuine—and, more than likely, so were her intentions.

I held my breath and thought about my daughter. I wanted her to have everything in life. All the things I'd never had. A mother included. But if everything Hadley had said was the truth, it was going to be a nightmare for me—my *worst* nightmare.

The amount of guilt I carried over that shooting. The huge fight I'd gotten into with my father that morning before I'd left for work. The secrets I still carried.

I'd have done anything to try to make things right for Hadley.

Anything except for potentially putting my daughter in harm's way.

"Shit, Caven. They're on the list."

My stomach sank, reality cutting me to the quick. "She was there, Doug. She was at the mall that day too."

"Son of a… Okay, listen to me. You don't owe her anything. I don't know where your head is right now. But I want to be very clear with you that this changes nothing."

"It changes everything and you know it."

"Not legally, it doesn't."

But this wasn't about the law anymore. "Listen, I'm going to take Rosalee and go to the beach house for a few days. I need time to think."

"Understandable. But promise you'll call me before that thinking turns into deciding."

Bile clawed at the back of my throat. "Can you do me a favor?"

"Anything."

"Talk to the prosecutor. See if they'll drop the charges against Hadley."

"What? Absolutely not."

"You said it yourself. The child endangerment charges aren't going to stick."

"No, but we can *try.*"

"At what cost, Doug? She's going to walk into that courtroom and be forced to use every skeleton I have in my closet to defend herself. She made a really bad choice but a very smart decision in the middle of a paralyzing PTSD episode. And speaking as someone who's been there too many times, there aren't a lot of good decisions to be found in that kind of darkness."

"You feel guilty. I get it. But—"

"I don't *feel* guilty. I *am* guilty. But I'm going to figure this out. I'm not handing over my daughter to this woman because I have a conscience. She's agreed not to file anything in court with hopes that she and I can work out something a little less *public.* I just have to figure out what that looks like. So I'm taking my girl and heading to the Outer Banks for a much-needed vacation."

"All right. All right. You know my number if you need anything. I'll hold the fort down with Ian while you're gone."

"Thanks, Doug. Send Nina my apologies for dragging you out of bed."

"I was kidding earlier. That woman was snoring so loud she probably doesn't know I'm missing."

"I'll be sure to let her know you mentioned that the next time I see her."

"Come on now. I don't have time for a divorce while dealing with all your messes."

I barked a laugh. "We'll be in touch."

"Have fun at the beach."

I wouldn't. But I'd be with Rosalee, so I'd at least be happy.

SIXTEEN

HADLEY

"**P**lease tell me that's not what you're wearing," Beth said when I opened my front door.

I glanced at my paint-covered overalls. "Hobo-chic is still a thing, right?"

"Oh, absolutely. And you must keep that purple glob of paint in your ponytail too. It really sets off the whole look."

I laughed and stepped out of the way for her to enter. She clipped in on stilettos. Her typical badass-lawyer attire had been peeled down to sexy lawyer, which included a black, high-waisted pencil skirt and a sleeveless, silk button-down that was really more of a button-*up* since she'd missed at least half of the actual buttons.

"Did you finish getting dressed before you came over?"

"Everyone knows you catch more flies with honey. My honey just happens to be my boobs, and before you hit me with one of your signature oh-so-witty-but-not-really-funny-at-all sarcastic jabs, let me just tell you to *shut it*. When you turn thirty-three and haven't had sex in over a year because you are married to your job and your job has no dick, you can decide what your personal choice of honey is and I won't say a word about it. M'kay?"

A smile I felt travel through my entire body stretched across my face. As a photographer, I'd been living in Puerto

Rico for the last three years, taking advantage of everything nature had to offer. And while the beauty of that island was unrivaled, it didn't have my best friend living a mere thirty minutes away.

Barefoot, I started down the hall to my studio with her following behind me. "You do realize it's eleven a.m. and we're going to *brunch*? You might literally catch flies rather than men with your *honey*."

"You can never be too prepared." She stopped at the doorway and gasped at the dozens of canvases lining the walls and four others drying on easels. "Oh my God. Did you do all this?"

"Yeah," I mumbled, gathering my brushes.

While it wasn't Puerto Rico, there was still beauty to be found in Leary, New Jersey. I'd taken hundreds of pictures over the last week, desperate to keep my mind busy and off Rosalee. Caven hadn't called or reached out, and it would be an understatement to say I was going crazy waiting. I'd lie in bed at night, scrolling through our texts from the week before, waiting for one more to suddenly appear at the bottom. It never did, and as the days passed, I was starting to lose my patience. Caven's house was only a fifteen-minute drive from mine and it was all I could do to stay away.

Beth hated the waiting too. Not surprisingly, my DNA had come back a match and she was chomping at the bit to get the proceedings underway. Since the prosecutor had dropped the child endangerment charges against me, there wasn't much else standing in our way.

But I'd promised him time. I owed him that and so much more. Even if it was slowly killing me to know she was so close yet so far away.

Beth kicked her shoes off and walked across the rainbow-splattered drop cloth to inspect my work. "These are incredible. Have you sold them already?"

I chewed on my bottom lip. "I haven't even listed them. I'm worried nothing will ever sell again without her."

"Oh, come on," she breathed, tracing her finger over the thick waves of oil paint applied with a palette knife over the blades of grass in my photo. "These are fantastic."

Three years earlier, my sister and I had started our own art company. It was therapeutic and something we could do together. She loved to paint and I loved photography, so we merged the two into our own unique style of art. At first, it was just something fun, but within months of opening our virtual gallery, we were slammed with orders.

We sold our first piece for thirty-six dollars with free shipping that actually cost me eighty-five dollars via FedEx.

We sold our last for one-point-two million, not including the seventy-five thousand dollars the buyer paid for it to be delivered escorted by an armed guard.

We'd become something of a phenomenon in the art world. Most of the people believed we were a fifty-five-year-old man who had once been a street painter in Italy before retiring to Puerto Rico to follow his dreams of becoming a photographer. We'd giggled ourselves sick writing that bio.

We'd worked hard to keep our identities hidden, and together, we were known as R.K. Banks, a pseudonym we'd chosen to honor our parents.

But now, I was just *Hadley*, lost in a business I loved but unsure if it'd ever be the same without *Willow*.

I walked past Beth as I carried my paint knives to the bathroom. The studio and dark room I was having built out back would have an oversized sink just for this task, but for now, I was using my downstairs bathroom.

"Why don't you let me update the website? I bet the one of the blooming Silver Bells would be gone before we had time to refresh the page."

"Silver Bells don't grow in Puerto Rico," I replied, dropping everything into the sink with a loud clatter.

"So you moved. People are allowed to do that."

"I'm going to take a shower. I'll be ready in fifteen." I headed to my bedroom, hoping she'd give me my space, but I should have known better. Beth would have stood in the shower with me if she had a point to be made.

She stepped in front of me, blocking my path. "You know my legal fees aren't cheap. You're eventually going to need the money."

I rolled my eyes. "I have plenty of money and you aren't charging me."

"I could though. And then I'd be the crazy-rich one and you'd be the poor, starving artist who needs to sell a picture."

"You're already crazy rich, and you wouldn't even let me buy dinner last time we went out. I'll take my chances on you sending me a ten-million-dollar bill that will break me."

"Fine. Then my rates just went up to eleven million an hour."

"In that case, you're fired. But I still need a shower if you want to get out of here anytime soon to show your honey off to the flies." I tried to dodge her, but the pushy wench once again blocked my way.

"What are you scared of?"

I shot her a pointed glare, and she waved me off.

"Right. Okay. Fine. Besides all of *that*, what are you scared of?"

Sighing, I gave up on my quest to my bedroom. "People will know it's not her. They'll see the strokes and they'll know."

"So tell them you're changing things up. We'll advertise it as a new collection. Oh! Oh! Oh!" She snapped her fingers and then tapped her nose. "Actually, we should start teasing the release now, and in a few weeks, bam! Put everything up auction-style and watch the all-out free-for-all that ensues."

I stared at her. God, she was crazy. Maybe having my best friend thirty minutes away had its downfalls too. "Look, if you want to go to brunch, you need to let me—" The ring of my doorbell interrupted me.

"Are you expecting someone?" Beth asked.

"Well, I did get an email from a Nigerian prince. Maybe he came to personally deliver my fortune."

"I'm serious," she hissed.

"Relax. You've lived with a doorman for too long. My neighbors do occasionally stop by sometimes. It's probably just cranky Jerry. He pops in a few times a week to bring me his recyclables. I tried to explain that all he has to do is put the bin next to the street, but he thinks I have some kind of magic that makes them disappear faster."

"Why would he think that?"

Walking to the door, I answered over my shoulder, "Because I put his recyclables into my big rolling bin and then hand his back to him empty. If only I could train Nancy and her brood across the street to do the same."

Just as I suspected when I opened the door, eighty-year-old Jerry Musgrave was standing on the other side, holding a green bin the size of a laundry basket. It was overflowing with various recyclables I'd have to sort later—my least favorite part of our arrangement—but it was the man standing a few feet behind him that made my heart stop.

He was wearing dark jeans, washed out at the thighs, and a gray fitted T-shirt that exposed black ink in the shape of feathers on his left arm, running from his wrist to his elbow. My mouth dried, and my skin flushed. It was seventy-five shades of wrong considering our situation, but I had two eyes and Caven was sexy as hell.

"I brought you the trash," Jerry announced.

Caven's stoic, blue gaze captured mine, ensnaring me until I was unable to look away. I frantically tried to get a read on his emotionless face to figure out if he'd come to deliver good news or bad. His scruff was longer than the last time I'd seen him, bordering on the verge of becoming a beard, and his cheeks and his nose were sun-kissed, but those were the only clues he was giving away.

"Would you…uh, like to come in?" I asked Caven.

Jerry's bin bumped my stomach. "No. Just take this crap so I can get it out of my house. It's too much. I don't see why I can't just put it in the regular bins like everything else."

On instinct, my hands came up to take the bin from Jerry, but I never tore my eyes off Caven. It was a warm day, but I felt his icy gaze travel down my body head to toe. Of course I was wearing my stupid overalls. Karma would have it no other way.

He could have called. He had my number.

Maybe he'd come to deliver the good news in person.

Or maybe he'd come to witness my agony when he told me he'd never let me see Rosalee again.

"Hurry up," Jerry chided. "I need my bin back. My sons came over for dinner last night and brought all their spawns.

My house looks like it was hit by a tornado. I'll have at least two more of these for you today."

Ignoring Jerry, I asked Caven, "Is everything okay?"

"You have a minute to talk?" he replied.

I had approximately the rest of my life to talk to him if he wanted. Luckily, I managed to get out a somewhat casual, "Sure."

But, first, I had to get rid of Jerry.

Making a mental note to buy him a rolling recycle bin first thing in the morning, I turned the container on its end, dumping plastic bottles, bits of wrappers, and cardboard all over my floor before handing it back to him empty. "I'll come by and pick up the rest later. Don't bring it to me. I'll come get it. Got it?"

He looked thoroughly confused, but when I turned my attention back on Caven, a smile was twitching the corner of his lips.

A smile.

A smile couldn't be bad, right?

Dear God, please don't let his smile be a bad thing.

I kicked the trash out of the way as best I could and then plastered on a grin that I hoped didn't look nearly as nervous as I felt. "Come on in, Caven."

He stood, patiently waiting until Jerry hobbled down my three brick steps. They exchanged macho chin jerks, and Jerry grumbled something under his breath as he passed that made Caven chuckle.

Oh, sweet baby Jesus, a chuckle had to be good news. No one chuckled right before ruining another person's hopes and dreams, no matter how funny a crochety old man may be.

I swallowed hard, rolling my thumb and my forefinger

together as he made his way up the steps. He stopped directly in front of me, so close that I could smell his cool and crisp cologne, the trail becoming woodsy and warm, purely masculine, just like everything else about Caven Hunt.

And then that magnificent lip twitch of his made an encore. "You still making up for our carbon footprint the other night?"

"I looked it up. Your SUV gets thirteen miles to the gallon. It may take a while."

He grinned.

I backed up, allowing him space to enter, tripping over an empty milk jug in the process.

"Shit," I cried as I fell backward.

With the speed of a cheetah—or a father with experience in dealing with a clumsy, accident-prone Banks girl—he caught my arm. My breath hitched and I felt every one of his fingertips branding the inside of my bicep.

Dazed and a tad bit hypnotized, I peered up at him.

God, how I'd dreamed about him over the years.

In those dreams, he'd never been scowling at me or shouting like he had in his backyard. Nor had he been riddled with guilt like he had been at the diner. No. In my dreams, Caven looked at me with tenderness and longing. This was neither of those, but I'd happily accept the gentle amusement he was currently aiming my way.

"Who knew recycling could be so dangerous?" he teased.

Like, actually *teased*, as though I weren't his archnemesis.

And because I was so lost in his dreamy, blue stare, I replied, "Some people believe recycling itself is actually a dangerous process that produces harmful byproducts and emissions."

His brows furrowed. "Interesting." Though he said it in a way that said it was not interesting in the least.

I couldn't blame him. It was a random fact I'd once heard. Why it had come to me in that moment, I would never know. But at least words had come out and I didn't look like a total imbecile.

"Is that paint in your hair?" he asked.

Strike that. I looked like a total imbecile in dirty overalls with damn paint in my hair.

Fan-fucking-tastic.

"Uh…yeah," I replied, raking my fingers through the top of my hair, like that was going to help. "Purple is my color." As I attempted to right myself, the back of my hand grazed the front of his shirt, leaving a lovely streak across the front of his gray shirt. "Oh my God," I breathed in horror. In the recesses of my mind, I knew it was oil paint—not, say, a dribble of ketchup I could just wipe away. But something in the embarrassment section of my brain told me to try anyway. "Shit. I am so sorry." Using my clean hand, I gave it a swipe, producing a yellow streak out of nowhere. "Shit," I cried, continuing my attempt to clean his uncleanable shirt with the heels of my palms.

It was ridiculous and I probably looked like a cat digging in the sand, but Caven just stood there, his chin to his chest watching me. That is until a red streak joined its primary and secondary friends.

"Holy shit," I gasped. "Where is all this paint coming from?"

And because my brain clearly could not accept that my hands had somehow magically transformed into paint brushes hell-bent on using Caven as a canvas… I. Just. Kept. Wiping.

"Hadley, stop," he said, gently taking my wrists. "It's okay. Really."

I could only imagine how red my face was because it felt like my cheeks had caught fire. "Oh my God. I'm so sorry. I'll buy you a new shirt. I swear. Just tell me how much it cost and I'll cut you a check." I paused my hysteria long enough to realize that *no one* had checks anymore, much less ones they "cut" like an old-school bookie. "That was a lie. I don't have a check. Do you by chance have Paypal?"

And that was when it happened. Caven Hunt didn't just grin at me.

Or twitch his lips.

Or even chuckle.

He laughed, deep and throaty.

Rich and brilliant.

Sexy and depressing.

Well…it was only depressing because I knew he probably wouldn't give those to Hadley the Terrible very often.

And that sucked because I liked it a lot.

"Relax. You don't have to pay for my shirt. It's not a big deal."

I shook my head, my wrists still held in his large hands. "That's not going to wash out. It's oil."

"I can afford a new shirt. And just think: Next time I have to paint the house, I'm all set for a wardrobe."

"You paint your own house?" I squeaked. Seriously. Because what the hell else would I say when I was already mortified?

I-M-B-E-C-I-L-E

"No. Never," he replied with a smile so bright that I swear I could feel its warmth.

I liked that a lot too.

"Now. Maybe you should hit the sink before we talk."

"Is it going to be a good chat?"

He shook his head and cut his gaze off to the side, tucking his lips like he really didn't want to be smiling at all. "Just... Wash your hands."

"Right. Okay." I looked at his fingers still curled around my wrists. "You gonna let me go?"

His gaze came back to mine, the strangest shadow passing over his face. "Yeah. Sorry."

But he didn't release me. He stood there for a minute, his blue eyes roaming my face, that shadow darkening by the second.

"Caven," I whispered.

"You look like her."

I offered him a tight smile. "I know."

"I mean, I knew you did, but I don't think I realized how *much* until I saw you again."

My stomach wrenched. "If you want the truth, she looks more like my mom than she does me." No sooner than the final word cleared my lips did I wish I could take them back.

The shadow on his face transformed into a storm of guilt, and in the very next beat, he dropped my wrists. "We should talk."

And just like that, the moment was gone.

His scowl returned, his body became hard, and angry Caven reappeared, leaving all the soft and gentle discarded on the floor with the rest of Jerry's garbage.

"Come on in."

He dipped his chin but only made it one step over the threshold before abruptly stopping.

Beth was coming at him full steam ahead.

And not my best friend Beth, trying to catch flies with her honey.

This was badass-*lawyer* Beth. Her shirt had been buttoned all the way up to her throat, her long, brown hair tied back in a bun. And I swear to God the woman was wearing a pair of glasses she had to have produced out of thin air.

"Mr. Hunt, allow me to introduce myself. I'm Beth Watts, Hadley's attorney."

Caven's face got hard. "You two working on something I should know about?"

"No!" I exclaimed, rushing forward to stand between them. "Beth is actually my best friend, not just my attorney. We've known each other since we were kids." I grabbed her arm and dragged her toward the door, not giving the first damn if my paint-covered hands ruined her shirt. "She just stopped by to see if I wanted to go to brunch. Unfortunately, I'd already eaten. So…" I snatched the door open and shoved her out. "See you later, Beth."

"Hadley," she growled as I slammed the door in her face. She'd forgive me when I called her later to fill her in on all the details. Right after she scolded me—*again*—for talking to Caven without legal representation.

Whatever. It was a risk I was more than willing to take.

"Can I get you something to drink?" I asked on my way to the kitchen sink.

"No. Thanks. I'm good," he replied, turning in a circle as he took in my living room.

I gave my hands a good scrub, all the while trying not to stare from the other side of the bar as he walked to the pictures hanging on the wall, thoroughly inspecting each before meandering to the next.

I hadn't had a lot of company since I'd bought the place, but even Beth had been in awe the first time she'd come over.

I might have lived in Jersey, but I'd brought the tropics of Puerto Rico with me.

My entire house had been decorated in varying shades of green and Caribbean blues. My furniture was rustic, distressed wood with cream cushions and throw pillows offering loud pops of color, and R.K. Banks originals hung on nearly every wall to the point that they almost looked like windows to the rainforest.

It was my own little private paradise. A sanctuary so bright and so relaxing that it was impossible not to smile when I walked through the door.

"Wow, this place is…"

"I know." I smiled, drying my hands on a bright-yellow dishtowel.

He did *not* return it. "Your credit's shit. How'd you afford this place?"

My back shot ramrod straight. "What?"

Shoving a hand into the pocket of his jeans, he quirked an eyebrow. "City records said you paid in cash. Where'd you get the money?"

I twisted my lips, feeling a little—okay, a lot—insulted. "I don't know, Caven. Where do *you* get money?"

"I work for it. But there's no traceable record of you having a job in the last five years, and up until two months ago, you had over a hundred thousand dollars in credit card debt. Care to explain where this sudden influx of cash came from?"

Discarding the towel on the counter, I crossed my arms over my chest and glared at him. I told myself not to be pissed that he'd pulled my credit. He had plenty of reasons to doubt me, and honestly, I'd have willingly given it to him if he'd asked.

But the fact of the matter was he *hadn't* asked.

Walking past him, I headed to my makeshift studio, waving over my shoulder for him to join me. "Have you ever heard the saying about what happens when you assume? You make an *ass* out of *you* and *me*."

"Answer the question, Hadley. I don't know a lot of unemployed people who can afford to drop that kind of cash. Where'd you get the money?"

I walked into my studio and waited for him to round the corner. He didn't follow me in, but rather propped his muscular shoulder against the doorjamb.

Standing in the center of the room, I spread my arms wide. "I work, Caven. That's where I got the money."

He scowled as he stated—not asked, but *stated*, "You said you were a photographer, not a painter."

"Are you *ass*-uming that a person can't do both?"

I was supposed to be winning him over with hopes that he'd let me see Rosalee, but I was not about to stand there and take his shit in my own damn house.

I advanced on him, not stopping until I was in his space, smelling his cologne all over again and pretending that it wasn't intoxicating. "Ask me a question, Caven, and I'll be happy to answer it. But every word out of your mouth since you dropped the sexy grin has been an accusation."

His eyebrows shot up and my stomach sank when I realized I'd mentioned the sexy grin, so by way of distraction, I persevered.

"Yes, I'm a photographer. Yes, I'm a painter. For your information, I even like to dabble in interior design and on occasion have been known to do a fashion sketch or two. I own a business, Caven. My sister and I were known as artist R.K. Banks before she passed away a few months ago. I'm sick of losing people I love. My parents are gone, their parents are gone, and now, my sister is gone too. Rosalee is literally the only thing I have left in this world. So yes, I sold my house in Puerto Rico, paid off all my credit cards that I'd been neglecting while…ya know, *grieving*. And then I paid over a million dollars *in cash* for a house so I could live fifteen minutes down the road from my daughter if and *when* I'm allowed to finally see her again." I pushed up onto my toes, tapped his hard pec with my finger to really drive home my point—not because I was dying to touch him or anything—and seethed, "And we could have calmly had this discussion like two grown-ass adults if you'd just *asked* the questions sans the accusations."

He stared at me for several beats, his head tilted down, his face unreadable. But I was not backing down. For Rosalee, I would beg and plead with this man for the rest of my life, but I wasn't going to be on my knees for him while I did it.

"Do we understand each other?"

"I don't know. Should I have *asked* these questions before or after I '*dropped the sexy grin*'?"

Heat bloomed in my cheeks, but I forged ahead. "Before. You're not as big of an ass when you smile."

I had no idea what was going on in his head as we stood there, our gazes locked, but neither of us moved. We were close enough to breathe the same air, and I fought to convince my hands to remain at my sides.

I was all too aware that Caven felt nothing but contempt for me, but the wild hum I'd had for him in my veins since I was only eight years old couldn't be tamed.

God knew I'd tried.

SEVENTEEN

CAVEN

Clearing my throat, I stepped as far away from her as I could get in a single stride.

Why did she always look at me like that? It was the most bizarre combination of anguish and adoration, like she couldn't decide if she wanted to burst into tears or launch herself into my arms.

And even more bizarrely, I couldn't decide if I wanted to run as far away from her as I could get or... No. There was no *or*. Not with her.

I didn't want to feel anything for Hadley, but in the week since she'd reappeared, she was the only thing I'd been able to think about.

Every day as I'd watched Rosalee playing on the beach, I'd done nothing but think about Hadley.

What if she took me to court?

What if she somehow won?

What if she managed to get custody?

Even the idea of joint custody where I'd lose Rosalee every other week and alternating holidays made me feel like I was burning at the stake.

It was a week spent in Hell, forcing smiles for my daughter while silently preparing for the worst. According to the team of attorneys Doug had gathered, losing Rosalee at least partially was a definite possibility. They were all in agreeance that Hadley didn't have much of a case at the moment, but eventually she would. She appeared to have money, owned a home, and had a good attorney. Hell, even the letters from her therapists, which she'd preemptively turned over to Doug, were glowing with just how well she'd been doing in the recent months.

But months weren't enough for me. Not when it came to Rosalee.

At night as I'd lie in bed, staring at my daughter, I'd wonder, had the roles been reversed, if I'd have had the foresight to leave Rosalee with her.

I would have liked to say I would have.

But nothing made sense when you were lost in the past.

When I was eighteen, just two weeks after I'd started college, the kids outside my dorm had set off a round of fireworks. I'd thought I was going to die. My visceral reaction trumped any kind of rational thought. I knew that it was fireworks. I could see them outside my window. Yet, at the sound of the first blast, I could smell all the food and blood as if I were right back in that mall food court again. Fireworks. Fucking fireworks, and I was a six-foot-four, one-hundred-seventy-pound young man hiding under a bed, convinced that it was the end.

I didn't know if I would have been able to separate that fear from reality long enough to focus on a baby, not even short-term to get her somewhere safe.

It took a lot of years, a lot of anger, a lot of medication, a lot therapy, and a lot of trial and error for me to figure out how to manage the reality of my past. It also required a lot of help.

Ian saved my life that night when he came home from a date and found his college roommate—a kid he'd only known for two weeks—hiding under the bed. He didn't ask a million questions or laugh the way he probably should have. He simply sat down on the floor and assured me that the world wasn't ending.

I didn't believe him.

But for the next half hour, as I worked my way out of the past, he never left my side. When it was finally over, Ian never asked why. He made us both a Hot Pocket and put a movie on. The credits hadn't started rolling before a dam broke inside me. The secrets I so closely guarded tore from my throat like rusty razor blades. I told him everything, from the abuse of my childhood to the shooting at the mall. He didn't say much as the filth of my life saturated that tiny dorm room, but I didn't need him to talk. I just needed someone to listen.

After that, he took to driving me to therapy twice a week and even sitting with me in a few group sessions. In all the years we'd been friends, he'd never looked at me the same way as he had before. He'd also never run for the hills, so I chalked it up as true friendship.

I wasn't sure where I stood on Hadley in relation to Rosalee. But the fact was that I didn't get the choice. Hadley was her mother. Full stop.

It wasn't right.

It wasn't fair.

But it was a fact.

The only thing I could think to do was to prepare for when I was no longer able to keep my daughter out of her reach.

And if that meant putting my personal feelings aside and becoming Ian, sitting on that floor in the middle of Hell, to ensure that my daughter never felt the blow back of my father's reign of terror, then so be it.

There was something to be said for the old adage *keep your friends close and your enemies closer.*

Hating Hadley wouldn't keep my daughter safe.

Pissing her off wouldn't make me the first person she called if anything went wrong.

And being a dick and driving her away would never stop her from coming back.

Even if I did decide to battle her in court for the rest of my life, she'd been right. One day, Rosalee was going to want to know her mother, and I wanted to know exactly who that woman was before that day came.

Standing in her living room and grilling her about her financial history probably wasn't going to win me any points, but accepting Hadley after everything we'd been through was going to come with a steep learning curve.

"You're right," I said.

"I am?"

"Yeah. You are. I assume a lot about you. But you have to understand—that's all I can do. We share a daughter and a dumpster-fire history, but I know absolutely nothing about *you.*"

"So talk to me. I have nothing to hide." She paused, swaying her head from side to side. "Well, except for the fact that I'm R.K. Banks. I'll need you to sign a nondisclosure agreement about that."

I smirked. "See, I don't even know if you're kidding right now."

"I am. *And* I'm also not. There are only about five people in the world who know my identity. I can't risk word getting out. I have a reputation to uphold." She grinned.

I forced a grin in return. Suddenly, the reasons she wanted

to keep a custody battle between the two of us and out of the press were a lot clearer.

"Are you a big deal in the art world or something?"

"I guess that depends on who you ask. R.K. is far from Picasso. I seriously doubt we'll end up in any museums, but rich people seem to have a real fascination with our work."

I looked at one of the pieces on an easel. It was a close-up of white flowers. If memory served me correctly, they were Silver Bells. The picture itself was beautiful, but the thick strokes of white and pink paint added highlights and dimension until the photo almost became abstract. I could see why they were popular. The flowers weren't my style, but leaning against the wall was a gray-and-white mountain scene that was incredible.

"How much do your picture-painting things go for?"

She rolled her eyes. "My *art* sells for anywhere from two hundred thousand to over a million. It just depends on the size and demand of the piece."

"Holy shit," I breathed.

She let out a laugh. "Trust me—no one was more shocked than I was when it first took off. It wasn't a career I planned. I just needed an outlet to keep my mind quiet while I was work-ing on myself."

I glanced around the room full of canvases two to three layers deep leaning up against the walls. "Why haven't you sold these?"

"Ah, well, I guess you could say I'm going through a... *phase*. I haven't sold anything in over a year, and since my sis-ter died four months ago, working without her hasn't felt right."

Christ. First, her parents. Now, she'd lost a sister too. "I'm sorry to hear about your sister."

138

Her head came up, a sad smile pulling at her pink lips. "I appreciate it. It was a car accident, so I wasn't in any way prepared for it. But I'm learning to cope."

"How'd you handle it when you heard the news?" It was a dick question no one should ever ask. But, for people like us, sometimes all it took was one tragedy to set us back years.

She looked me right in the eyes when she replied. "I hit my knees. But I managed to get back up." She swept her arms out, indicating the dozens of pictures surrounding her. "And here I am, moving on. One manageable second at a time."

I nodded, unexpected pride hitting me. My chest got tight as I stared at her staring at me, her eyes shimmering with vulnerability.

She wasn't as close anymore, but nothing about the way she was looking at me had changed.

And nothing about the way I felt it, deep in places Hadley Banks had no business being, had changed either.

I cleared my throat. "We need to talk about Rosalee."

"Yeah. We do. You sure I can't get you a drink?"

I laughed. "You got any Scotch?"

"It's eleven thirty."

"Is that a no?"

Her lips twisted. "Depends. Are you trying to get *me* tipsy to soften the blow, or are *you* trying to get tipsy to work up the courage to tell me that you've finished the thinking part of your process and you're here to deliver good news?"

"I'm not actually sure yet."

She smiled, radiant and genuine. "In that case, I have mimosas."

"Better than nothing, I guess."

She giggled, brushing my shoulder as she passed, and I

silently cursed the fact that my body responded to such insignificant contact with her.

She went straight to the fridge and pulled out orange juice and a bottle of champagne as I settled on the barstool overlooking her galley kitchen.

"Your place is nice," I told her.

A quiet pop sounded as she removed the cork with a dishtowel. "Thanks. That means a lot coming from Social Worker Hunt. I'm assuming this is my surprise home visit?"

"I've heard assuming is bad, ya know? But yeah, something like that."

She poured the bubbly into two flutes, topping them with a splash of orange juice before sliding one my way. "Well, if you'd like to take a look around, go for it. There's not much to see upstairs. The rooms are furnished but sparse since I decided to decorate from the bottom up. I can assure you, though, everything is by the book. I have alarms on all the doors and windows, a child-proof latch on both the medicine cabinets, cleaning supplies are out of reach, and just in case"—she bent down and pulled a red fire extinguisher out from under her sink, plopping it down on the marble counter with a loud thud—"I'm a rock star in the kitchen, so I don't expect this baby to get any use. But you can never be too safe."

I drained over half the mimosa in one long sip. "Did your *friend* Beth help you prep for a home visit?"

"No. My *attorney* Beth helped with that." She rolled the stem of her glass between her fingers. "We knew you weren't going to be happy with me showing back up, so I wanted to be prepared for whatever you could throw at me."

I shook my head and sighed. "I don't want to throw anything at you. I just want to protect my daughter."

"I get that."

I rested both of my forearms on the counter and leaned toward her. "I don't think you do, so I'm going to be blunt here. I don't trust you, Hadley. I don't trust your motives. I don't trust your ability to care for a child. And, most of all, I don't trust that you're going to stick around long enough to justify telling Rosalee that you're her mother."

Her mouth fell open and hurt flitted across her features.

I hated it but I didn't let it slow me. "*But*…that doesn't change that fact that you *are* her mother. Biologically speaking anyway. So I've come to the conclusion that I'm going to have to learn to accept this. But *you* are going to have to work with me."

The hurt faded away as her mouth stretched so big that it was a wonder it didn't split her face. "Done. Whatever it takes. I'm game."

"For the next year, you and I can get to know each other. You can prove to me that not only can you handle having a child in your life, but that you actually plan to stick around long term. Then…maybe we can introduce you to Rosalee."

She did a slow blink. "I'm sorry—did you say *a year* before introducing me to Rosalee?"

I had. And I'd also known there was no way in hell she was going to agree to it. But nobody started a negotiation with their best offer. She'd counter with something absurd like two weeks, I'd counter at nine months, and we'd keep going back and forth until we landed on six months. And only then would I concede.

"You're a stranger to me. It's going to take more than just a few days before I trust you with my daughter."

"Oh, really?" she drawled. "So her preschool teacher had to wait a year to meet her too?"

"You're hardly a preschool teacher, Hadley."

"You're right. Because I'm her *mother*."

"A mother who abandoned her," I shot back. "So that makes *you* a *stranger* to *us*. One year. I get to know you first before she even enters the picture. That's my deal. Take it or leave it."

"Uhh…I'm going to leave it. Because it's a crap deal and you know it."

I shrugged. "What did you expect? That you'd just waltz back in and have her calling you mommy by the end of the week? That's not the way this is going to work."

"I'm not asking her to call me mommy at all. Introduce me as Hadley. Your friend, your maid, the gardener, the babysitter, the—" Her eyes flared wide as she exclaimed, "Oh my God, let me teach her art!"

I already had my mouth open, ready to shut her down, when she rushed around the counter and grabbed my arm, tugging at it as if dragging me off the stool would somehow make me agree.

"I could teach her about painting and drawing at first, then graduate up to photography as she got older. Come on, Caven. It's perfect. I'd get to spend time with her, teaching her all the things I love. And you could be there too. You could see me in action and how I interact with her. You'll feel comfortable. She'll feel comfortable. And I'll get to spend time with her."

No was poised on the tip of my tongue.

But she had a point.

In my house, Rosalee would always be safe.

I'd be there if anything happened.

And I'd be there if nothing happened—i.e. Hadley decided to hit the road again and left my girl hanging.

"And this is your long-term solution? You just become her art teacher? We all live happily ever after?"

She stopped bouncing and tugging on my arm and glared at me. "No. This is my solution to your ridiculous one-year-wait deal. I may not be a preschool teacher, but I'm damn qualified to teach her art."

The gears in my head began to spin in every which direction. Hadley had agreed not to do anything with the courts… yet. But I wasn't going to be able to hold her off forever. According to Doug, there was nothing I could do to keep her from walking in with her DNA test and having her name added to Rosalee's birth certificate. And when she did, my options became even smaller, a nasty custody battle being my only way out.

That wasn't exactly ideal, but I'd go to all-out war for my daughter…

Unless I didn't have to.

"I want it in writing," I announced, rising to my feet. "Legal and binding. Six months. Supervised visitation *only*. Supervised by *me*. In *my home*. Two days a week. One hour—"

She gave my arm another shake, her fingernails starting to bite into the feathers on my tattoo. "Two hours. I need two hours."

"Two hours and you'll agree to everything else?"

"Yes," she breathed. "Absolutely. I promise."

The day I'd seen her talking to Rosalee at the party, I'd been terrified. That hadn't changed over the last week, but for the first time in the last seven days, I felt like I was finally in control.

Lying to my daughter and spending two nights a week with Hadley for the next six months was not my idea of a perfect situation, but it didn't scare the absolute hell out of me the way the idea of Hadley's picking her up every other weekend did.

So, with that in mind, I extended my hand toward her and muttered, "Deal." And then my body turned to stone when she threw her arms around my neck, her whole front becoming flush with mine, her breasts pillowing between us in a manner I *never* should have noticed.

"Oh my God! Caven, thank you so much!"

I sucked in a sharp breath, unsure of what to do—or how I felt about being that close to her. Only that wasn't totally true. I felt more for Hadley than I ever should have—even if I didn't understand why.

Maybe it was because I felt like I could relax now that I'd bought myself six months of security.

Maybe it was because, after everything that had happened in the past, I liked seeing her happy.

Maybe it was because I secretly liked the way she felt in my arms.

Whatever the reason, I didn't set her away as she celebrated her victory.

"I swear to you. You won't regret this. I'm going to make this right," she promised, tightening her arms around my neck.

I wasn't positive she was right, and a part of me still very much wished she'd take off and never look back.

But as I stood in the middle of her tropical oasis, her deep-red hair complete with purple paint streaked through the top tickling my nose as she bounced and laughed, not crying, not afraid, not haunted by the past, I felt a hint of victory too.

Fucked. Totally and royally.

But victorious nonetheless.

EIGHTEEN

HADLEY

"**S**he's going to love you," I told myself as I stood at Caven's front door, smoothing my unwrinkled fitted T-shirt for the tenth time. The nerves buzzing inside me probably could have been measured on the Richter scale. Given the security gate he'd left open for me, I was sure he had cameras aimed at his front door, but I couldn't bring myself to care.

I was freaking out.

Over the four days since he'd left my house with paint covering his shirt, I'd been beside myself awaiting this moment. But, now that it had arrived, I couldn't bring myself to lift my fist to knock.

Beth had drawn up the papers agreeing to six months of supervised visitation and had them couriered to Caven's attorney before she'd fired me as a client. She'd rehired me about ten minutes later when I'd told her I'd finally grab a martini with her at this God-awful hoity-toity bar she'd been talking about for weeks.

Caven had texted me two days later with our new schedule. He hadn't asked if it worked for me, but I worked from home and didn't have much of a life outside of catering to Beth's best-friend-and-wing-lady needs, so my schedule was wide open. He'd decided on Wednesdays from five to seven and Saturdays from one to three.

It wasn't enough. But it was a start.

Flexing my hands at my sides, I practiced what I would say when he opened the door. Funny enough, I wasn't really all that nervous about seeing Rosalee. She'd been an absolute angel when I'd met her at her birthday party. Even if she was a spoiled brat, I already loved her with my entire soul.

It was seeing Caven again that had me on edge.

I wasn't sure what version of the man I'd get that night. I hoped like hell it was the one who laughed and smiled. Or even the one who gave me lip twitches and chuckles as I dealt with my crochety neighbor.

But the one time I'd seen Rosalee in his presence, I'd gotten nuclear Caven.

I wasn't real eager for a repeat performance from that guy.

My palms were sweating as I reached for the doorbell, but before I had the chance to press it—or, more than likely, chicken out again—the door swung open.

Ian nearly plowed me over. "Shit. Sorr—" He didn't finish as his face filled with recognition—and disgust.

"Hi," I squeaked. "I'm Hadley."

"So I've heard."

When he didn't move or invite me in, I prattled out, "Is, um…Caven here?"

"He is."

Again. No moving. No inviting. Just lots of judgmental staring.

"Any chance I could talk to him? He's expecting me."

He cocked his head to the side. "Why are you here?"

I knew what he was asking. I also knew I was going to pretend I didn't.

Pointing to my bag filled to the brim with new arts and crafts supplies, I replied, "I'm here to teach Rosalee about art."

"*Why*?" He stretched that one syllable out as if he thought I was hard of hearing or just plain dumb.

Again. I knew what he was asking, but…

"Well, because art is known to bolster creativity in children. And I know what you're thinking—that seems pretty obvious. But did you know it also improves academic performance, enhances fine motor skills, and has even been shown to strengthen decision-making skills and focus? With the cutbacks in art programs in schools all across our country, hiring a private instructor is the only way to ensure your child is exposed to the arts as early as possible. Truly, I applaud Caven for making such a wise and bold decision for Rosalee's wellbeing." I finished with a grin to really sell it.

Unfortunately, Ian wasn't buying it that day—or possibly ever.

"Don't think because you scared the shit out of Caven and got him to agree to this charade that the rest of us don't see it for what it truly is. I don't know what the fuck you're up to, but there is nothing I wouldn't do for Rosalee. It'd do you well to remember that."

Surprised, I rocked back on my heels—and not because of his threat. "I scared the shit out of Caven?"

He shot me a blistering scowl but offered no explanation. Leaning into the house, he yelled out, "Cav, you got company!" Then he marched past me to the driveway.

I was watching him fold into a convertible Mercedes when I heard Caven's voice behind me.

"He's usually the nicer of the two of us."

"Well, he didn't call the cops this time. I'd consider that

progress." I turned back around.

He was in dark slacks and a white button-down that was tucked in, but the sleeves had been rolled up to his elbow, revealing that tattoo of feathers again. One day, I'd gather the courage to ask him about it. Today was not that day though.

"Hi," I breathed.

"Hey," he mumbled.

Then nothing. Much like Ian, he stood there, not moving, not inviting me in. But thankfully unlike his friend, there wasn't any judgmental glaring. I couldn't read his expression at all.

Oh, but I felt his gaze as it traced over me, my body heating under his scrutiny.

"What happened to the overalls?"

I glanced at my jeans and simple tee and smarted, "I guess I didn't realize there was a dress code."

"I'm kidding. Come on in. She's been excited since I told her you were coming earlier."

My chest warmed. "Good. I'm excited too."

His smirk grew into a mischievous grin. "I know. I've been watching you gather up the nerve to knock for the last ten minutes. I really thought you had it a few times there."

Dammit! I'd been right about the cameras.

"Well, it was sweet of you to come out here and put me out of my misery... Oh, wait, that didn't happen."

He chuckled. *Oh, thank you, God.* It was chuckling Caven. I could deal with chuckling Caven.

Out of the corner of my eye, I caught sight of a blur of pink polka dots as she came sliding around the corner, colliding into her father's legs. Caven caught her arm before she had the chance to fall.

Seeing her again stole my breath. How was it possible to love someone so much that I felt it all the way down to the marrow in my bones?

"You're the nice lady from my party," she stated with red sauce smeared across her mouth. "Did you help the police?"

I shot Caven a questioning look.

"She did," he replied. "Saved the day and everything. That's how I found out she was good at art."

It made zero sense. But, as a testament to how much Rosalee trusted her father, she didn't question it.

"Can you draw a unicorn?" she asked. Obviously, the true test of my skills.

"I can," I replied, squatting in front of her, thinking there was a solid chance my heart was going to explode—tears already welling in my eyes.

"With wings?"

I smiled, looking off to the side long enough to clear the emotion from my face. "Well, that's a Pegasus. But sure. I can put a horn on anything that even resembles a horse. Goats included."

"Yesssss," she hissed, pumping her fists in the air. "Did you bring paint? I love to paint, but Daddy won't let me use it anymore because I accidentally got some on the chair—"

"Accidentally?" Caven interjected. "You painted the entire chair pink."

She tilted her head back and peered up at him. "I tried to clean it up."

"It was nail polish, baby. There was no saving that. I had to buy a new chair."

She gasped and looked back at me with huge eyes. "Is painting nails art?"

"It can be. Maybe I can bring some polish over next time?"

Caven shook his head. "Wow, fired before you even step foot in the house. That must be some kind of record."

I made the eek face at Rosalee. "Okay, so no nail polish. Sorry, sweetheart."

She crossed her arms over her chest and let out a harrumph, but a rascally grin curled at the corners of her mouth.

Caven had been right. She did look a lot like me—mainly in her coloring. But there was still a bit of him in there too. Especially when he'd been younger. She had the subtle curve of his mouth and his lips so full in the center that it caused a permanent part. I thought she might have had his chin too, but I couldn't be sure because his was now masked by scruff.

Either way, she was beautiful beyond all reason.

"So, did you?" she asked, her green eyes dancing with excitement.

"Did I what?"

"Bring paint?"

"Paint, clay, *and* crayons."

She twisted her lips adorably. "Okay, but I already have crayons."

And then I blew her little four-year-old mind. "Have you ever melted them and dripped them over a canvas though?"

Dogs in a hundred-mile radius could have heard her squeal.

Caven laughed, and I took the second to relish in the sound.

I liked seeing him like that. Happy, content, guilt-free.

And more than anything I loved that he'd made a life for himself after everything he'd gone through.

He deserved it.

He'd *always* deserved it.

Which was why my decision to come back had almost never happened.

"Invite Ms. Banks in, Rosie."

Rosie. Be still my heart, he called her Rosie. How freaking cute was that?

She reached out and grabbed my hand, tugging on it as I returned to my full height.

It was crazy the way children could heal a broken soul.

As I walked through that door, I wasn't just following a little girl with wild, red curls.

I was following my mother.

My father.

My sister.

Our whole family was holding my hand for the first time in eighteen years.

And Caven, the boy who had saved my life, was right there, his smile small but his warmth consuming me all the same.

I paused before she pulled me past him. "Would it be okay if she calls me Hadley? Ms. Banks always makes me feel like my mother."

His face filled with apology. "Of course. I'm—"

"Don't say sorry." It was a risk. But everything, including coming back, had been a risk. That was a big part of living in the seconds. So, without concern for how he might react, I reached out and caught his hand, giving it a tender squeeze.

He glanced at our connection, something dark flashing across his face, but he didn't pull away. He just stared, heartbreaking and lost. But for the first time ever, I stared back at him with hope for a better future—for all of us.

I released his hand and succumbed to Rosalee's relentless tugging, allowing her to drag me through the house.

And through it all, I felt Caven's gaze on my back.

She held my hand as we entered a large open-concept living room, kitchen, and dining combination that smelled of garlic and oregano. It was set up similarly to my place, but everything was nicer. *A lot nicer.* Mine was decorated better though. His was all muted grays and browns, not a primary color in sight unless I counted the few rogue building blocks that had tumbled out of the wicker basket in the corner. Everything was clean and tidy—again, something we had in common. My attention was on the tall built-in bookshelves on either side of his fireplace ,where several rows of children's books lined the bottom, when a woman's voice surprised me.

"Rosalee," an older Hispanic woman with beautiful raven hair called as she walked toward us.

I braced for more of the detest Ian had slapped me with, but she offered me a kind smile.

"Hi, I'm Alejandra. Can I borrow Rosalee for a few minutes?"

"No!" Rosalee whined. "She's going to let me melt crayons, Ale."

"Well, that sounds…messy. I'm sure Ms. Banks can—"

"Hadley," Caven corrected. "We can all call her Hadley. Even you, Rosie Posie."

Rosie Posie.

Dear. Lord. Forget about crayons. I was the one who was going to melt.

"Okay, then," Alejandra said. "I'm sure *Hadley* can wait a few minutes to get started. I need you to pick out a dress for picture day at school this week. Your dad bought a few new ones today that you can choose from."

Her whole little body jerked like she'd been struck by lightning. "Are they *pretty* dresses?"

"Uhhh…" She pointedly avoided Caven's gaze. "Well… He tried. That's the important thing."

I bit back a smile at the idea of Caven Hunt strolling through the dress section for his baby girl's picture day at preschool.

"Ugh," Rosalee groaned. "Cats again?"

"What's wrong with cats?" Caven defended. "You begged for that cat dress a few weeks ago."

"But now I like ferrets."

"You don't even know what a ferret looks like."

"Yes, I do. They look like my very favorite animal in the world."

I slapped a hand over my mouth to stifle a laugh.

Rosie saw it.

Caven too.

But they were too busy in a heated debate over ferrets to pay me any mind.

Caven planted a hand on his hip. "Maybe you should have Hadley teach you how to draw a ferret tonight."

She planted her hand on her hip right back. "I don't need her to teach me. I already know."

And that's when I really saw it.

She looked like my mom.

She had her father's lips.

But her attitude? That was a hundred percent my sister.

"Then you know it's a long weasel-looking rat, right?" Caven argued. "Just like that stuffed animal Uncle Ian got you."

"Nuh-uh."

"Afraid so, baby doll."

She crinkled her nose. "Have you ever even seen a ferret?"

"Yes," Caven answered decisively. "And it looks like a rat."

"No!" She stretched her hands high above her head. "It's tall and has a long neck and curly hair and big lips."

"A giraffe?"

She huffed. "No. A ferret."

Setting my bag on the floor, I pulled my phone out and Googled: *tall long neck curly hair big lips.*

I added the word *animal* when a dozen images of hair models popped up.

"A llama?" I asked, causing three pair of eyes to swing my way. After tapping on a picture, I turned the phone to Rosalee. "That?"

"Yeah! A ferret!"

"Jesus," Caven breathed. "That's a llama, Rosie. Big difference."

Her anger morphed into an angelic smile, and then she batted her eyelashes like a trained professional in the art of conning her father. "Can I have one of those, then?"

The side of Caven's mouth hiked up, but his voice remained stern. "No. And now that I know you're talking about a llama, you can't even have one when you move out and get your own apartment."

"What? Why not?" she squealed.

Caven bent over, scooping her off her feet and planting her on his hip. "They live on a farm, baby."

"Then we need a farm," she countered.

In that moment, there was no way I could have forced the smile from my lips.

Standing there with them.

Listening to them talk.

Watching them interact.

It was beautiful on a very basic level, and it made my fingers twitch for my camera.

Caven shook his head, his lopsided smile growing. "Do me a favor and go upstairs with Ale and try on the dresses I got you. They aren't all cats. I think there was a pink-and-purple one too."

"Oh, okay," Rosalee reluctantly agreed before looking to me. "Don't leave to help the police this time, okay? I'll be right back."

"Come on, Rosie," Ale said, taking her hand.

I peeked at Caven out of the corner of my eye. But he wasn't looking at me. It was more than just his eyes anchored to that little girl; he watched with his entire being, a wide smile on his face.

God, a person could suffocate in the density of love he had for his daughter. And witnessing it up close was an experience all of its own.

It had been less than two weeks since he'd called the police on me, and now, I was standing in his house, getting ready to introduce Rosalee to the Banks family passions. It was the most surreal feeling of my life.

Swiping my finger over my heart in an x, I replied, "I promise, sweetheart. I'll be right here."

I watched her walk away, her short, little legs trotting to keep up with Alejandra. As soon as they hit the stairs, Caven erased my euphoria with my least favorite four words in his vocabulary.

"We need to talk."

"Oh, goodie," I deadpanned.

He moved with long, purposeful strides behind the bar

that divided the kitchen from the rest of the house. "I signed the visitation agreement your attorney sent over, but I had a few things I wanted to add before we went any further." He retrieved a manila envelope from a drawer and withdrew a single sheet of paper. "I came up with a list of rules. Most of them are pretty straightforward, but I wanted it in writing to ensure that we were both on the same page about what's happening here." He handed me the paper before digging a pen out of his pocket. "I'm going to need you to sign that before *art classes* can start." He threw a pair of air quotes my way.

I threw them right back. "I do plan on *teaching* her, you know? Art is a big part of who I am and who my family was. I'd really like to pass it down to her too now."

"Even better. Now, just as soon as you sign that, you can start setting up." He propped his hip against the counter and crossed his arms over his chest, but it appeared about as uncomfortable as a person could get.

I'd have bet fifty dollars that, much like me at the front door, he'd practiced this conversation, including that casual, completely-not-casual lean at least a dozen times before I'd arrived.

Something about him being nervous too set me at ease.

The paper was written in legal jargon, but I gathered the gist.

No telling Rosie that I was her biological mother and/or family member, implied or otherwise.

No telling her about the shooting at the Watersedge Mall, including any reference to how my parents died.

No telling her who Caven's father was, his name, or his role in the shooting.

And last but not least, no mentioning that she'd been left on his doorstep or abandoned at any point.

He was right; all of this was *very* straightforward. Which was why I was so confused when I looked up and found him watching me with a hard expression.

"She's too young," he said. "For all of this. I hate lying to her, but she's *four*. It's my job to keep this kind of sludge from seeping into her life." He paused and let out a groan. "And I don't mean to insinuate that you're sludge, but our past most certainly is."

"Caven," I whispered, closing the distance between us. "I understand."

He didn't even flinch as I placed my hand on his forearm, that hum in my veins becoming deafening at the contact.

I had to stop touching him all the time.

He was starting to get used to it.

And I was starting to crave it more and more.

I'd work on that the next day though, because in the moment, I'd have done anything to ease the guilt carved into his handsome features.

"You don't need to explain anything to me. You're right. Everything from the moment we met has been covered in sludge. But not her. I know you don't trust me, but I swear I'm on your team. We can work together to make sure it *never* touches her. I'm completely content being Hadley the art teacher. She doesn't need to know anything else." With that, I released his arm, picked up the pen, and signed my name.

Beautiful relief sifted through him, all the way down through his tall, muscular frame. "Thank you."

I didn't want his thanks.

I hadn't earned his gratitude.

But I would eventually.

Until then, all I could do was try to make this adjustment

easier on everyone involved. A little levity went a long way in the middle of a raging storm.

Slapping a hand over my chest, I swung my gaze around the empty kitchen, talking to no one as I asked, "Did he just thank me? *Me.* Hadley the Terrible?" I replied for no one too. "I think he did."

He glowered as he slid the paper back into the envelope and sealed it with the brass clip. This particular glower though was packed with only slightly more heat than Rosalee's.

Meaning he did it with a sly curl to his lips.

Also meaning it stole my breath.

He shoved the envelope back in the drawer. "Maybe. But I also locked up my computer, tablet, and wallet in the safe, so I'm not sure we're out of the woods yet."

It wasn't funny. It was actually sad. But it gave me hope that we were making progress.

"And he made a joke?" I told my invisible friends.

He tipped his head to the side, still smiling, thus still wreaking havoc on my heart. "Oh, that was no joke." He stopped just on the wrong side of close—the right side being pressed against me—and dipped his head so his lips were painfully close to my ear. "I hope you're serious about this, because if you break her heart, I will ruin you."

As his breath drifted across my neck like a feather, drawing a chill from my skin, it wasn't Rosalee's heart that I was worried about.

But that was my problem.

He didn't know how often I'd thought about him since the shooting or dreamed of him every night for the majority of my adolescence.

Or how, in the middle of a raging storm, it was his eyes

that would flash on the backs of my lids.

And if I was careful, he never would.

"We were both ruined a long time ago, Caven. Maybe it's time for us to clear the wreckage and rebuild. Starting with her."

NINETEEN

CAVEN

"**O**h my—"

"Don't say God," I corrected Rosalee from my spot at the end of the dining room table, where she and Hadley had set up art station central. I had my laptop open and was going through some of the data Ian had sent over from the Lance Goodman deal. The man had been blowing up my phone wondering where his money was, and while legal was still going through all the contract and bank statements, something just didn't feel right.

"Why not?" Rosalee argued. "Molly says 'oh my God' all the time."

"I'm not Molly's dad."

"I know. Her dad lets her eat donuts for breakfast when it's not even her birthday."

"Her dad is also essentially sending her dentist's son through Yale. So there's that."

"What?"

I waved her off. "Nothing. Why don't we just stick with 'oh my goodness' for a while?"

"Can I say oh em gee?"

I lifted my gaze to her. "What? No."

"Is it a bad word?"

"No. But it makes you sound like you're thirteen and I'm

160

thirteen years away from being ready for that. Stay four until you are at least twenty-one. Okay?"

I glanced at Hadley, who had her head down, a pencil in hand. Her shoulders shook with silent laughter.

Rosalee's second "art class" was well underway, and as if the melted-crayon crap wasn't enough, Hadley had brought glitter this time. It didn't matter that she'd laid a drop cloth down on the floor beneath them. If I so much as stepped foot at that end of the table for the next month, I was going to look like a platinum member at the strip club. Glitter was only one step above the plague in my house. But I had a little girl. So, as long as she wasn't using it as body lotion to work at the aforementioned strip club, then I was going to have to get over it.

What I couldn't get over, though, was how much she loved Hadley.

From Wednesday to Saturday, all I'd heard from Rosalee was Hadley, Hadley, Hadley.

And it fucking sucked because my brain was already stuck on Hadley too.

How the whole damn room lit up when she smiled.

How she always managed to find a way to touch me.

And, worse, how I always managed to find a reason to let her.

The last two times I'd seen her, she'd been in jeans and a T-shirt. But there was no hiding that body. She couldn't have been over five-five, but her legs were long and her ass was round—not that I'd been looking or anything. That would have been fucked up on epic levels, considering how I felt about her.

Or how I was *supposed* to feel about her.

And let's not forget how goddamn cute she looked in those ridiculous overalls. They should not have been sexy.

Then again, *she* should not have been sexy in my mind, either.

Though I guess there had been a reason she and I had made a baby together. Attraction had never been our problem. I could still remember seeing her from across the bar.

I'd spent years avoiding redheads.

They all reminded me of that shattered little girl the day of the shooting.

But Hadley had been different. Come to find out that was probably because she had been on a mission to steal my computer, but whatever. It'd happened and it had given me the greatest gift of my entire life, who was currently covered in what had to be a gallon of glitter while decorating a unicorn she and that same gorgeous redhead had drawn together.

"Daddy, look!"

I lifted my head from my laptop. "Oh, wow! That's awesome, baby."

"Look at its horn. I did its horn all by myself."

"Well, duh. The horn is my favorite part. Of course you did it."

Glitter fell everywhere as she shook the picture at me. "Look at its butt. Hadley did its butt. Isn't it a good butt, Daddy?"

It was. It really fucking was. Not that I'd looked one of the four times she'd bent over to get something out of her bag that night.

Also, not that I'd been counting how many times she'd bent down or anything.

Christ. I had to get laid. This was ridiculous. I hated the woman. Kinda.

My sex life had both changed a lot and not at all since I'd

become a father. Interactions were limited to one-night stands. But they were so infrequent that they were more like once-a-year stands. And it was starting to feel like we were creeping up on day 364.

"Tail," Hadley corrected. "She's talking about its tail." She laughed, trapping her teeth between her lips.

My phone started ringing, Trent's name flashing on the screen. Standing up from my chair, I looked back to Rosalee. "It's almost three. Hadley should probably start cleaning things up."

"Noooooooooo," Rosie cried. "She just got here. We were going to make a Pegasus next."

I flicked a pointed look to Hadley, and she quickly backed me up. "You know what? I have to get going anyway. What if I outline the Pegasus for Wednesday? That way, we can spend more time decorating it."

"Without the horn. I wanna draw the horn."

She smiled at my girl, who immediately smiled back—the whole damn room becoming ten watts brighter. "Okay, so I'll just draw its butt and wings, then. Deal?"

They continued talking, but I gave Alejandra a chin jerk as I lifted my ringing phone in her direction. She was standing at the sink, washing dishes for the tenth time. She didn't usually work on Saturdays, but I could tell she was worried about Rosalee, so I hadn't said anything when she'd popped in minutes before Hadley was slated to arrive.

She gave me a curt nod in understanding, and I headed for the front door, lifting the phone to my ear.

I hadn't talked to Trent in weeks. I'd been trying to get in touch with him since Hadley had shown up at the birthday party, but admittedly, I hadn't been trying hard. Trent and I didn't have that kind of relationship. We talked twice a year whether we needed to or not, and he and his wife, Jennifer, would come down to visit two other times. The calls usually aligned with the visits for planning purposes. And since they'd left our place less than two months earlier, it wasn't time for either.

"About damn time you called me back," I grumbled as a greeting while walking outside to wait for Hadley—and get out of earshot.

"You rang," he droned in his best Lurch impression.

"I rang *twice* in the last two weeks."

"Does rich, neglected Caven need me to hang up and call back to make up for the second time?"

I rolled my eyes. "You're an asshole."

"But you have to admit I'm really good at it."

Jennifer shouted in the background, "Hey, Cav!"

I sank to the cold brick step. "Tell her I said hey."

"He says fuck off. I think he's mad at you for not calling him back last week," Trent told her.

"That is not what I said."

Jennifer knew better. Laughing, she replied, "He didn't call my phone, smartass."

"Ah, right," Trent said. "So, what's up, little brother. How's Rosie?"

"Pretty good. She's just cleaning up the glitter in the dining room with Hadley."

"Did you fire Alejandra?"

"Nope," I said, waiting for her name to click in his head.

"You got a new girlfriend?"

"Nope."

"Then who is Hadl—Oh, shit!" Yep. There it was. "Are we talking about Hadley *Hadley*? Rosalee's womb donor Hadley?"

"Hadley Banks. And yes."

I heard his recliner snap as he no doubt jumped to his feet. "What the fuck, Cav? When the hell did she get back?"

I put my elbows to my knees. "About two weeks ago."

"And I'm just hearing about it now?"

"I called."

"Twice. In two fucking weeks. That says to me you stubbed your toe on a stack of cash, not that the mother of your child suddenly reappeared out of nowhere. Goddamn it. Did someone amputate your thumbs? You could have sent a fucking text letting me know it was urgent."

"Yeah. Sorry. It's been a fucking mess over here."

If I knew Trent, he was pacing as he demanded, "Dammit. Start from the beginning. But give me the abridged version so we can get to the part to why she's in your goddamn house and not the city's jail."

There was only one part of the long, sordid story he was going to care about, so I went there first. "She was at the mall. Her parents died there."

"What. The. Fuck," he breathed before his voice grew to a shout. "What the fucking fuck! How is that possible? You met this woman in New York, right? Does she know who you are? Does she know about Dad?"

"Yeah. She came looking for me after she saw Kaleidoscope on the news and wanted pictures of her dead parents."

"Right, so obviously the way to get that is through the dick of the man responsible for her parents' murder. Makes perfect sense."

My back shot straight, the hairs on my arms standing on end. "I'm not fucking responsible for that shit."

It was a lie. I was absolutely responsible, but he didn't get to blame me. No one got to fucking *blame me*. God knew I blamed myself enough without owning someone else's feelings as well.

He groaned. "That's not what I meant. I know you're not responsible. Dad did that shit. No, strike that. *Malcom* did that. But I've been a cop long enough to know that victims need someone to blame. It wouldn't matter if you were Malcom Lowe's mailman. Victims will still rationalize a way to hold you responsible for doing your damn job delivering the unmarked package of ammunition to his house. This is why we changed our last name. To avoid the stigma of being related to that piece of shit. So this makes no goddamn sense that she would come to you knowing you were related to that man. I bet she's fucked up in the head. Probably has a shrine to Malcom at her house."

I glanced over my shoulder to make sure the door was still closed and kept my voice low. "She's not fucked up in the head. Well, no worse than I am."

"It's been two weeks. You can't possibly know that. Why the hell did you let her in your damn house? Does Rosie know she's her mother?"

"No. Relax. Rosalee doesn't know anything. Look, I'm not happy about this, either. But she showed up squeaky clean. She's got money, a good lawyer, no record."

"Do not give me that bullshit. She lifted over ten grand worth of property from your apartment."

"Yeah, but her prints weren't a match to any that the cops took from my place. They couldn't even charge her with that."

"See. I'm telling you. That bitch knows what she's doing. She knew enough to cover her damn tracks that night. What about child endangerment, abandonment—hell, neglect? Hang her from the rafters for that shit."

"Right. So she can walk into the courtroom and defend herself by explaining, on record, that she was suffering from a PTSD episode, reliving the day *my father* killed *her parents* when she made the decision to give me the baby?"

"And how many hospitals, police stations, and fire stations did she pass on the way to your place that night? There are legal and safe ways to do what she did. And she picked none of them. I wouldn't trust that woman with a goldfish, much less my daughter."

"You do not have to tell me shit I already know. I don't trust her. Which is why a custody battle scares the piss out of me. What the hell am I supposed to do if a judge orders me to give her to Hadley even every other weekend? You know good and damn well how much the legal system favors mothers over fathers. That is not a risk I can afford to take. And let's not even pretend that the rake through the coals I would get after the public found out about Dad and her parents wouldn't play into that decision. I could be father of the fucking year and I'd still be the villain."

"Shit," he mumbled. Forget about being my brother, Chief of Police Trent Hunt knew I was right about that.

"Look, I'm playing this smart. She volunteered for six months of supervised visitation. So far, she's been agreeable and understanding. I'm not sure how long that will last, but I've got my fingers on the pulse over here. We haven't told Rosie anything, so right now Hadley is just… Hadley the art teacher. If she hangs around long enough, we'll cross that bridge of lies when we get there."

"I don't like this. I don't like it at all."

"You are not alone in that. But it is what it is at this point."

"How's your husband handling it?"

I barked a laugh. "Ian is scared to death about me being scared to death. I've decided to be nice to her to avoid any further conflict. But he's under no such obligation, so I'm pretty sure he's angling at being a dick to see if he can run her off."

"For the record, I'm on his team."

Grinning, I rose to my feet when I heard voices on the other side of the door. "I'd be disappointed if you weren't. Listen, I gotta go."

"Do me a favor and use some of your fancy money to buy a set of prosthetic thumbs so you can keep me in the loop. I don't have good feelings about this."

The door opened and Hadley and her overflowing bag-o-crap appeared on the other side.

"Will do. We'll talk soon. Tell Jenn I said to fuck off."

He laughed, and as I pulled the phone away from my ear, I heard him call out, "Jenn, Cav said hi!"

Tucking my phone in my back pocket, I plastered on a smile. It should have disturbed me at how easy that smile was when I saw her. "You guys done?"

Hadley pointed at her invisible watch. "Three o'clock on the dot."

"Perfect. I'll walk you to your car."

Her body sagged. "Oh, God. Are we going to have another *talk*?"

"No, smartass. I was just trying to be nice."

She brought a hand up to her chest. "Oh, wow. I knew the unicorn butt was good, but I didn't expect all this fanfare."

I shook my head. She was funny.

I fucking hated that she was funny.

Predominantly because I fucking *loved* that she was funny.

She turned around to where Rosalee was standing in the hallway, holding Alejandra's hand.

"Bye, Rosalee. See you in few days, okay?"

"Don't forget. I want to draw the horn."

"No prob, Bob."

Rosalee cackled. "My name's not Bob!"

I couldn't see Hadley's face, but I could hear the smile in her voice. "All right, all right. See you later, alligator?"

Rosalee beamed up at her. "I'm not an alligator, either!"

"See you soon, baboon?"

"Hadley!"

"Gotta go, buffalo?"

My girl doubled over in laughter. "Buffa-what?"

Hadley kept going. "Take care, polar bear? Better shake, rattle snake? Be sweet, parakeet?"

Rosie was laughing so hard that she couldn't even get a reply out.

"How about this, then?" Hadley cleared her throat and bowed low. "I'll see you soon. Have a g-*llama*-rous day."

Okay, fine. She was funny…and a touch weird.

Rosalee loved it. After rushing forward, my little girl threw her arms around Hadley's legs, squeezing her tight.

I sucked in a sharp breath, my whole body coming alert. It wasn't long and lingering the way she hugged me, but it was huge no matter what package it came in.

At least in my eyes.

Rosie sprinted away, casually calling, "Bye, Hadley," over her shoulder.

Alejandra came forward with wide eyes and her signature gentle smile, closing the door.

Hadley and I stood there in silence for several beats. She

had her back to me, her chest rising and falling with labored breaths, the emotion swirling around her nearly choking me.

"Hadley?" I whispered.

Her red ponytail swayed, and she slowly pivoted. A huge smile showed on her face along with a stream of tears.

"Are you okay?"

She swiped at her cheeks. "Yeah. I just… I really love that kid."

I had a daughter; women crying were my kryptonite. Or that's what I told myself as I shoved a hand into my pocket to keep from reaching out to her. "She seems to be pretty fond of you too."

She pointed to her face. "See, this is why you can't be nice and walk me to my car. Some walks of shame are best done alone."

Shame. Shit. She thought crying because her daughter had hugged her was somehow filled with shame. If she only knew all the times Rosalee had cut onions in my eyes over the years.

"Why's it a walk of shame?" I asked. "You just drew a phenomenal unicorn butt. It should be a walk of pride."

She laughed, using her shoulder to dry her face. "You're right. Maybe I've missed my artistic calling all these years. R.K. Banks is nothing but an imposter for the real UK Bottoms."

My brows shot up. "UK Bottoms, really?"

"Eh. It was the best I could come up with on short notice. I didn't want to go with the obvious Hairy Butts."

I blinked, and her only reply was a shrug.

Hefting her bag up on her shoulder, she started toward her car.

I fell into stride beside her. "Well, I'm glad we could help you sort that out. You can mail my consultant fees directly to my office."

"Oh, please. You haven't seen my bill for the art classes yet. Let's just assume they cancel each other out."

"Fair enough."

When we reached her car, she leaned inside to put her bag on the passenger seat. Then she propped her arm on the door. "Can I ask for a favor?"

Here it was. The moment Ian and Doug had warned me about. A week of good behavior and she was now going to ask for a favor. A loan maybe, though I'd looked up her paintings online and she'd been telling the truth. They sold for a hot penny even at resale.

"Sure," I replied tightly.

Her gaze drifted from the house to the ground before coming back to me. "I was wondering if you'd be okay with me calling her Rosie sometimes."

My head snapped back. "What?"

"The last thing I would want to do is upset you or her. And I promise you I would never dare tread on Rosie Posie. That's special and all you. But I've heard Alejandra call her Rosie a few times and I like it. My family was big on nicknames." She swallowed hard and chewed on her bottom lip before continuing. "I don't think I ever remember my dad saying Hadley. It was always Haddie. Anyway...I completely understand if you'd rather me not. It hasn't been long but I thought—"

That all-too-familiar guilt settled in my stomach as she prattled on and on about a damn nickname. To my knowledge, no one had ever *asked* me if they could call her Rosie. It was simply the logical shortened version of Rosalee.

"Hadley..." I trailed off, unsure of how to say, *Holy shit, you don't have to ask me permission for something so small,* all the while maintaining boundaries because the next thing she asked for might not be so small.

"You know what, forget I asked. We can have this discussion in a few months when things aren't so...new." She climbed into her car and started to shut the door when I caught the top of it.

"Wait."

She stabbed the start button before fumbling with her seat belt. "Caven, it's okay. Really. I understand. I shouldn't have asked."

Walking around to the opening, I rested my forearm on the roof and bent down so I could see her. Her chin was to her chest as she peered at her lap.

"Hey," I said softly. "Look at me." I blanched when her bright-green eyes came up, tears filling them all over again. "I don't mind if you call her Rosie. And I hate that you had to ask me that, and worse that you were notably nervous while you did it. But I *appreciate* it. I know this isn't easy on you. And the fact that you recognize that it's hard on me too, well...that means a lot. So, thanks."

"I'm trying, Caven. It's such a weird position to be in. I feel like she's mine in my heart, but then I know she's yours in every other way. The lines are all so blurry."

I dug my wallet out of my back pocket and slipped out the picture I always carried inside. I updated it every year on her birthday, and despite Hadley's reappearance, that year had been no different. It was the first picture my baby didn't look like a baby anymore. Laughing in the backyard with bubbles all around her, she resembled a teenager more than the eight pounds of terrifying I'd held in the hospital.

Passing the laminated photo to Hadley, I said, "She's not

blurry though. I think, no matter what happens, as long as she's our focus, everything else will be clear."

She bit her bottom lip, more tears welling in her eyes. "Can I—"

"You can keep it."

Her shoulders rounded forward as she clutched the picture to her chest. "She's an amazing kid, Caven. You should be so proud."

"I am. Every single day."

"Thank you for this. It's the greatest gift anyone has ever given me."

"Yeah, well. The same could be said about you giving me her."

The tears finally fell as she nodded.

I nodded back, patting the top of her car and knowing it was time to go.

And then I stood there.

Staring at her.

Like.

A.

Fucking.

Idiot.

Again.

Much like the last time my legs had broken free of my brain, she put me out of my awkwardness. "Have a good day, Caven."

I shut her door, mumbling, "You too." Then I watched her drive away with the strangest feeling of dread settling in my stomach.

TWENTY

HADLEY

I put my car into park and looked at the clock on my dash.

Four-fifty. Great I had ten minutes to kill before I could go inside. That was going to be nothing short of torture to my kid-on-Christmas-morning soul.

Three months ago, I'd have been cursing Hump Day and its unfair distance to the weekend. Not that a photographer worked set hours or days of the week, but gallery buyers who would never pay R.K. Banks prices, marketing experts with no real experience, and all-around general spammers seemed to take a few days off. So, on the weekends, my life was blissfully quiet.

But now on Wednesdays, I saw Rosalee. Save for Saturday, when I also saw her, it was my favorite day of the week.

For the last three months, my life had been blissfully dull. Beth came over every Thursday morning and Saturday afternoon to get an update—a.k.a.: to interrogate me—on how my visits were going. She didn't trust Caven. She didn't trust this agreement. She was convinced that he had a nanny cam aimed at me, waiting for me to slip up and say or do something he could use against me in court.

She was right. He probably did.

At least, if he was smart, he did.

I didn't care. I wasn't slipping up with Rosie.

During my time *"teaching"* her art—yes, even I was using air-quotes now—I'd highly underestimated a four-year-old's attention span. We'd made it through Roy G Biv and… Well, that was about it educationally speaking. But she was still learning, even if it was things like tie-dying T-shirts and making friendship bracelets. Come on. Braiding was a necessary skill for a child. Especially one with hair like mine who would look like she'd stuck her finger in an electrical socket if she didn't dry it before going to bed. Trust me, last-minute braids came in handy.

Besides, I loved doing all the silly arts and crafts with her. When I was a kid, my mom used to make a big deal out of our projects. She'd kept boxes upon boxes of all the knickknacks we'd made together over the years.

Now, I had boxes and boxes of stuff Rosalee had created. We made two of everything, sometimes three, so sneaking one out in my bag at the end of our time together wasn't a big deal. I had big plans to decorate my studio with her work as soon as the contractors were finished. Which, let's be honest, at the rate they were going, it might have been never.

Though that would give me time to gather more pieces from the Rosalee Hunt collection. I just hoped it wasn't long enough for me to add her high school diploma.

If I'd thought I'd loved her the first time I saw her, nothing had prepared me for getting to know her. She was so damn smart.

And sweet.

And funny.

And bright.

And…*everything*.

My heart was so full when I was with her that it actually hurt.

And then, when I inevitably had to say goodbye for a few more days, it hurt even more.

It was ridiculous, but I cried pretty much every time I left her. I'd missed so much time with her, and two days a week was *not* enough.

But I was going to roll with it.

I'd given Caven my word.

Surprisingly, Caven and I were getting along too.

Things were still tense, and he never left me alone with Rosalee. But he no longer sat at the end of the dining room table as we worked. He hovered—always within eyesight or earshot, which was relatively easy in his open-layout living area. But, now, he gave us our space, or at least the illusion of it. Either way, I was grateful.

I turned my car off and started inspecting my nails. I missed the days when I could keep a manicure. Painting was hard on my hands, but if I was going to master the R.K. Banks strokes now that I was a one-man team, it required a lot of practice. Like, every-waking-moment-I-wasn't-with-Rosalee practice.

My phone vibrated on the seat beside me.

Caven: You can come in. No use sitting in the car.

Of course he'd seen me when I'd pulled up. He left the gate open when he was expecting me. I'd been early before, once by about fifteen minutes, and he'd never texted to invite me in.

See? Progress. Sweet, sweet progress.

I smiled and typed out a reply.

Me: Are you sure? I didn't realize I was so early.
Caven: What project did you bring for tonight?

Me: Paper flowers? Is that okay?

Caven: Glitter?

Me: No.

Caven: More of that slime shit?

Me: Nope.

Caven: Dye that's going to stain my back deck again?

I rolled my eyes. It was literally three droplets that had splashed off my tarp.

Me: No. Just coffee filters, markers, and pipe cleaners.

Caven: Then yes. You can come in early. She's been frothing at the mouth for you to get here, and just a heads-up, Ian picked her up from preschool today. They went out to an early dinner and she had her first and last Coke. She's been bouncing off the walls since she got home. If you can get her to sit down longer than ten minutes, I'll be impressed.

Me: Challenge accepted.

I'd barely gotten my bag out of the back before I heard her voice.

"Hadley!" She sprinted down the driveway at a full gallop.

Smiling, I cupped my mouth and yelled back, "Rosie!"

She ran all the way over to me, careening into my legs and giving me one of those tight squeezes I adored.

"Guess what?" she shouted, her voice echoing off the brick driveway.

"What?" I replied just as excitedly.

"I drew a picture of a unicorn at school and my teacher said it was the best unicorn she has ever seen so she hung it on the wall and I get an award next week!"

177

My mouth fell open in both real and exaggerated surprise. "You're getting an award?"

"Yes!" she screamed, throwing both arms over her head.

I set my bag down and squatted in front of her. "What kind of award? Best drawing? Best artist? Best all-round?"

She shrugged. "I don't know."

She wasn't a baby anymore, but she was still so young.

And she was already getting a freaking award.

In art.

Just like her mother.

Hell, just like her grandmother too.

I opened my arms wide and she didn't delay in coming in for a long hug.

"Oh my goodness, Rosie. I am so proud of you."

She kept her arms around my neck as she leaned away. "Can you come? When they give me my award? Will you be there?"

My stomach knotted when I saw Caven standing on the front steps, watching us with his expression unreadable. There was no way he was going to let me go to something like that.

Our sweet progress was not nearly up to inviting me to school functions yet. No matter how much I wanted to go.

"Oh…um, I'm not sure. I might have to work that night."

Her whole beautiful face fell. "Noooo, I want to come."

"I know. I, uh…" God, her puppy-dog eyes were going to be the end of me. "We'll see, okay?"

Her smile returned. "Okay."

The loss was staggering when she backed away.

She went straight to my bag and started rummaging through. "What'd you bring today?"

I stood up. "Well, I brought paper flowers, but that was before I knew I would be working with an award-winning artist. Would you like to teach *me* anything today?"

She giggled and took my hand, leading me to the front door. "I could teach you to make bath bombs. I got a kit for my birthday, but Daddy doesn't like bath bombs."

I shot a smile to Caven when we got close. "How in the world does your daddy not like bath bombs?"

His lips hiked into a distant relative of the smile family. "Because Rosie opened the bath bomb kit someone gave her for her birthday alone in her bathroom, without permission, and spilled the powder that you use to make them all over the floor. Then, instead of telling me that she'd spilled it, she covered it with her rug and replaced the crap with kinetic sand. She also failed to mention to me that it was kinetic sand when we made the bath bombs and tried to use them, thus clogging the drain in her tub to the tune of six hundred dollars."

"Oh, wow."

He glowered down at Rosalee, who had suddenly become fascinated with her shoes. "So, yeah. It's safe to say: I do *not* like bath bombs anymore."

I gave her arm a slight tug. "Sorry, kid. I'm with your dad on this one."

She gasped and craned her head back, the word traitor— if she'd known it—written all over her face.

I had to muffle my laugh, but Caven didn't even try. "You hear that, Rosie girl. Hadley agrees with me."

She swung a scowl to her father. "When I have my farm and make bath bombs with my llamas, you are not invited."

He clutched his chest. "Oh, how you wound me."

A laugh sprang from my throat, the warmth and happiness radiating through my entire body. I loved watching Caven with her. There was nothing sweeter—or, coincidentally, sexier—than a daddy with his girl. Not that I was still obsessing about Caven or anything.

Like every day.

Every night.

And all the times in between.

No. I was over that.

Except for on Wednesdays and Saturdays when I could feel his presence like fingertips gliding up my spine.

"Can we make lots of flowers?" Rosalee asked, snapping me out of my Caven Hunt stupor.

"Absolutely. We can make a whole bouquet."

She tugged on my hand, dragging me past Caven, straight to our usual spot at the end of the dining room table. I got to work unloading all the supplies and doing my best to ignore the eighteen-year-old ache I felt in my chest for her father.

An hour later, Rosalee and I had made not one bouquet of flowers, but two. Caven was not wrong. The caffeine and sugar Ian had given her were running through her baby veins at full force. She was all over the place. Up and down getting a snack or a drink. Playing with the reversible sequins on her shirt. Talking at a million miles per minute. Had it not been for the fact that my time with her was already so limited, I would have given up on the flowers for the night.

But I feared that if I packed up, Caven wasn't going to let me just hang around for another hour and play with her in the backyard where she so desperately needed to burn off some energy.

So we kept cutting coffee filter paper flowers. Well,

mainly I kept cutting them, while she climbed in and out of her chair after picking up and dropping markers repeatedly.

"Hadley, look at me," she mumbled around the markers hanging out of her mouth like walrus teeth.

"Whoa! I thought kids were supposed to lose their teeth, not grow bigger ones." I plucked them one by one from her mouth. "Well, what do you know? I was right."

She laughed wildly. "I need a pink. This flower needs to be pink," she declared, standing up in her chair and putting her elbows on the table to reach across for the basket of markers.

"Sit down. I'll get—"

Her socked feet shot out from under her.

My heart slammed into my ribs as I saw it happen in slow motion, her lower body slipping off the chair, her torso sliding across the table as she struggled to cling to the flat surface. My mind screamed as panic ignited inside me. Dropping the scissors, I dove toward her, catching her before she hit the floor.

Though not before her mouth hit the edge of the table.

I slid off the chair with her in my arms, landing hard on my knees, chanting, "It's okay. You're okay."

And she was. I knew it, even as her big, green eyes filled with tears and a cry tore from her throat.

But that's when I realized *I* was not okay.

Because blood—oh my God, so much blood poured from her mouth.

The world in front of me tunneled, including the child crying in my arms.

But no matter where I was, the past or the present, one thing remained the same.

"Caven!" I screamed.

Eighteen years earlier...

"Dad, no!" he yelled just before the pain sliced through my side.

My ears rang from the sound of the gunshot echoing in the tiny kitchen, and the scream I'd been holding since I'd watched my father collapse finally ripped free from my chest, shredding my throat on its way out.

The boy protecting me fell backward, taking me down with him and causing my head to crack against the door. We both landed on the tile, his heavy body hitting me like another bullet, stealing the breath from my lungs.

I couldn't move.

I couldn't run.

I couldn't even scream again.

I was trapped beneath him, his body limp, our warm blood mingling and pooling at my side.

Everything hurt, yet as his father prowled closer, the fear was the most painful of all.

"No," I groaned before resorting to begging, but the word *please* wouldn't come out.

Squeezing my eyes shut, I turned my head into the boy's neck, ready for the horror to finally end, even if that meant dying.

At least then my mom would have been there.

And my dad.

Anyone who could make the fear slaying me from the inside out *stop*.

There was a grunt before the boy jerked, my heart lurching with him.

My eyes flew open just in time to see him land a kick in

his dad's stomach then scramble drunkenly to his feet. I was able to breathe again, but I was also left completely exposed.

Hot tears rolled down my cheeks as the gunman went tumbling down. My hero took early control, landing his fists across his face. But the bloodstain on his back from the bullet that had gone through us both was growing by the second.

My side was on fire, but I had to move. My boy wasn't going to win this fight. His dad was too strong. But there was nowhere to go. The way out was to get past them, and as they exchanged punches and banged into walls before rolling onto the floor, it was impossible.

I found my voice with another scream when the sound of the gun rang out once more, deafening me all over again. I scrambled on all fours, slipping in my own blood as I wedged myself into a corner.

The fighting continued.

The grunts. The groans. The sound of my sobs.

He was losing.

He was on his back.

That man was going to kill my boy, the only safety I had left. And just like with my mother, I had no idea how to save him.

Drawing my legs up to my chest, I begged the universe, the stars, the gods, and Jesus himself to help us.

And then, just as quickly as my hero had arrived when I'd been lying on the floor in the middle of the food court, holding my dead mother's hand, our savior appeared in the form of the big tattooed guy I'd seen hiding behind one of the tables.

Blood roared in my ears as I watched him enter the kitchen. He no longer looked like a frightened child, but rather a murderous man on a mission. His face was tight and his eyes were hollow pits, but his steps were filled with dangerous purpose that broke the dam inside me, flooding my system with hope.

Without hesitation, he dove into the fighting, tackling the gunman off my boy.

I tried to keep up, but it was all happening so fast.

My boy shouted for someone to get the gun.

His father cussed.

But the tattooed man said nothing.

Fists against flesh, heads against tile, and then a second later, just as it had started, a single gunshot ended it all.

The room fell silent, my pulse pounding in my ears was the only sound I heard.

The tattooed guy rolled off the pile first, the gun in his hand.

And I waited, holding my breath and praying to gods I wasn't sure existed that my boy would be next.

I rose to my knees, searching for any sign of life.

But he was so torturously still.

As far as I knew, I'd lost my entire family that day. But I still had him and I needed him to be okay.

If it was truly over, I needed him to be okay.

"Oh, God," I cried when he suddenly pushed up to his knees—swaying and unbalanced—revealing the gunman dead beneath him, a puddle of red haloing around him.

My boy's face was covered in blood, and it had already swelled to the point that he was unrecognizable. But his blue eyes felt like spotlights when they landed on me. "Are you..." He fell over to the side, catching himself on a hand, his other going around his bloody midsection.

My whole body shook, but nothing could have stopped

me from getting to him. I rushed toward him and threw my arms around his neck, holding him up as he tried to fall over.

He didn't return my embrace as he burst into loud sobs, his body shaking with every breath. "I'm sorry. I'm so sorry. I'm sorry. Oh, God, I'm so sorry."

He'd saved my life. I had no idea what he could possibly be sorry for.

"Stop," I choked out during my own hysterical fit of relief. "Please stop."

He never stopped though.

Not until the paramedics rushed in and dragged us apart.

TWENTY-ONE

CAVEN

The sound of Rosalee's cry hit me hard but it was Hadley's scream that shot straight to my central nervous system.

"Caven!"

I was up off the couch before my eyes found them across the room. Hadley was on her knees, beside the table, her face so pale and filled with fear that it nearly stopped me in my tracks. It was my baby girl crying in her arms that pushed me faster.

"What happened?" I barked.

Hadley shook her head, her eyes unfocused as she pushed to her feet and lifted our daughter in my direction.

"Daddy!" Rosalee cried as I plucked her into my arms. "I fell down." Blood seeped from her mouth, spiking my pulse, but she was alive and crying.

After years of practice, I could deal with the rest.

After marching her to the kitchen, I set her on the counter and snatched a paper towel from the dispenser. I dampened it before pressing it to her upper lip to clear away some of the blood.

"Tilt your head back so I can look at it." I instructed, and though she was still wailing, she did as she'd been told.

There was a nice gash on her upper lip, but her teeth were fine and the blood was already starting to slow.

"You're fine. Just breathe." I kept my hand on her thigh as I stretched toward the closest cabinet and retrieved a coffee mug. Filling it under the faucet, I gave her a reassuring smile. "You're good. Just a little busted lip. Let's rinse your mouth out. Cold water will help stop the bleeding."

Rosalee swished water around like she did after she brushed her teeth. When she repeated the process, the water came out almost clear this time, and I finally took a second to look for Hadley.

My heart stopped all over again the moment I saw her. A semi-truck's worth of guilt and understanding slammed into me. Her face was still so white, a stark comparison to her green eyes, that it made her appear almost supernatural. Her arms were drawn close to her chest, and her trembling hands were covering her mouth as she stared at Rosalee so intently that I wasn't sure she knew anyone else was in the room.

I actually wasn't sure she realized she was in that room anymore, either.

And I was terrified about where she could be.

"Hadley," I called.

Her eyes snapped to mine.

"Why don't you sit down, babe. You look like you're about to pass out."

She shook her head.

"Hadley," I repeated soft and slow. "She's good. Nothing to worry about. But I need you to go sit on the couch while I get her some ice. Okay?"

She just blinked at me for several seconds. "I... I just... I was... I didn't..." She looked back at Rosalee, who had now stopped crying and was watching Hadley with strange curiosity.

"Go sit down and I'll be right there."

Her vacant gaze ping-ponged between Rosalee and me, and then all at once, she darted through the living room, straight to the bathroom, and quietly shut the door behind her.

Rosalee looked at me, holding the paper towel to her mouth. "What's wrong with Hadley?"

A vise in my chest cranked down. "I think you scared her when you fell," I mumbled. "Listen, are you okay?"

She nodded and then ratted herself out. "I stood in the chair again."

I brushed her hair out of her face and kissed her forehead. "Do you see now why I always get on to you about that?"

She sighed. "Yeah."

I lifted her off the counter, putting her on her feet, and turned to the freezer. "Bunny or bear?" This wasn't my first accident rodeo. I had a whole selection of mini animal-shaped ice packs ready for moments like these.

"Bunny."

I passed her a frozen gel pack in the shape of a pink cartoon rabbit. "Why don't you take that up to your room for a little bit while I check on Hadley?"

"Can I watch my iPad?"

It was a school night, so she knew better. But I had no idea what was waiting for me on the other side of that bathroom door. "Yeah. Sure, baby."

"Yessssss," she hissed, taking off for the stairs at a full sprint, all blood and injuries forgotten.

"Hold on to the rail!"

She groaned, switching the ice pack to her other hand before taking the rail and disappearing to the second floor.

With nerves rolling in my stomach, I made my way down the hall to the bathroom, knocking with two knuckles when I arrived. "Hadley?"

Not even a door dividing us could hide the tears in her voice. "I'll...be right out."

Knowing she was hurting on the other side was enough to make me tear the damn thing off the hinges. Luckily, when I tested the knob, I found it unlocked.

"I'm coming in," I announced.

"What? No. Caven—"

But it was too late. I pushed the door open in time to find her scrambling off the floor. Black makeup and tears were streaming down her cheeks, but at least some of the color had returned to her face. It was red now. Anything was better than the ghostly white.

I shut the door and put my back to it. "She's okay."

"I know," she chirped, turning on the faucet to wash her trembling hands.

"It was just a busted lip. It happens with kids. More than you'd expect, actually."

"I'm sure... I've never done well with blood though. Even before...ya know. You can look it up. It's actually a common problem for a lot of people. I just get a little woozy when I see it. That's all."

That could have been true.

But we both knew it wasn't.

Her breathing was ragged and her movements were jerky, like she didn't have full control over her body yet. I knew all too well how that felt and it was killing me to see her trying to fight it back alone.

"Come here, Hadley."

She swiped under her eyes, refusing to look at me by focusing on the mirror. "It doesn't affect my ability to take care of her or anything. I would have been fine if—"

Shit. She thought I was questioning her ability to care for Rosalee. If that wasn't a gut punch, I didn't know what was.

"Come here, Hadley," I repeated, this time taking a step toward her.

Emotion clogged her throat as she forced out, "I would have been *fine*." A sob hit her and she supported herself with her hands on the vanity, her head hung low as she finished with, "Really."

After everything we'd been through, Hadley and I did not have the best relationship.

But there was something about her that made me *feel*.

I told myself that it was only because we had a connection far deeper than the one we'd made the night we'd created Rosalee.

We were two people who had experienced the inside of Hell and lived to see the other side. Every once in a while, the flames would still devour me. The least I could do was try to extinguish hers.

"Come here, Hadley," I whispered once more, pulling her into a hug.

She didn't resist, not for a second.

I'd seen this woman cry far too many times over the last few months.

The tears that had filled her eyes the day I'd first seen her at Rosalee's party.

The tears that had streamed down her face that night at the diner.

The tears that had dripped over her smile each and every time she left my house, still even three months later.

These tears were different though. They were formed in a place so dark that only a few people knew it existed. They were born in urgency and filled with fear, torn from your soul, leaving a gaping hole behind until it eventually felt like you were going to disappear altogether.

But you didn't disappear, no matter how much you wished you could.

And that made them the most terrorizing emotion of all because there was no escaping those tears.

The only thing you could do was hope there were enough pieces of you left to pick up when it finally passed.

So yeah, we didn't have the best relationship.

But I owed her. So, for Hadley, I'd stand there for the rest of the night, picking up the pieces while she was devoured by the task of losing them.

She cried into my chest, her arms circling around my waist and her hands fisting the back of my shirt.

"Caven," she murmured.

"Shhhh, I've got you. It's all right. Everything's good. You're good. Rosalee's good. Everybody's good," I whispered into the top of her hair.

"I froze, Caven. I just stood there. She was bleeding and I did nothing."

It made me an asshole, but relief washed over me like a warm summer wave. She wasn't lost in that mall. She was very much in my arms, in that bathroom, and filled with regret for something she couldn't control.

I slid a hand up her spine, pressing between her shoulders to bring her closer. "You didn't do nothing. You called for me."

"And then I stood there."

"Yeah. You stood there fighting back demons after you *knew* I had her. Don't twist this up in your head."

She suddenly tilted her head back, beautiful surprise registering in her red-rimmed eyes as she searched my face. "What?"

I didn't let her go purely because I wasn't sure I was done picking up her pieces yet—not because I liked the way the curves of her body felt flush with mine.

No. This was Hadley.

None of that mattered at all.

Or so I pretended as I peered down at her, so close I felt her every exhale.

"When she was nine months old, Ian and I were watching the Jets game. She'd just started pulling up on everything. I'd paid a company to come in and baby-proof my place. They were thorough. Seriously, I couldn't open the cabinets for a week." I smiled at the memory, but it was the almost imperceptible hitch of her mouth—which I was definitely not staring at—that eased the ache in my chest. "I had this big coffee table that they told me to get rid of because she could hit her head on the corners. So, being a good dad, I replaced it with a giant leather ottoman and bought a wooden tray to hold the remotes and stuff. Anyway, Ian and I were watching the game, and she was crawling around, playing at our feet. The next thing I knew, she started screaming, and when I looked up, she had blood in her mouth and smeared all over her face."

Hadley went solid in my arms, but I gave her gentle squeeze and kept talking.

"She'd somehow pulled up on the other side of the ottoman, and when her little legs gave out, she smacked her mouth on the tray." I closed my eyes, feeling the bile crawl up my throat. "I lost it. Seeing her. My baby girl covered in blood, I couldn't… I just shut down. I couldn't form a rational thought about how to fix it, but I knew I had to do something. So I jumped up, scooped her off the floor, and did the only thing I could think of to make her better." I cleared my throat to buy myself a second for the emotion to clear my voice. "I passed her to Ian."

Her face got soft. "Oh, Caven."

"Yeah. It was bad. I mean…it wasn't *bad*. She was fine two seconds later, eating little puffs out of his hand. But I was not okay in any way, shape, or form. And most of that was because I felt like I'd failed her."

She stared up at me with nearly hypnotizing understanding. So much so that I didn't move a muscle when her hand slid over my chest, the smooth pads of her fingers curling around the back of my neck, where she used her thumb to trace the underside of my jaw. "Oh, Caven."

Why did she keep saying my name?

Why did I fucking love hearing *her*, of all people, say my goddamn name like the vowels and consonants had been strung together for the sole purpose of rolling off her tongue?

I needed space.

I drew her impossibly closer.

"We're not normal people, Hadley. We won't ever have normal reactions to things like her busting her lip or cutting her finger. But we love her, and I've found that a very basic part of me will always ensure she's safe. Even if that means not being the one to fix things for her."

"What if I don't have that part?"

"You do. Because four years ago, you handed her to me."

She sucked in a deep breath, and just like that, the spell was broken. She blanched, and her arms fell away. It was the right thing to do—absolutely, one hundred percent, for both of us. We needed the distance to remember who the hell we were and, better yet, who the hell we *weren't*. And that was two people standing in a bathroom, minutes away from doing something seriously stupid—and, more than likely, seriously incredible.

Hadley had always been gorgeous, and I knew I'd always feel a certain draw to her, knowing what we'd shared in the past.

But that wasn't who Hadley and Caven would ever be in the future.

Regardless of how much my body objected when I released her.

"We should probably go check on her," she whispered, backing away.

"Yeah." I hooked a thumb over my shoulder. "I'll give you a few minutes. Let me know if you need anything."

I turned and pulled open the door.

"Hey, Caven?"

I didn't have the strength to look at her again. "Yeah?" I replied, my gaze trained on the handle of the door.

"Thank you." Her voice broke and the jagged edges of her gratitude raked across my skin.

I didn't deserve it, but I could make damn sure she knew I would always be there.

Putting my chin to my shoulder, I caught her gaze. "Anytime, Hadley. If you ever need someone who can understand, I'll be there. And not just about Rosalee."

She nodded, her eyes sparkling with the most profound

regret. "You too, okay? I'm here if you ever need to talk…or something."

Or something. That was what I was scared of.

As I forced myself out of that bathroom, I definitely wanted to take her up on the *or something.*

Fuck. My. Life.

TWENTY-TWO

CAVEN

"**D**addy, look!" Rosalee yelled when I reached the top of the stairs. She had her arms and legs stretched between the doorjambs, scaling to the top.

"Get down from there," I rumbled, closing in on her.

"Did you know I could do this?"

I folded her over my shoulder and carried her into her bedroom. "I know you just busted your lip, and I'm hoping not to add a broken leg to tonight's laundry list of injuries."

She bounced on her twin bed when I gently tossed her onto it. "Did Hadley leave?"

"She did. She told me to tell you bye for her."

"Why didn't she tell me herself?"

Because she'd been crying and neither of us wanted to explain to you why. Oh, and there was also the tiny little fact that I hadn't been able to keep my hands off her and nearly suffocated in the desire to kiss her in that damn bathroom. So, when the door opened, we both sprinted out of there in opposite directions like two feral cats. Ya know. The regular stuff.

I sat on the edge of her bed, knocking off approximately twelve stuffed animals in the process. "She…had an emergency and had to go."

"What kind of emergency?"

"Art."

"What kind of art?"

I pinched the bridge of my nose. My head was still a mess after my coulda, woulda, shoulda moment with Hadley. I was not prepared for an inquisition. "Paint."

"What happened to her paint?"

"Her…cat knocked it over. It got all over her carpet and her alarm went off and she had to rush home to clean it before it dried. Fingers crossed everything works out."

She narrowed her eyes. "Hadley doesn't have a cat."

I poked her belly. "You don't know that."

She squirmed, laughing. "Yes, I do. She's allergic to them. So I'm never getting one on my farm. But she's not allergic to llamas or emus, so I can have as many of those as I want."

"What the heck is an emu?"

"A really big bird."

I leaned back on the bed, spreading my arm wide in invitation, and she didn't delay in curling into my side. "I thought you were scared of birds. You once dove into shark-infested waters to escape a seagull at the beach."

"There weren't any sharks." She popped her head up, worry crinkling her nose. "Were there?"

"Nah. I'm kidding."

She lay back down, draping her arm across my stomach, going straight for the scar on my side.

She'd had an obsession with the two scars on my abdomen since she was a baby. She would lie on my chest or at my side, rubbing her chubby little fingers back and forth over the puckered flesh.

I'd hated it at first.

I hated those scars and the nightmares that accompanied them.

And I'd hated that something as pure and good as my Rosalee would even touch such filth.

But God was doing something right, because my baby girl loved them. Over time, I'd stopped associating them with how I'd gotten them and instead connected them with the perfection and comfort I felt as she fell asleep in my arms while stroking them.

And still, four years later, it didn't matter if I was wearing a shirt or not. That was where her hands always went.

"Did you know Hadley had a guinea pig when she was little?"

I kissed the top of her head. "Really?"

"Yeah, her sister named it Bacon. She thought that was a funny name, but I don't know why because she said it didn't eat bacon or anything. A guinea pig isn't a real pig. Did you know that?" She didn't take a breath long enough for me to answer. "It's a little guy with lots of hair. Well, not all of them have lots of hair. Hadley showed me a picture of one on her phone and it had no hair at all. It looked kinda gross. But I told her if she comes and visits me on my farm that I'll let her keep a guinea pig there."

"Wow, you are racking up some serious animals. Maybe you should start a zoo instead of a farm."

"Zoos have snakes. I hate snakes."

"But it will be *your* zoo, so you can have whatever animals you want."

She stopped rubbing my scar and contemplatively tapped her chin. "But then where will Hadley keep her guinea pig? I bet the elephants would step on it."

"Ah. Excellent point. Maybe stick to the farm."

"Yeah. Okay." She went right back to rubbing the scar. "Daddy?"

"Right here, baby."

"I love Hadley."

I closed my eyes, feeling the all-too-familiar squeeze in my chest. I had to clear the emotion from my throat before I could reply. "Oh, yeah?"

"Yeah. She's kinda weird sometimes. Like, she told me she dips her brownies in ranch dressing and she wraps her chicken nuggets in pickles."

"Say what?" I laughed.

"But she's really funny and good at art. And she always has her toenails painted. She told me that maybe soon we could ask if you would let her paint my toenails as long as we did it outside. And she told me not to let Jacob kiss me on the playground at school anymore because he might have cooties."

I sat up enough to look down at her. "Jacob kissed you?"

"Yeah, but don't worry. Hadley gave me my cootie shot."

This time, I bolted upright. "She gave you a shot?"

My girl took my hand, serious as a heart attack, and traced her fingers over my palm. "Circle, circle, dot, dot, now you've had your cooties shot."

I breathed a sigh of relief and fell back against the bed. "Don't scare me like that."

She was quiet for a second. "Hadley was scared tonight."

"Yeah. She's okay now though."

"What was wrong?"

I ruined her life. "She just doesn't like blood."

Rosalee and I had these types of conversations a lot. Not necessarily about Hadley, but since she was old enough to talk, we'd lie in her bed and shoot the shit. The conversation would start at point A and then jump to Y before heading back to J. Majority of our chats zigzagged through every letter of the alphabet before she got bored of cuddling with her old man and got up to play. This one would be no different.

I just didn't realize she'd jump to point Z so fast.

"Why don't you like Hadley?"

My chin snapped to my chest, where I found her peering up at me. "What? Who said I didn't like her?"

"When she came to my birthday party, you yelled at her. And then when she came to teach me art, you used to sit at the table and give her the mean daddy face. Now, you look sad when you look at her from the couch when you pretend to work."

Jesus. Kids noticed *everything*.

I rolled to my side and dragged her up to share the pillow. "I don't hate Hadley, baby."

"Then do you love her? Because tonight you called her babe. That's what Jacob calls me sometimes."

I blinked "Okay, first of all, I need Jacob's last name because toddler Rico Suave and I are going to have a long talk."

"Who's Rico Sway-vay?"

I shook my head. "It doesn't matter. Listen, I don't want you worrying about me and Hadley. I like her just fine." This included her body. Her hands. Her lips. Her... Son of a bitch. I had to get my shit under control when it came to that woman.

"Are you friends?"

Shit. I had no idea how to answer that. Things had been going well with me and Hadley; we were casual and courteous with each other. Despite the urge to rip her clothes off, I wasn't sure that would categorize us as friends.

But Rosalee didn't need to know any of that.

"Yeah. Hadley's my friend."

She suddenly sat up and crisscrossed her legs. "Oh, good. Then can you invite her to my awards thing at school? She told me she had to work. But if you ask her, I bet she'll come. She always looks at you like this." She folded her hands in front of her chest and stared dreamily into the distance while batting her eyelashes. "I think she likes you."

It shouldn't have mattered. After all, my kid was four. She was hardly qualified in deciphering human emotions attached to expressions. But tell that to the spike of my pulse like fucking Jacob on the playground.

"She looks at me like that?"

"Yep. When you look at your computer, she looks at you. And when you look at her, she looks at me. And then, when you both look at each other, her cheeks get pink and she looks down at the table and smiles. Jacob told me at snack that she probably loves you."

My jaw slacked open. "You were talking to Jacob about me and Hadley?"

She gave me a duh side-eye that did not bode well for me during her teenage years and replied, "He's a love expert, Daddy."

Fuck. I was going to have to find a way to convince Jacob's parents to have his lips surgically removed—or at the very least pay for his tuition at the preschool across town.

I toyed with the replica of my mother's heart necklace around her neck. "What if we make a deal? You stop worrying about how Daddy and Hadley look at each other and I'll invite her to the awards ceremony."

"Yesssss!" she hissed, all but diving off the side of the bed.

Clearly, our conversation was done and she was off to

other caffeine-induced shenanigans. But as I stared up at her ceiling, my mind drifted back to Hadley and the way she'd breathed my name while stroking the curve of my jaw.

It was the most ridiculous, asinine, and flat-out idiotic thing that had ever passed through my head. But dammit...

I should have kissed her.

TWENTY-THREE

HADLEY

I held my palm less than an inch away from my face. "He was this close."

"You were freaking out about Rosalee bleeding. He was trying to calm you down. I think you're reading into this a tad," Beth said before squirting water into her mouth like a professional soccer player while sitting on the other end of my couch.

I'd texted her that it was an emergency when I was on my way home. She'd arrived covered in sweat, straight from the gym, but I had to give it to her. She'd nearly beat me to my house.

"I'm not reading into anything."

"He still won't even leave you alone with the kid, but now, you think he's trying to get in your pants?"

"I didn't say anything about my pants. I just said he was looking at me like he wanted to kiss me. And then possibly eat me like a snack."

She arched an eyebrow. "I know you've been out of the business for a while, but that usually requires no pants."

I sighed. "I'm serious, Beth. There was something there tonight. And not just on my side of the equation. He was feeling something. I know he was. I should have kissed him."

"You should *not* have kissed him."

"I should have. God, why didn't I kiss him?"

She leaned back against the cushion and gaped at me. "Jesus, what are you thinking right now?"

"He was two seconds away from doing it himself. I could have sped the process up for both of us."

"Are you listening to yourself? Because this is insane. And the fact that you wasted my time by calling me over here instead of telling me to meet you at the loony bin, where you so obviously need to be, is just rude."

I stared off into the distance, a chill pebbling my skin as I thought about his hard body. "It was like a magical bathroom. He walked in there and brought this whole ocean of calm with him. Which is funny because Caven is usually the storm. But then he hugged me. It was so sweet and so real."

"You know what else is real? Your delusions."

"You weren't there. You didn't see the look on his face. It was like he couldn't stop himself. He was sta—" A blast of cold water struck me in the face. "Shit!"

She lowered her water cannon/water bottle and glared at me. "I'm sorry! But someone had to do it."

Using the bottom of my T-shirt, I patted dry my face. "What the hell is wrong with you?"

"You, *Hadley. You* are what's wrong with me." She rose to her feet and loomed over me. "You promised me you could handle this. You swore up and down when I brought you back from Puerto Rico that you could handle being around him without making eight-year-old googly eyes at him. And here we are, a little over three months later, arguing about whether you should have kissed him?" She scoffed and crossed her arms over her chest, luckily not aiming the water bottle at me again. "He is not fifteen-year-old Caven Lowe anymore. He's Caven *Hunt*. The father of *your* daughter who, thanks to the bullshit agreement you signed, owns your time with Rosalee for the next three months. Literally and figuratively: Do not screw this up."

"What if he kisses me? What if *he* screws this up?"

She rolled her eyes. "Please just let me set you up with a guy. A few orgasms and a big dick would go a long way in diluting the case of the sexual insanity you've currently got going on."

"You know what? I changed my mind. Go home. I need a better best friend."

"No. What you need is a dick…and not the fictional one that belongs to Caven Hunt in your secret little fantasies."

"He produced a child. I'm ninety-nine percent sure his dick is not fictional."

"It could have fallen off in the last four years. You don't know."

I cut my gaze to the wall, my face blooming with heat. "He tucks to the left."

She gasped dramatically, as only crazy-ass Beth could. "You've been checking out his cock."

"No!" I chewed on my bottom lip. "Well…maybe once… on accident though."

"Explain to me how one *accidentally* checks out a man's cock?"

"He was wearing particularly fitted slacks that day. It showed when he sat down. What was I supposed to look at?"

"Uhhh…his face?"

"Trust me. If you saw the way he was looking at me tonight, you'd know that his face is far more dangerous than the outline of his penis."

"Ew, don't say penis. You're ruining my mental image of Caven tucking his *cock* to the left."

My mouth fell open. "You did not just say that."

"What? He's a sexy man. I'm allowed to imagine. You should try it next time instead of gawking like a perv."

"Yep. Time to go." I unfolded off the couch and headed to the door. Snatching it open, I waved her out like a flight attendant pointing to the nearest emergency exit. "As my attorney, can you please draw up the paperwork ending our friendship tonight?"

She followed after me, stopping short of the threshold. "I'm only trying to be real here. You two hooking up has the worst kind of bad news written all over it." She placed her hand on my side and pointedly gave me a squeeze over the round scar that, instead of disappearing with time, had been stretching and growing with me. "Don't make this any more complicated than it already is."

My shoulders sagged as disappointment rained over me. Deep down, I knew she was right. He wasn't Caven Lowe anymore, but the problem was: The longer I got to know Caven Hunt, the more I was starting to like him too.

He was a good dad with a tough exterior, but on the inside? His girl made him all soft. And let's be honest, his sense of humor was as dry as the Sahara, but his subtle smiles and lip twitches were going to be the end of me. I loved that he didn't laugh at everything. The rich and deep sound was so rare that it felt like I'd struck gold when he gave it to me. Sure, I hated it when he apologized, but I adored the way he wasn't too proud to show vulnerability. And most of all, I was addicted to the way he could not only read my emotions, but understand them too.

In a lot of ways, I wished he weren't Caven Lowe, because then it wouldn't have mattered that I wanted to crawl into his arms and never leave.

But it did matter and wishing had never gotten me any-where before. This time would be no different.

"I hate when you make sense."

"I know. But one of us has to." She pulled me in for a chaste hug. "What about this? If you happen to be right about the way he was looking at you tonight and he tries to kiss you in the future and you are physically unable to dive out of the path of his lips, I give you permission to kiss him back for eight seconds before shoving him away, telling him he's lost his mind, and storming out. Okay?"

I smiled big. "Eight seconds, huh?"

"If a bull rider can do it and walk away without a broken heart, so can you."

"Awesome. Me and the bull riders."

"Speaking of bull riders, there's this country bar we should hit for your birthday. Jeans so tight you can be a little perv and check out what side all the cowboys tuck on."

I rolled my eyes. "I already told you I'm not celebrating my birthday."

"Well, if you change your mind, you know I'm here." Waving over her shoulder, she walked toward her car, shout-ing, "Get some sleep tonight! You look like shit!"

I probably did look like shit after having lost it at Caven's, but that wasn't why she'd mentioned it. The concern on her face every time she'd *stopped by*—a.k.a.: checked on me—over the past few weeks had been obvious. She hated that I was spending so much time in my makeshift studio trying and failing to make one single piece that didn't feel like a fraud.

I needed sleep in the worst kind of way. She didn't need to point it out to me.

After locking up my house and dragging my tired body

up the stairs, I barely managed to wash my face and brush my teeth before collapsing into bed. It was just past nine and I had a hot date with the backs of my eyelids when my phone chirped on my nightstand.

Caven: She's finally asleep and I've banned all caffeine from the house.

Uhhhh… What was happening? Caven didn't text me unless it had something to do with Rosalee's "art classes." Things like, *Why the hell is there glitter on my egg carton?* or *You spilled tie-dye on my deck!* But never, not once, had he reached out to me to tell me she was asleep.

Me: Hey, I think you meant to send that message to someone else. This is Hadley.
Caven: I know who it is.

Okay, so that theory was out the window. The problem was: Without reading into this far more than the I'm-going-to-kiss-you smolder he'd given me in the bathroom, I was out of other theories as to why he was texting me.

Me: Oh. Okay.

Yep. That was all I could come up with to reply. *Oh. Okay?*
Idiot.

Caven: I just wanted you to know that she was okay. She didn't even mention her mouth again after you left.

Holy smokes. Was he reaching out to me because *he* was worried that *I* was still worried? How freaking sweet was that? Sitting up in bed, I propped a pillow behind my back and grinned at the phone.

Me: Aw, thank you for that. I hate that she got hurt, but I promise it won't happen again.

Caven: Oh, it will absolutely happen again. Maybe not from standing on the chair, but she'll do something else. We haven't had stitches yet, but with as accident prone as she is, it's only a matter of time.

Me: Yeah. Sorry about that. She got that from my side of the family. I broke my arm when I was five after slipping on a banana peel.

Caven: A banana peel? You're kidding, right?

Me: Nope. True story. My mom was making banana bread and one of those death traps fell off the counter. My dad was pretending to be a monster, chasing me around the house. I didn't see it before it was too late. It was a scene straight out of The Three Stooges.

Caven: Wow, The Three Stooges? How old are you again?

Me: 26.

Caven: I know how old you are. I was making fun of your Three Stooges reference. Clearly it was a fantastic joke.

And he was now making jokes.
Via text.
To me.
His archnemesis.
Only I wasn't his archnemesis anymore.
I was a woman he was texting and telling jokes to at

nearly nine p.m. because he was worried about me worrying about Rosalee.

Oh, Beth was *so so so* wrong about me reading into that situation in the bathroom.

I bit my bottom lip to suppress my smile as if he could see me.

Me: Yeah. My parents didn't let us watch TV when I was growing up, but every now and then, my dad would sneak us down to the library when they were showing The Three Stooges on the big projector.

Caven: No TV at all?

Me: Nah. They were old school. If it plugged into the wall, we weren't allowed to have it. We had books and art. That's about it.

Caven: How'd you get into photography then?

Holy shit. We were having a conversation. Complete with questions and everything. My fingers couldn't fly across that keyboard fast enough.

Me: Well, young whippersnapper, back in the Dark Ages, there was this thing called film. It didn't operate on a fancy-schmancy screen or require any technology, so Mama Banks couldn't say no.

Caven: Smartass.

Me: My mom was into photography long before I was. She was the most talented photographer I'd ever seen. Unfortunately, she died while I was still taking pictures on a disposable, so she didn't teach me much more than the basics, but I figured it out in the end, I guess.

His reply was much slower that time, and I watched the text bubble dancing on the screen for well over a minute.

Caven: Shit, Hadley. I'm sorry. I shouldn't have brought up your parents.
Me: You didn't bring them up. I did. And it's okay. I like talking about them. The memories fade slower that way.
Caven: I still feel like an ass given the circumstances.
Me: Yeah, well. You shouldn't. If anyone should feel like an ass, it's me. I dry-heaved into your toilet today without even lifting the seat. So rude.
Caven: Jesus, you were dry-heaving?

Okay. So that hadn't gone as planned. I'd thought I could distract him from feeling guilty for bringing up my parents only to make him feel guilty about me dry-heaving in his bathroom.

Me: What? Who said anything about dry-heaving? Did Rosie calm down after I left?
Caven: Nice change of subject. And no. She was a wild woman all night. The only time she settled down was to tell me about Jacob being a love expert.
Me: Awwww. That's so cute.
Caven: Jacob is not cute. But I appreciate you giving her the cooties shot. I'm trying to keep my medical expenses down this year. I'll need the bail money for when I go toe-to-toe with Jacob's father.
Me: Did she happen to mention that Jacob's dad is a former professional heavyweight boxer turned stuntman?
Caven: Oh please. I could take him. Wait...are you serious?

Me: Maybe. I can't remember exactly what she said. It was either former professional heavyweight boxer turned stunt-man or proctologist. Definitely one of the two.

Caven: Rosalee knew the word proctologist?

Me: No. I was just trying to save you from the horror of hearing, "Jacob's dad is a doctor who looks at the inside of people's butts."

Caven: How big of a box would I need to mail a four-year-old boy to China?

I laughed, my smile so wide that it was almost painful. God, this felt good. Easy and comfortable, the way I'd always secretly hoped it could be between me and Caven. I sucked in a deep breath, holding it as if I could inhale this moment and engrain it into my subconscious to revisit in the future when things inevitably got hard again.

Me: I don't have much experience in that department. But I have faith you could take the butt doctor toe-to-toe. So maybe a talk with his parents would be the safer choice.

Caven: Good point.

Me: Hey, did Rosalee finish the paper flowers I left for her?

Caven: Sorta. She colored an entire roll of toilet paper then tried to hide it by flushing it down the toilet along with two markers. The plumber just left.

Me: She did not.

Caven: Oh yes she did. But I was kidding about the plumber. I was able to fish everything out with a wire coat hanger from the dry cleaner. Not my finest hour, but it didn't cost me six hundred dollars either, so I'll chalk it up as a victory.

Me: Wow.

Caven: Yeah. So that was my night. How was the rest of yours?

I blinked at the phone.

Okay… So, *now*, we were just two people chitty-chatting via text at nine p.m. like this was any given Wednesday night and not the first time in…*ever.*

I inhaled through my nose. Okay. I could do this. Not a problem.

Me: It was good.

Yes. That was the smart and intriguing response that would surely incite hours of conversation, break down the barriers between us, and kick off a whole new future.

He'd reached out to me and I'd given him the riveting answer, *It was good.*

Outstanding!

I leaned my head back against the headboard and cursed my near-superhero abilities to notice what side a man tucks when he dresses, but not reply to a text message with more than three words. It was as if my brain had no idea there was a damn delete button.

Caven: Good. I'm glad you're feeling better. Listen, Rosalee has this end of the year awards ceremony at her preschool on Friday. I promised her I'd invite you. Don't feel obligated to come or anything.

I sat straight up in bed, nearly dropping my phone.

Me: I'll be there!!!

My brain screamed a reminder to write more than three damn words.

Me: I mean… I would love to come. Thank you so much for inviting me.

Me: She told me she was getting an art award and I desperately wanted to come, but I didn't want to make things weird if you didn't want me there. I know things are still tense between us, so I couldn't blame you.

Me: I just love her so much and I'm trying really hard not to make any waves with you.

Me: And I think for the most part it's been going really well.

Me: Well, except for tonight when I was dry-heaving in your toilet without lifting the seat.

At this point, my brain screamed that one-hundred and two words was probably too many, and I threw my phone on the bed to force my damn non-deleting fingers to stop.

My phone vibrated, and I did a ten count of breathing exercises before gathering the nerve to look at his response.

Caven: Who said anything about dry-heaving?

I laughed, pure giddiness swirling in my head.

I'd mentioned dry-heaving. *Again.* Because I was still an imbecile.

But I was an imbecile who had just been invited to Rosalee's school, where I could watch her get an art award.

Me: You have no idea how much this means to me.

Caven: I'm starting to figure it out.

Caven: It's Friday at six thirty. I'll forward you the invite the school emailed me. And every kid in the school gets an end of the year award. So, don't get too excited.

Too late for that.

Me: Thanks, Caven.

Caven: No problem. Have a good night.

Me: You too.

I didn't have a good night. I didn't even have a night at all. Because no sooner than I realized he wasn't going to text me again, I threw the covers back, got dressed, and drove over an hour away to share the good news with my family.

Including leaving one of Rosalee's paper flowers on each of their graves.

TWENTY-FOUR

CAVEN

"Your daughter is a natural," the woman gushed over Rosalee's crooked tree painting hanging on the wall. She slanted her head from side to side while cupping her chin like we were standing at The Met and not the auditorium of a preschool.

"My girl's definitely talented." I smiled, glancing a few rows up to where Rosalee was giggling with her friend Molly. I was glad she was having fun, but I wished she didn't look so damn happy so I could use her as an excuse to make a break for it.

The woman clutched her pearls with her left hand, showing off her empty ring finger for at least the tenth time since she'd approached. "I don't think we've officially met?" She extended the limp fish of handshakes my way. "I'm Marilyn. Like Monroe, only a brunette." She laughed nasally, patting at the bottom of her short bob.

Unfortunately, her name was the only resemblance she had to the late American icon.

As the only single father at Rosalee's school, I didn't find it unusual for women to stop by and chat with me at school functions. But Marilyn was extra special, assuming you defined being a Grade-A bitch as special. She was the president of the PPTA (Preschool Parent-Teacher Association.) As if one of those were remotely necessary in a school with a five-to-one student-teacher ratio. But if there was ever a shortage of cray-ons, Marilyn was all over it. I'd been avoiding her like the plague since I'd heard her divorce from her plastic surgeon husband had been finalized. She was currently living on her alimony and never missed a Sunday service at the church where her ex and his new girlfriend attended services.

In short: She was drama in every sense of the word.

I took her hand in an awkward up-and-down shake that would have felt more natural had she been a Labrador retriever. "I'm Caven."

"Ooohh, how unique. I love that name." She trailed her finger down the front of my shirt in what I thought was sup-posed to be a seductive gesture.

"Thanks. I should probably go check on Rosalee."

Just Rosalee though. Not to see if Hadley had shown up yet.

For the tenth time.

In so many minutes.

I'd decided that, at some point of the last three-ish months, I'd suffered a stroke. My condition included: thinking about a woman I supposedly hated twenty-four-seven, imagining her ass as she bent over while I was in the shower, and waking up to her on the backs of my eyelids, naked and calling my name. Those symptoms hadn't produced many results on WebMD though.

But, dammit, there had to be a medical explanation out there somewhere.

Marilyn grabbed my arm, inching closer. "Don't be silly. We have ten minutes before the awards start. Come on. Let me buy you a drink." She burst into laughter, pointing to the water station in the corner. "I only wish they served alcohol at these functions. It would make them a lot more *interesting*, that's for sure." More loud obnoxious laughter, and her hand tightened on my forearm.

Gritting my teeth, I sent up a silent S.O.S. Though, as God's least favorite sinner, I wasn't expecting any kind of response.

Until…

"Sorry to interrupt."

I spun, finding Hadley behind me, a camera hanging around her neck and an uncomfortable grin splitting her mouth.

"Hey," I said, standing straighter, my entire body coming alert, reacting to her presence. I'd have to add that to my list of symptoms when I got home.

"I'll be out of your way in just a second. I was just wondering if you have a preference where I sat. I don't want to intrude or anything."

I blinked at her, because she had literally just intruded and I owed her a miracle for it. "You can sit with me and Ian."

Her eyes flashed wide, and her mouth formed the most ridiculous fake smile, showing off every one of her white teeth—and not in a good way. "Ian's here?"

"Well, not yet. But he's on his way."

"Oh, fun," she mumbled, focusing on her camera. Her long, red waves curtained her face off and I had to stop my hands from brushing them away.

"Come on. He's not that bad."

She peeked up. "The only time he's ever spoken to me, he told me there was nothing he wouldn't do for Rosalee and it'd do me well to remember that."

"Yeah, but he meant like egging your house or filing a

complaint with your homeowners' association because you left your recycle bin out overnight."

"I'm not so sure about that."

That time, I didn't bother trying to stop my hands. I gave her forearm a squeeze. "Relax. I'll protect you from Ian."

She tilted her head back and stared up at me, her cheeks turning the most brilliant shade of pink. "I know you will."

I smiled.

She smiled back.

Neither of us moved as the auditorium filled around us.

"Hi, I'm Marilyn." She shifted around me, my AB line segment with Hadley suddenly becoming a triangle. "Who are you?"

She smiled big and kind. "I'm Hadley."

Marilyn's face pinched as she gave her a quick once over. "Girlfriend?"

"No," Hadley and I answered in unison.

Marilyn's eyes narrowed, and her lips curled. "Sister? Secretary? Personal assistant?"

I had to give her credit. Hadley didn't have a hint of attitude as she replied, "Nope, nope, and nope."

"We should go sit down. It was nice meeting you, Marilyn." I rested my palm on Hadley's lower back and started to guide her out of the awkwardness, when Marilyn pulled the pin on my grenade.

"Are you Rosalee's mom?"

Hadley and I both froze midstep.

Before caving to my daughter's nagging to invite Hadley to come to the awards ceremony that night, I'd considered the possibility that someone would notice the resemblance between the two of them. I'd never imagined a scenario where anyone would have the gall to actually ask.

But I never should have underestimated the nosy and imprudent Marilyn Not-Monroe.

"You are," she breathed, wonder filling her eyes.

Hadley turned to stone. "I…uh…" She looked up at me and her panic made me hate Marilyn that much more.

"You know, we've always wondered why you were never around. My guess was that you died. Guess I won't be winning that betting pool." She smirked, slimy and arrogant.

Oh, this was not fucking happening. Nope. No fucking way.

"The betting pool?" I took an ominous step toward her. "Are you fucking kidding me?"

Her dull, boring, brown eyes flicked to mine. "It was a joke." She circled her long, pointed fingernail at Hadley. "But *you* have definitely been the topic of many a playground debates. Wait until I tell the other moms that you actually do exist."

Annnnnd I was done. All patience gone. All social courtesies out the window. The last thing I needed was the entire school gossiping about Hadley being Rosalee's mom. All it would take was one bratty kid parroting their mother to rock my daughter's world.

If and when that conversation happened, it wasn't going to be because of a rumor at fucking preschool.

"From here on out, Marilyn, you keep my family's name out of your mouth on the playground and everywhere else."

Her head snapped back. "Excuse me?"

Hadley tugged on my forearm and whispered, "Let it go, Caven."

But I couldn't let it go; too much was at stake. "You heard

me. Stay out of my family's business. Who she is or isn't does not make one bit of difference to you. And please, by all means, run back to your minions and let them know that I'm not fucking around about this. I hear one damn word about Hadley or Rosalee and I promise it won't end well for any of you."

"Well, then," she scoffed, thoroughly affronted.

I couldn't count the amount of fucks I did *not* give about Marilyn's porcelain feelings. "Say you understand."

She pursed her lips. "I understand you are an extremely rude man."

"Then you can only imagine how much ruder I could get should you not heed my warning to keep your mouth *closed*."

Grabbing Hadley's hand, I stormed off, dragging her behind me. The nerve of that woman was astounding. I knew I'd hate that damn school from the moment I'd pulled up and every single car in the parking lot was top-of-the-line luxury. Not to say that my vehicle wasn't, but I hadn't grown up with money, so I'd never acquired the sense of entitlement or holier-than-thou mindset that so often accompanied it.

Marilyn clearly had.

My vision was still red as I caught sight of Ian holding Rosalee on his hip in the middle of the aisle.

Concern crinkled his eyes. "Everything—" He paused and traced my arm down to where my hand was linked with Hadley's. "Okay?"

Hadley tried to pull her hand away and I told myself to let her. The last thing we needed were rumors about us being in a relationship adding fuel to the already burning gossip train.

Yet I didn't let go.

I forced a smile when Rosalee's gaze swung our way, though her eyes weren't for me.

"Hadley!"

"Hey, pretty girl."

Ian's concern transformed into a disapproving scowl as he set Rosalee on her feet.

She ran straight to Hadley. "You brought your camera."

Hadley started to squat, tugging on the arm in my grasp before shooting me a pointed glare. It was only then that I managed to convince my stubborn brain to release her hand.

"I did," she breathed. "I was hoping your dad would let me take pictures of you getting your award tonight."

Two sets of matching green eyes expectantly peered up at me. The beauty of seeing them together momentarily rendered me speechless.

I'd seen the two of them huddled over my dining room table numerous times over the last few months, but this time, it was different. Okay, maybe it wasn't different. But my undiagnosed stroke that made me a dripping sap made it *feel* different

We were out in public. The three of us. Together. At something so normal as my baby girl's end-of-the-year awards ceremony.

Rosalee was smiling.

Hadley was smiling.

And if it weren't for the steam still working its way out of my system thanks to Busybody Marilyn, I would have been smiling too.

It all just felt so comfortable, right down to holding her hand.

God, what was happening?

"Yeah. Sure. Pictures would be great."

Rosalee squealed with delight, throwing her arms around her mother's neck.

Shit. Her mother.

Sooner rather than later, I was going to have to tell her who Hadley truly was. Luckily, school was about to be dismissed for the summer, so I figured I might be able to hold the rumors at bay for a little while. Hadley still had three months left of the supervised visitation she'd agreed to, but she'd made it known she wasn't going anywhere.

And, as fucked up as it was, I liked that idea too.

A woman's voice came over the sound system. "Attention, parents. If we can have everyone please take their seats. All of your precious little ones should meet with their teachers in the back of the auditorium. Don't worry. We'll bring them back shortly." She giggled, and while it wasn't quite as nasally as Marilyn's, it was up there. Not at all like Hadley's smooth and…

Fuck. Me.

"Kiss!" Rosalee declared and pulled at the sleeve of my suit coat.

I bent down and she pecked my cheek. "I'll see you in a few when you're a star, baby."

"Don't forget the little people!" Hadley called after her as she jogged to the line of children forming at the back of the auditorium.

Hadley watched her, pride beaming on her face—something that was usually my job.

And, this time, I couldn't even be mad about it.

I loved that she looked at my baby girl like that.

I loved that she'd never been late to see her.

I loved that she cared enough to come to a damn preschool with her camera in hand, ready to take a dozen pictures like a doting parent.

None of that made up for the four years she'd been gone, but it was a start.

Maybe it was time I started letting those four years go too.

"Caven, can I get a word?" Ian snapped.

I arched an eyebrow. "Any word or are you looking for one in particular?"

He lowered his voice to a hiss. "Specifically, one that means *what the fucking fuck are you doing?*"

I did not have the energy to answer that question—and sure as shit not with Ian. It was no secret that he was not Hadley's biggest fan, and while talking to him and allowing him to be the voice of reason would have been the right thing to do, blissful ignorance was my choice for the evening.

I gave his chest a shove, forcing him into the row of seats ahead of me. "Come on. We should sit before someone takes our seats."

"Please tell me you're not sleeping with her."

Despite the negative answer, the *her* in question was entirely too close for this conversation. I glanced over my shoulder and found Hadley still smiling and watching Rosalee's class file out of the room. "Mind your own damn business."

His jaw became hard. "Say that to me again. Go ahead. Tell me your life and that little girl aren't my business, because for the last fifteen years, it sure as hell has been."

I stepped close enough so no one could hear our conversation in the quickly quieting room. "What is your problem?"

He laughed sans all humor. "Let me ask you this question? How'd it work out last time you slept with her?"

"Well, I lost a computer but got Rosalee, so…"

"Hey, Caven," Hadley called, and I spun to face her the way Rosalee did when she was sneaking cookies from the pantry.

"Yeah?"

She hooked a thumb over her shoulder. "I think I'm going to stand in the back so I can get a better shot of her on the stage. Can you keep an eye on my camera bag?"

"Absolutely." I took it from her.

She tucked a wave of red behind her ear. "Nice to see you again, Ian."

"Yeah. Fantastic," he mumbled.

After a tight smile, she hurried away.

Setting her bag on the seat on the aisle, I sank into the chair beside it. Ian followed suit on my other side.

"Do you even remember the head trip you went on those first six months after she dropped Rosalee off? You were a wreck, but now, you're willing to forget about all that just to—"

"Would you shut up? I'm not sleeping with her." He did not need to know about the stroke-induced dreams. Best friend or not, I was not required to check in with him any time my cock got hard. "I'm being nice. Something you should really try. Like it or not, she's going to be a part of *our* life forever. Rosalee, me, and yeah, you if you'd stop being a dick long enough to get to know her."

He scoffed. "Unless she leaves."

"Then she leaves. And like the first time, there is nothing you or I can do about that. But let me tell you this: As long as she stays this version of Hadley, the one who has her shit together, the one who loves our daughter, and the one who actually shows up and works with me and not against me, then maybe her being a part of Rosalee's life isn't so bad. God knows I'd have given anything to have a mom growing up."

"Oh, okay. Should I call Doug now and tell him to draw up the joint custody papers?"

Pivoting with my entire upper body, I sliced him with a glare. "Say another word, Ian. Swear to God—say one more word."

"Oh, I have a lot more to say. But I see the way you look at her, so I don't think any of it matters anymore."

"Are you...*jealous*?"

"I'm worried, you asshat. I know you. With her past..." He glanced around before lowering his voice to an almost inaudible level. "When she came back, you were hell-bent on keeping her away from Rosalee. Then she told you she was at that mall and now she spends two days a week hanging out at your house. And then, when you factor in that she's sweet, and beautiful, and good with Rosalee... It doesn't take a rocket scientist to see where this is headed."

I smirked. "She's sweet, and beautiful, and good with Rosalee, huh? God, she sounds terrible."

He shook his head and faced forward, where a line of kids were filing across the stage. With her red hair in a sea of brown and blond, my girl was easy to spot. She found us almost immediately and giggled as she waved at Ian and me with both hands.

We excitedly waved back, not a cool or dignified bone in either of our bodies.

Still smiling up at Rosalee, he whispered out of the side of his mouth, "Do me a favor and wear a condom this time. The next one might look like you and then we'd have to sell it to the trolls."

My smile never faltered as I elbowed him in the chest.

He let out a grunt but said no more.

I loved Ian like a brother. And it was completely fair for him to be worried about me. Hell, I was worried about me too.

I didn't understand the draw I felt to Hadley. When I'd first met her at the bar, it had been purely physical, but since she'd come back, it was something else altogether. That woman got under my skin.

Yes, I felt responsible for her past and the nearly paralyzing need to make it right. But as much as I tried to deny it, ignore it, and fight it, there was something else about her. Something that struck me with the familiarity of déjà vu or a whispered secret I'd once heard as a boy. Deep down, I felt a truth that couldn't be untold, yet it was blurred to the point that it had become unrecognizable.

But it was always there.

Every time I saw her.

And it was getting stronger every day.

TWENTY-FIVE

HADLEY

Short of a few evil side glances from Marilyn, the program was relatively boring.

I'd never been so happy to be bored in my entire life. Seeing Rosalee walk across the stage made tears hit my eyes as though she were graduating from high school.

And then tears fell from my eyes when the reality sank in that I'd actually be there to see her graduate high school. And then college.

Those tears turned into rivers when I imagined her coming over to my house to introduce me to the boy who had stolen her heart.

And those rivers became waterfalls when I thought about seeing her in a wedding dress, walking down the aisle, her surprising me with the news that she was expecting, and then her call on her way to the hospital to tell me she was in labor.

They were all the things I'd missed and would continue to miss with my own mother.

But no matter the cost, I'd be there for Rosalee, and that made them the happiest tears of all.

By the time I snuck back to my seat next to Caven, my cheeks had dried.

He still noticed.

"Everything okay?" he whispered.

"Everything is fantastic."

His eyes twinkled in the dim lighting, our stare lingering for a beat too long. His drifted away first, but not before sweeping over my lips.

We sat in silence for the rest of the program, his arm pressed against mine, our elbows sharing a narrow armrest, both of our loving gazes locked on Rosalee, who was squirming and fidgeting while she was supposed to be paying attention to the teachers.

Not surprisingly, when it ended, Rosalee was the first one charging off the stage.

"Daddy, look!" Rosalee shouted, a paper certificate stretched out in front of her.

Caven scooped her off her feet as all the other parents hurried to wrangle their own children.

"What's it say?" she asked, handing it to me as he settled her on his hip.

I was in awe of how fluidly he handled her. "It says exactly what your teacher read when she handed it to you."

"Read it again!"

"To Rosalee Hunt, Best Unicorn Artist of the Year."

She squealed and put her hands on either side of Caven's face, squishing his cheeks. "I'm the best unicorn artist!"

"I heard," Caven mumbled through duck lips.

"Does this mean we can go to Mo's? Please, Daddy. Please. Please. Please."

"Are you going to let go of my face?"

"Are you going to say yes?"

"Yes. Fine. We can go to Mo's."

I laughed when she threw both hands in the air.

"Hadley, you want to come to Mo's?"

Yes. Yes. God, yes. I didn't even know what Mo's was, but I wanted to go wherever she was.

Unfortunately, sweet progress, warm hugs, and sharing an armrest didn't equal an open invitation. I looked to Caven. "Oh, I don't know." But I watched in fascination as his lips split into a breathtaking smile.

"Come on, Hadley. It's a pizza place just around the corner. They have the most incredible pies you can find in Jersey."

"Pies are pizza," Rosalee added.

I bit my bottom lip to keep from grinning like The Joker. "Well, what do you know? I love pizza."

Rosalee's hands shot right back up in the air. "What about you, Uncle Ian? Are you coming?"

His dark gaze flicked between Caven and me, his disapproval tangible. "Nah. I'm going to have to pass tonight." He rubbed her back as she sat in Caven's arms. "But listen, maybe you and I can go grab lunch again next week?"

"Can I have another Coke?"

"No!" Caven growled.

Ian winked. "Maybe."

The four of us braved our way through the crowd together.

Thankfully, Caven missed it when Rosalee sneakily pointed out Jacob to me. He was a cute kid, though I noted to give her another talk when he blew her a kiss as we passed by. Something I was also thankful Caven missed.

Ian left without so much as acknowledging me again, and I did my best to pretend like it didn't sting. After all, Beth wasn't sold on Caven, either. It was his job to be skeptical of me. Maybe with less glaring, but whatever. I could handle Ian.

I followed Caven and Rosalee to the restaurant. He wasn't kidding; it really was just around the corner. It was also a glorified shack that I swear the roof was going to cave in any moment. I couldn't imagine successful businessman/multimillionaire Caven Hunt walking into that place voluntarily. He was far from a snob, but even I was hesitant about this place. I decided to check the food inspector's score before ordering anything.

They were waiting for me at the entrance by the time I'd convinced myself that this wasn't a practical joke and climbed out of my car.

"Your face is priceless," Caven said as I walked up.

"I'm just a little shocked, that's all."

"It's good. I promise. They bring out all the ingredients and you get to make your own pizza. Well, *you* won't get to make anything. Rosalee does it all, but it keeps her busy."

"And it has…" She grunted, pushing at the chipped wooden door with both hands, her feet slipping on the gravel as she fought to get it open. Caven put a hand to the top and sent her stumbling inside, where she finished with, "Video games too."

"Video games," I gasped, clutching my heart. "Why didn't you say so?"

Surprisingly, the place was busy, but after a whispered request and a handshake that I'm almost positive contained cash, the hostess seated us at a round booth in the corner near the arcade. Rosalee went in first, settling at the curve. Then Caven and I slid in on either side of her.

"What's your favorite topping?" she asked, pretending to read the giant folding menu. "I'm getting pepperoni, cheese, and olives. And Daddy is getting pepperoni, sausage, those spicy things, and the gross stuff."

"Oh." I looked at Caven. "Is the gross stuff good here?"

He smirked. "Some of the best."

"Ewww," Rosalee cried. "It's vegetables!"

"Even better. I don't eat meat." I tickled her side.

She squirmed out of my reach. "Then get pepperoni."

I laughed. "That's meat, crazy."

"It is?"

We both looked at Caven, but his curious gaze was stuck on me. "You're a vegetarian?"

"Yeah. When I was eleven, my grandfather fed me undercooked chicken and it made me so sick I swore off meat."

His lips twisted. "But you'll eat leftover pork egg rolls?" He pointedly tipped his head to Rosalee.

Ah, yes. The night she'd been conceived and the leftover Chinese out of his fridge between rounds two and three.

My stomach rolled as I forced a smile. "Egg rolls don't count. My dad used to trade the man who owned a Chinese restaurant next door to his bakery every Saturday. A loaf of sourdough and one bear claw got him eight egg rolls—two for each of us. I make the occasional exception for other nostalgic foods too."

He nodded sheepishly. "Sorry. I didn't mean to—"

A young waiter in a red-and-white-checkered half apron suddenly appeared at our table. "Hey, guys. What can I get you to drink tonight?"

"Lemonade, please," Rosie said.

Caven signaled for me to go next.

"Water, please."

"IPA, whatever you have."

"Actually, you know what?" I said. "Make that two. I could go for a beer."

"Yes, ma'am," the waiter replied. "I'll just need to see your ID."

My mouth fell open, and Caven barked a laugh.

"What? Why? You didn't card him?"

He shrugged. "I have to card anyone who looks under forty."

"Hey!" Caven objected.

It was my turn to laugh. I dug my ID out of my purse and handed it to the kid.

He gave it a quick glance before handing it back. "Oh, hey! Happy Birthday."

"Birthday?" Caven said at the same time Rosalee yelled, "Birthday!"

She scrambled around the booth until she was right beside me, pushed up onto her knees. "Today's your birthday?"

"Yeah, but it's not a big deal. I don't really celebrate anymore."

She completely ignored me. "Dad! Does that mean Hadley gets her dessert first?" She didn't wait for him to answer before she looked back at me. "What did you have for breakfast?"

"Um…peanut butter toast? Why?"

"Nooooo! It's your birthday. You get donuts on your birthday."

"I must have missed that memo." I flared my eyes at Caven, but he was watching me with quiet contemplation. "What?"

"Why aren't you doing stuff with your friends tonight?"

I shrugged. "I am. I went and saw my favorite unicorn artist get an award. Now, I'm about to eat pizza with her and her dad."

He stared at me as he leaned to the side to retrieve his wallet. After pulling out a five-dollar bill, he handed it off. "Rosalee, go play some games for a minute."

She snatched the money. "Will you call me when it's time to make our pizzas?"

He turned his head a fraction to the side, where we could see the line of arcade games and three different claw machines across the aisle. "Yeah. Baby. I'll *call* you."

I started to slide out when she suddenly ducked under the table and sprinted to the video games, nearly knocking our waiter over as he returned with our drinks.

Caven didn't say anything, but I felt his gaze roaming over my face as I watched Rosalee feeding her money like a skilled professional into the change machine.

When the waiter walked away, he laid into me. "Why didn't you mention that tonight was your birthday?"

I took a sip of my beer. "Because it doesn't matter."

"You didn't have to skip your birthday to go to the school tonight. Now, I feel guilty for even asking you."

"You should really let some of that guilt go. I didn't go tonight because you invited me. Well, I guess I did, but I went to see *her*. I've had twenty-six birthdays… Twenty-seven now. But never once had I seen her walk across a stage to get an award. I've missed a lot, Caven. I have no intention of missing anymore."

Her loud laugh captured our attention. She was sitting on a stool, playing an old Ms. Pac-Man game—and not well.

"I should go help her." I started to slip out of the booth when his hand came across the table, landing on top of mine.

"Rosalee asked me if we were friends."

I froze, his touch causing the hum in my veins to sing at deafening levels. "Okay?"

"I didn't know what to tell her."

I breathed a deflated, "Oh."

Using his thumb, he stroked the back of my hand. "Because we both know you're more than that, and one day, she will too.

We're unconventional, but the one thing I want my daughter to always remember is that she has a family who loves her. And that includes you."

"Caven," I whispered, my heart feeling as though it might explode.

Family. It was all I'd ever wanted and why I'd come for Rosalee. That little girl was all I had left. But now, in some strange way, I felt like I had Caven too.

His lips thinned into a tight smile. "Life is short, Hadley. I know I don't have to remind you of that. So I'll just say this. Today's your birthday. And, in my family, we celebrate on birthdays." He slipped his palm off mine, stopping with just his index finger resting on top of mine the same way he had in that mall all those years earlier.

I sucked in a sharp breath, the onslaught of those memories hitting me at full force.

But not the terrible ones that paralyzed me with fear.

Or the bloody ones that made my stomach revolt.

No, the memories that washed over me were of his blue eyes staring back at me.

A three-count to safety.

His hand holding mine as he guided me through Hell.

They were memories of Caven Lowe—the fifteen-year-old boy who had protected me with his own body before he'd ever known my name.

Tears welled in my eyes.

"Don't cry," he murmured. "Please. No more crying."

Using my free hand, I pointed to my eyes. "Good tears." Turning my hand over, I curled my fingers so the tips of his locked with the tips of mine. "Life isn't lived as a whole."

His forehead crinkled. "Huh?"

"We aren't given a hundred years all at once. Time is doled out one very manageable second at a time. If all you focus on is the big picture and worry about tomorrow, you lose the happiness that can be found in the seconds." I covered our linked fingers with my other hand. "Thank you for this second, Caven. And for all the other ones you've given me in the past."

Shaking his head, he breathed, "Jesus, Hadley. Don't thank me."

"I am. And you're going to take it without feeling guilty or being filled with regret. Because, for this second in time, we're going to be happy. Okay?"

His handsome face softened as his gaze held mine.

And we just sat there. Holding hands. Staring at each other.

Living in the second.

Happy.

Well, at least we were.

"Aw, man!" Rosalee yelled. "The ghost ate me again!"

Caven smiled first, bright and wide, and mine followed almost immediately.

The loss of our connection as he pulled his hand away was staggering. The hollow ache left behind morphed into laughter—another second I'd always remember—as he lifted his hand in the air, signaling to the waiter as he called out, "We've got a birthday in the house. I need three brownies over here to start." Humor sparkled in his eyes as he turned his gaze back on me. "And one side of ranch dressing."

There were a lot of laughs over dinner that night. First, as Caven and Rosalee pretended to gag as they watched me dipping the corner of my brownie in ranch with each bite. Then as Rosalee chanted "Ew!" as she made Caven's and my pizzas with the *gross stuff*—which turned out to be sautéed onions, mushrooms, and red peppers. Caven paid for dinner, but neither of us were in a rush to leave, so by the time we finally stood up from the booth, it had been over three hours and twenty dollars spent at the video games.

Hands down, it was the best birthday I'd had in over a decade.

At that point anyway.

TWENTY-SIX

HADLEY

'd just finished washing my face and changing into my white tank top and baby-blue sleep shorts when my phone pinged.

Beth: If you don't answer my texts, I'm sending a team of Navy SEALs out to search for you. They might be birthday strippers though, so I'm not sure how effective they will be.

I plodded out to my kitchen to grab a bottle of water before bed.

Me: I'm alive. I just got home a few mins ago. No strippers needed.
Beth: How was your night with Caven?
Me: Do you really want to know?

A banner notification fell from the top of my screen.

Caven: Did you get home okay?

Dear. God. My heart. He was checking on me.

Me: I did. Thanks again for dinner, and the brownie, and especially the ranch.

Caven: Let's not mention the ranch again, or I'm going to be the one dry-heaving this time.

Me: Who said anything about dry-heaving?

Beth's message slid down on a notification. I read it without switching conversations.

Beth: Yes. I want all the perverted details. Including, but not limited to, what side he was tucking to tonight.

I was laughing as Caven's reply came through.

Caven: Rosalee is planning an elaborate surprise birthday party for you tomorrow. Spoiler alert: It won't include glitter, bath bombs, or llama fur.

Me: One, awwwwww. Two, llama fur?

Caven: She thought it would make a good decoration for the table. Kind of like confetti but hair shaved off a filthy barnyard animal.

Me: That sounds like perfection, so now I'm seriously disappointed.

Caven: Please don't tell her that tomorrow. She'll have me hopping the fence at the zoo with a set of clippers before the cake is served.

Me: Oh! There's going to be cake! What kind?

Caven: As soon as we got home, she barged over to Alejandra's and asked if she'd help her bake one in the morning. I overheard something about funfetti.

Me: My favorite!!!

Caven: Any particular salad dressing dip you'd like to request?

Me: French goes with funfetti. Now, if it was red velvet, that would be thousand island.

Caven: Stop it. Stop it right now.

Me: I'm kidding.

Caven: Good. I might actually be able to sleep tonight.

Another message notification slid down the top of the screen.

Beth: Hello! I'm waiting.

She could continue waiting too. I typed out another message to Caven.

Me: Me too. Thanks again for tonight.

Caven: You're welcome. See you tomorrow. Act surprised.

Me: Will do. Night, Caven.

Beth text again, just as Caven's last message popped up.

Caven: Sweet Dreams.

Beth: Okay! That's it SEAL Team Sex is on the way.

Grinning like a maniac, I clicked on the notification and typed out a message to Beth.

Me: Calm your tits. Caven was texting me.

Me: For your impatient information, tonight went amazing. Like amazing, amazing. Rosalee was adorable as usual. But Caven… Oh my God, that man does it for me so hard. Screw your eight seconds. If he ever kisses me, I'm not coming up for air. Possibly ever.

Those three little dots bounced at the bottom, but I was done with her lectures about keeping my distance from Caven.

Me: OMG, stop typing and just listen! I know all the reasons this is a bad idea, but you don't understand what it feels like when he touches me. Or looks at me. Or…seriously, he walks into the damn room and my whole body goes on high alert. And it's not just because he's gorgeous. He's sweet and thoughtful too. He found out it was my birthday tonight and ordered me a brownie with ranch. I mean, what guy does that?

Me: Don't say a gross one! It was ridiculously sweet. And he told me I was part of his family. I mean, sure, it was in a roundabout way. But he said it. And it was like he knew how badly I needed to feel that again.

Me: And he's so funny. Even when he isn't trying. When was the last time a man made you laugh, Beth? Like truly laugh? God, I can't do this anymore. I feel like I'm sinking in quicksand while tiptoeing around him, when all I really want to do is crawl into his lap and never leave.

Me: You were so damn wrong the other night. I should have kissed him in that bathroom. I swore to my entire family that I'd live my life in the seconds. I'm not letting another one pass me by.

I was typing another message listing all the things I should have done to Caven over the last few months when another text notification dropped down from the top of my screen.

Beth: Fine. Don't tell me about your night. I didn't care anyway. Just kidding… Text me all the details by the morning or I'm kicking down your door. Nighty night.

My.

Heart.

Stopped.

I read and reread her message over and over again, toxic dread settling in my stomach. If Beth's text was showing up as a notification, who the hell had I just spilled my guts to?

But I knew the answer. I just really didn't want to know the fucking answer.

Nerves and embarrassment roared inside me, dueling like the winds of a hurricane.

With a heavy weight in my chest, I ever-so-slowly pushed up on the notification to reveal the name beneath it.

Caven.

Oh, fuckity fuck.

Caven.

My mind went into irrational panic mode. Well, not that the panic was irrational. That was very, very rational after I'd just accidentally poured my heart out to the man I was lusting after. But ideas my brain was throwing off to fix this fiasco were completely and utterly irrational.

Things like: Maybe he hadn't read it.

Then I remembered the bouncing text bubbles when he'd started to reply, more than likely to tell me I'd texted the wrong person. Ya know, like a decent human being. But I'd told him to stop typing and just listen.

Then I considered that maybe he'd rolled over on his phone, which had caused the text bubbles, when in actuality he was already asleep. Thus giving me time to sneak over to his house, find his phone, delete the texts, and then give it back.

Then I remembered the cameras.

Finally, my brain landed on the most irrational but somewhat believable excuse of all.

Me: Shit. Sorry. That was meant for Beth. I was telling her about this other guy I know named Caven. Weird, right? Who knew it was such a common name?

With my stomach in knots, I paced a path in my living room, watching the bottom of that text for over five minutes, but the bubble never appeared. So I decided to give it another shot because that was clearly a great idea.

Me: You didn't think I was talking about you, did you? HA! That would be crazy.

I stared holes in that phone for another solid five minutes with no response. Dammit. He knew I was lying. Real shocker there.

Me: Okay, look. I'm mortified. What will it take for you to forget this ever happened?

I sank onto my couch and put my elbows to my knees. This couldn't be happening. Not something so stupid and preventable. But no. I hadn't sent Caven one accidental text that could be brushed off or explained away. I'd sent him the text version of an autobiography. Outlining in great detail all the bullshit that had been swirling in my head over the last few months.

I had no idea how he was going to react to finding out I had feelings for him. Based on the way he looked at me, I was sure he was harboring a few feelings of his own. But admitting it out loud and not in the middle of a lust-filled stare-off was a lot like accepting it. Three months ago, Caven had thought I was Hadley the Terrible. We'd come a long way, but now, I was expecting him to be able to look me in the eye every Wednesday and Saturday knowing *If he ever kisses me, I'm not coming up for air. Possibly ever.*

I could handle the rejection.

Hell, I was *expecting* the rejection.

But there was a very big, very real part of me that worried this would change things between us. What if he was uncomfortable or mad and went back on his deal to let me see Rosalee? That was the one thing I couldn't risk. Yet there I was, staring at my phone, waiting on pins and needles, nerves rolling in my stomach for judgment day.

Me: Please. I'm begging you. Put me out of my misery here.

Me: If you're mad, I'll totally understand. We can talk about it. I can explain. Just don't take Rosalee away from me.

The more I typed, the more frantic I became, the possibility of losing her sinking in until it felt like a foregone conclusion.

Me: Caven, please. I take it back. I take all of it back. I'm sorry. Please just say something.

My head snapped up when there was a knock at my door. It was past eleven and my elderly neighbors never braved the night.

It was him.

I could feel the hum in my veins.

Damn that fucking hum.

Steeling myself for the absolute worst, I stood up, and crossed the room, and while holding my breath, I opened the door.

It was the most disheveled I'd ever seen Caven. His button-down was untucked, his sleeves were rolled up haphazardly, and his hair was a mess, as if he'd been running his hands through the top of it.

None of this made me feel any better.

"I'm sorry," I whispered, because what the hell else was there to say?

Silently, he stared at me, his gaze heavy and his jaw hard. His Adam's apple bobbed before he licked his lips. "You should *not* have kissed me that night in the bathroom."

I wrung my hands in front of me. "I know. I know. I know. And I—"

In a low gruff voice, he rumbled, "But that doesn't mean I shouldn't have kissed you."

My shock or relief didn't have time to register before he took a long step forward, his arm hooking around my hips. Dragging me against his chest, he crashed his mouth down on mine, hard and punishing, filled with all the desperation of a starving man.

Chills exploded on my skin as the start of every sexual fantasy I'd ever had played out in front of me.

It was Caven.

Caven Lowe.

Caven Hunt.

It didn't matter.

It was just Caven, his mouth opening, his tongue sweeping with mine, his strong arms holding me tight against his chest. His heart pounded out a sweet and devastating harmony to my own.

Slanting his head, he took the kiss deeper, our lips sealing like puzzle pieces clicking into place. He tasted like nothing and everything at the same time, my senses too overwhelmed with the fact that he was there to concentrate on any one thing.

Not his velvety tongue tangling with mine, seeking control as he swallowed my surrender.

Not his hand sliding down my ass, my skin catching fire as he palmed one cheek, grinding me against his thickening cock.

Not the way his other hand gripped the back of my neck, his fingers biting into my flesh as he ravaged my mouth.

"Fuck," he murmured, lifting me off my feet, my legs dangling as he carried me inside my house and kicked the door shut. He turned, setting me down while pinning me against the wall with his strong body. Nipping at my lips, he growled, "Tell me to stop."

I laved my tongue over his bottom lip. "I promised I'd never come up for air."

He pulled his head back to catch my gaze, blue flames burning in his eyes.

That should have been the moment I told him the truth.

That should have been the moment I spilled three months of secrets and lies.

That should have been the moment I threw on the brakes, confessed to eighteen years of loving him, and made him understand why I'd done all the things I had.

But I'd spent every agonizing second of those eighteen years wanting him.

Longing for him.

Dreaming of that moment.

My life was lived in the seconds.

And in that second, I wanted to touch every inch of Caven Hunt while he touched every inch of me.

"Please, Caven," I whispered.

And that was all it took.

TWENTY-SEVEN

CAVEN

It was the worst idea I'd ever had.

After reading her texts, I'd sworn to myself that I would never let something happen between the two of us.

I'd continued swearing it to myself as I'd paced my living room while I waited on Alejandra to show up to keep Rosalee.

I'd sworn it again as I'd pocketed two condoms before leaving my house.

And I'd sworn it every minute of the drive to her place, the thought of her naked body writhing beneath mine making my foot heavy on the accelerator.

I'd known that those texts weren't for me, and I'd resigned myself to a cold shower and fisting my cock as they kept rolling in.

But then she'd typed it. The one thing that had me rethinking my entire fucking life.

I swore to my entire family that I'd live my life in the seconds. I'm not letting another one pass me by.

I didn't know why I felt the way I did about her. It sure as shit wasn't the way I'd felt the first time we'd spent the night together. I could have said that it was because we shared a child now and, most recently, I'd found out we shared a pained past at that mall as well. But it was more than that. I felt a pull to her that I couldn't explain any more than I could extinguish it.

So, yeah. Bad, horrible, stupid choices aside, after reading those texts and finding out that she was just as enamored as I was, I wanted to live in the seconds too.

And when she opened that door in that sexy little white tank top, her nipples showing through the thin fabric, and those shorts that revealed her toned legs just long enough to encircle my hips as I took her fast and hard, I wanted those seconds to be spent inside her.

"Please, Caven," she whispered.

That was all I needed to hear.

"Bedroom?" I murmured, sucking my way up her neck.

"Upstairs," she panted.

"Fuck, that's far away."

She hummed, rolling her hips, the friction against my cock making it throb.

"Point made," I groaned, starting toward the stairs.

With our mouths fused together, we kissed, bumping into walls and nearly falling as she tried to unbutton my shirt. By the time we reached the top of the stairs, I'd shimmied her shorts off, leaving her in nothing but that thin tank top and an equally thin pair of pink panties. It shouldn't have been as mouthwateringly sexy as it was.

But on her...

We hadn't made it to her room before I hooked a finger in her panties, tugging them to the side and teasing through her wetness.

She gasped, folding her arms around my neck for balance as we stood in her hallway, only yards from her bed but physically unable to make it any farther.

I dipped the tip of my finger into her opening, gliding it up until I found her clit. "Is this what I do to you, babe? Is this what you were talking about in those texts?"

She rested her forehead on my pec as her body sagged. "Yes."

I circled her clit. "And you want more, don't you? You remember how good it felt—"

Her head suddenly snapped up. "I don't want to remember anything, Caven. This is now. Me and you. I just want you to touch me." She pressed up onto her toes, ghosting her lips across mine. "And kiss me and—"

I fulfilled that wish, rough and needy. She was right. This wasn't about the past—a road neither one of us needed to get lost down.

Keeping our mouths connected, I backed her through the open door.

Her room was dark, the light in the hall dimly illuminating her tropical escape, complete with decorative mosquito netting draped across the top of her bed. But that was the only thing I noticed about her room in our frenzied path to the mattress.

As she sank onto the bed, I finished her efforts on my shirt and threw it off to the side then toed off my shoes and socks and stepping out of my pants, but not before retrieving a condom from my pocket.

While I rolled it down my shaft, she trapped her bottom lip between her teeth as her eyes, wide and filled with surprise, made the slow trip over my hard cock before landing on my scars. The bullet through my stomach had shredded my left lower ab. Women always stared at that one. I couldn't blame them; it was a mangled wreck. Hell, Hadley had stared at that one the first time too. But it was the one at my side that was nothing more than a circle the size of nickel that had captured her attention.

She could do a full inspection later for all I cared, but I was done waiting. I stripped her panties down her legs, throwing them off to the side. Then I took her mouth again, swallowing her moan as I climbed on top. Her legs opened, allowing my hips to fall through, her hot, wet core pressing against my straining cock.

"Caven," she breathed, clinging to my neck as I rocked against her.

"I fucking love the way you say my name."

Kissing her way up to my neck, she raked her teeth over my earlobe and repeated, "Caven. Caven. Caven."

Fuck me, I should have brought more than two condoms.

Inching back, I tugged the front of her tank down, a perfect, round breast popping free.

As I swirled my tongue around her peaked nipple, her back arched off the bed, which pressed her deeper into my mouth.

"Yes, oh, God, Caven, please."

I traced a hand down her side and pushed up on her shirt. "Take this off."

"No," she panted, spreading her legs wide.

It was an offer I couldn't refuse.

Gripping the base of my cock, I guided myself inside her tight heat.

And when I say tight, I mean, *fucking tight.*

"Jesus, Hadley," I groaned, deliberately stretching her inch by inch.

Peering down at her, I seated myself at the hilt. Her eyes were closed, her mouth gaping open, a full spectrum of ecstasy coloring her face.

"You are so fucking beautiful."

Her lids fluttered open, and I'd wished like hell I'd turned the lights on because there was a soft emotion on her face that I couldn't quite make out in the dimly lit room.

But I felt it. Somehow, someway. I had no idea what it was, but my chest got tight and the muscles in my arms and back tensed. "Hadl—"

"Shhh," she purred, lifting her head to kiss me. "Don't ruin this with words." Her body wrapped around me, her arms around my neck, her legs around my hips, her core squeezing me in a long, needy pull.

I kissed the side of her throat as I began a slow ride that had lost its frenzy but consumed me with something else altogether. I worked her with rhythmic thrusts, her body rolling with mine like waves lost at sea.

She kissed me like she was drowning in us—her lips panic-stricken, touching and tasting anywhere she could reach as if she couldn't get enough. But it wasn't about sex. She wasn't lost in desire, chasing down an elusive release.

She was trying to inhale me, and fuck if I didn't love that more.

As my thrusts became more urgent, her nails bit into my flesh, her hand traveling down to the exit wound from the bullet on my side.

The second she found it, her whole body sagged beneath me as if she'd just come home. "Oh, God, Caven," she cried, her voice cracking as she clung to me.

I needed to see her face. I had no idea what the hell was happening in her head, but she felt too damn good beneath me.

"Come on, babe," I growled, driving in hard.

She cried out again, but there was no mistaking this one for anything other than pleasure.

A tide of raw physical need overtook me and I drove into

her deeper and faster, dropping my fingers to her clit, desperate to take her over the edge with me.

She moaned while I whispered blessed curses, the licking of our flesh playing the bassline to our erotic symphony.

She broke first, the sound of my name tumbling from her lips in a drunken slur. The world crumbled around me, nothing but her and that bed existing outside of that second as she pulsed around my length, stripping the release from my body.

"Fuck," I groaned, burying my face in her neck as I rode my high out with lazy strokes.

As my sated mind wandered down to the present, she gently scratched my back with one hand, but she never moved her other from my scar.

I could have slept there for a dozen years—inside her, on top of her, her fingertips lulling me into oblivion. That wasn't an option though. The fact was that, while I'd had the most incredible sex, physically and bleeding into emotionally, it'd been with Hadley—the mother of my child.

But feeling her curled around me, her heart racing and her breathing labored, I didn't regret it. Not for a second.

And that might have been the most terrifying part of all.

Lifting my head, I peered down at her, my chest constricting at the sight of her hooded eyes.

I pecked her lips. "Hey."

"Hey," she whispered back.

Unable to stop myself, I dipped to take her mouth in a languid kiss.

She smiled when I finally pulled away. "I could do that all night."

"I've got one more condom. But, first, I need to get rid of this one and we need to talk."

She squeezed her eyes shut, her arms suddenly falling to the bed. "Noooooooooo. No talking tonight."

I chuckled against her lips before slowly withdrawing. "Trust me. It's low on my list too."

She gasped at the loss, and as I stood up, she closed her legs before I could catch a glimpse of her glistening pussy. It was probably for the best since the thought alone made my cock thicken again.

By the time I got back from her bathroom, she was sitting up on the far side of the bed, pillows propped behind her, the tank top still on, and her tan comforter pulled over her waist. But it was the way she nervously picked at the edge of the blanket that caught my attention.

I didn't bother with clothing or the blankets as I settled beside her on my stomach in bed. "You want to clean up before we talk?"

"I used the one in the guestroom."

I smirked and lifted the edge of the blanket for a not-so-subtle peek. No panties. Okay, so she was nervous, but not nervous enough to put on pants and rule out round number two. I could work with that.

"Good girl," I praised, kissing her shoulder. Draping my tattooed forearm over her stomach, I shifted closer and propped my head in my hand with an elbow to the mattress. "So tell me about these feelings you have for me."

Her body flashed solid. "What? No."

"Come on. In your texts, you were telling Beth all about them. Surely you can tell me."

"Well, I can tell you Beth thinks my *feelings* are a horrible idea and would probably have a coronary embolism if she saw us naked together right now."

I brushed two fingers over her covered breast, her nipple hardening immediately. "Technically, I'm the only one naked. You're still wearing clothes."

She was breathy when she replied, "She's a lawyer. I'm not sure that defense will hold up with her."

"Touché."

"Besides, what about Ian? He doesn't seem to be on Team Hadley, either."

Fascinated by the tight nubs showing through her shirt, I didn't look up as I replied, "Don't worry about Ian. Nobody needs to know about this until we figure out what's going on here."

"Wait." She grabbed my hand and moved it to rest on her stomach. "I can't think when you're doing that."

"That's kinda the point." Grinning, I looked up at her. My smile faded when I saw the anxiety on her face. "Hey, hey, hey. Don't look at me like that. What's going on?"

"I don't know. I guess that's the real question. What *is* going on here?"

I let out a heavy breath. "I don't have an answer to that yet. An hour ago, I didn't think I'd be sitting here." I inched closer and cupped the side of her neck. "I'm going to be honest with you: This was the most epically stupid thing the two of us in our situation could have done. Wouldn't you agree?"

She cut her gaze to the wall. "I know."

"Good. Now, that's out of the way." I released her neck and moved my attention back to her nipple.

Her mouth fell open, but her skeptical gaze jumped back to mine. "That's it? That's our talk? *We did something epically stupid. Now, let's burn through that last condom?*"

"Well, I mean, it's not actually the *last* condom. As far as I know, the apocalypse hasn't happened since I got here. The drugstore will have more."

She once again stilled my hand at her breast. "Caven, I'm serious. I panicked tonight after I accidentally sent you those texts because I was afraid you'd be mad and take Rosalee away from me. You have all the control in this situation, and as much as I loved every single second of what just happened between us, the not knowing what you're thinking scares me."

The idea of her being scared or thinking I was going to use Rosalee to punish her if I got mad felt like a punch to the gut. "Look, it's been a long time since I've had any kind of relationship. I don't even know what kind of guy I am anymore. But I know I'm not that kind of father. Whatever happens between us or whatever doesn't, I'll never use her as a pawn."

"I didn't mean to insinuate that you would, but I just can't get a read on you all the time. It's like you can't decide if you hate me or if you want to tear my clothes off."

"Yes. It's exactly like that." I flipped onto my back, draped an arm around her shoulders, and jostled her into my side. "A few weeks ago, I didn't know how I felt, either. I haven't felt in control of any part of this situation since the day I saw you in my backyard. And for a guy like me, whose entire life has been defined by chaos, that was a paralyzing feeling. I didn't want you to have anything to do with Rosalee because I was scared. It's my job to protect her and you were the one person in the entire world with the ability to take her away from me."

Her head tipped up as it rested on my shoulder. "Caven, I told you I would never—"

"I know what you said, but in my experiences, words are worthless. The man who taught me to ride a bike and kissed my skinned knees…" I paused, moving her hand to my ugly and scarred ab. "He tried to kill me."

She slid her hand to my hip and gave me a reassuring squeeze. It was sad, but it didn't feel like pity coming from her.

"Trust is hard for me. I took a leap of faith to let you have visitation against everyone's advice because that was something I could control. I was prepared to hate you until the end of time. I know we didn't spend a lot of time together the night we met at the bar. But I didn't realize this is who you were." I kissed her forehead. "Fuck me, I was not ready for *you*. And I mean that as a compliment. You're sweet. And kind. And generous. When I showed up at your house that day and you dumped that man's recyclables on your floor because he wouldn't leave until you took them…" I laughed at the memory. "And the paint. I still have that shirt, ya know? I can't bring myself to trash it because it makes me smile every damn time I see it."

Her voice was filled with emotion as she replied, "If you're going to keep it, I rescind my offer to PayPal you for it. Though, if you ever decide to leak my identity as R.K. Banks, it would probably be worth a fortune."

I laughed, the high that woman gave me going straight to my head. "And that. Just that. Your smartass answer for everything. You asked Beth on that text when was the last time a man made her laugh. And I thought about it. I couldn't remember the last time a woman made *me* laugh."

She beamed up at me. "Really?"

"Don't play coy with me. You're funny. *Weird.* But funny. And you're good with Rosalee. She loves you. She did however notice that we eye-fuck across the room during art."

She sucked in a sharp breath. "Please tell me she did not say eye-fuck."

"No. But it won't be long if we don't address this Jacob issue. Apparently, he's a love expert."

"We?" she squeaked.

"Huh?"

"You said *we* need to address the Jacob issue."

I knew what she was asking, and I'd meant it when I said it, but that was a conversation for another day. "You won't let me mail him to China. So, yeah…*we* are going to have to find an alternate solution for that little shit."

She tipped her chin down so I could no longer see her face, but the slight shake of her shoulders gave her tears away.

I put my lips in her hair and whispered, "I'm going to keep talking, but I don't want you to cry through it."

"Good tears."

"Ah, okay then. Carry on."

She giggled just the way I'd hoped and it affected me the way it always did by stretching a smile across my face.

I didn't speak for several seconds as I relished in the rare taste of happiness I'd found with another adult. I had friends. I had Ian. But nobody truly understood the sour in my life to realize how huge the sweet was when I finally tasted it.

For four years, Rosalee had been my only sweet.

And she was enough. She would always be enough for me.

But it was a different kind of sweet with Hadley.

"I'm happy that you know about my past," I rushed out like it was a dirty little secret burning the back of my throat. "It makes me a horrible human being, but knowing you were there and that you understand me on a different level has been the most liberating experience of my life. I think it's why we're lying here right now. I feel this undeniable connection to you that I can't shake, and a big part of me doesn't want to shake it at all because, while I'm almost positive we are a disaster waiting to happen, knowing that someone else actually gets the clusterfuck in my head without me having to explain every agonizing detail, it's…addicting."

Her face snapped up so fast that it ignited the guilt inside me. Shit. Why had I confessed that to her? My fucking father killed her parents because of *me*, and like a selfish bastard, I'd told her that I was glad she'd been there that day because I appreciated that she could understand *me*.

What a fucking piece of shit I was. "I'm—"

"Don't do that. Don't you dare apologize to me." She rolled so she was half on top of me. The light in the hall illuminated her as she supported herself on an elbow, bringing her face only inches from mine. "But what if we're not?"

"What if we're not what?"

"What if we're not a disaster waiting to happen?"

I blinked, utterly in shock. "How do you do that? How did you hear everything I just said and know everything about me and just overlook it? Like it's nothing."

"Because it is nothing, Caven. You were a kid in a mall with a monster. Same as me."

A lump formed in my throat. *Jesus. This woman.*

"It was different."

"No, it wasn't. That's just a game you play in your head. The facts are you were a fifteen-year-old boy alone at a mall the day a sick individual decided to take his frustrations with life out on innocent victims. But we got out. It hasn't been easy. It will never be easy. But you have to learn to stop apologizing for something you could never control in the first place."

And that was where she was wrong. I should have been at the police station that day, turning over the stash of my father's trophies I'd found to the authorities. And if that's where

I'd gone that day instead of going to work first, forty-eight people, including her parents, would still be alive.

"I don't want to talk about this anymore." I went in for a kiss, but she easily dodged it.

"You will always have that free pass with me. *Always*, Caven. But let me say this before you take it. There's a reason time only marches in one direction. You can choose any second to start over again."

I stared at her, green eyes sparkling and red hair falling in messy waves over her shoulders. I wanted to believe her. To believe that I choose to shed the overwhelming burden I'd taken on that day in Hell all those years earlier.

But I didn't believe her.

And I never would.

Rolling her to her back, I pulled the covers out from between us. "You said it scared you not knowing what I was thinking. Well, here's what I'm thinking. We're two consenting adults who both know that this thing between us might blow up in our faces, and because of that, we're both going to tread in these uncharted waters with caution. But I swear to you our daughter is not a factor in what happens in this part of our lives. Neither is Beth. Neither is Ian. Outside of this room, we're going to keep on figuring out our life the same way we have been for the last three months." I traced my hand from her stomach, down the silken length of her thigh, gently guiding her legs apart to reveal her wet core.

She threw her head back as I dipped a finger inside her opening, her slick heat causing my cock to stir to life all over again. I moved my mouth to hers, teasing her with a kiss and allowing our lips to brush as I finished with, "But inside this room, I want to fuck you. I want to make you come on my fingers and on my mouth. I want your ass in the air when I take you from behind, and I want all of your hair fanned out over my stomach when you take my cock to the back of your throat." I added a second finger and flicked my tongue over her lips. "And that's *all* I'm thinking about right now."

She hissed, her hand flying up to grip my ass.

Conversation.

Over.

A few minutes later, she came on my hand.

Shortly after that, she came on my cock.

And three hours later, when I crawled out of her bed in order to get home to my daughter, the only regret I had was that she was still wearing that fucking shirt.

TWENTY-EIGHT

HADLEY

"**B**eth, I have to go!" I whisper-yelled as I stood in Caven's driveway.

"So, that's it? You just went out to dinner, he ordered you a brownie with ranch, and then you came home and didn't answer any of my texts?"

No. He'd come over. We'd had amazing sex, after which—or, depending on how you looked at it, *before* the second doubly incredible time we'd had sex—we'd agreed not to discuss it with Beth or Ian. And then, when he'd kissed me long and slow at my front door, he'd promised me again that whatever happened between us would not affect Rosalee. I had no idea how that was possible, but I trusted him enough to take it at face value.

"For the millionth time, *yes*. That's all that happened. I was tired."

The amount of sleep I'd gotten the night before was easier to measure in minutes than hours, but my lips were bruised and I had an intoxicating ache between my legs, so I was still riding the peak of a sexual high.

I couldn't lie. I was a nervous wreck about seeing him that day. I'd started getting dressed at six in the morning even though I wasn't supposed to be at his house until one. I'd torn everything out of my closet in search of something that said,

Hi, I'm here to teach your daughter art, but I'd also like to see you naked later tonight. So look at my tastefully revealed cleavage as a sample of the goods while we wait for the hours to tick past.

I'd always attempted to look cute but casual when I went to his house.

But this was different.

This was bigger.

It was also exactly the same, which pretty quickly allowed me to rule out my favorite little black cocktail dress.

Jeans seemed…blah.

And shorts seemed *too* casual.

So, eventually, after two hours of trying on clothes and my bedroom being declared a national disaster zone, I'd decided on a lilac maxi dress that made my body look like a dream.

"I don't believe you," Beth said.

"I don't care if you believe me or not. I still have to go." I'd brought my art bag despite the fact that he'd warned me that Rosalee was going to throw me a party. I wasn't sure how I was supposed to act today. Was I allowed to just hang out with them for two hours? Or was there an expectation that, after a quick round of happy birthday, I was to break out the tissue paper mosaics I'd brought as the day's craft?

When I was alone with Caven, I was comfortable and free to be myself. But the man who had been in my bed last night was *not* the standoffish, scowling man who usually greeted me when I arrived to spend time with Rosalee.

There was a huge difference between Caven the dad and Caven the man. And as I saw him walk out onto the front porch, barefoot with jeans slung so low on his hips that my mouth watered, I hoped it was some mixture of the two.

I ended my call with Beth without so much as a goodbye.

"Hey," I whispered to him when I got close enough.

His face was hard, but the slide of his gaze from my breasts to my lips was gentle as a feather. He reached out for my art bag, taking it off my shoulder. "So, we have a little change of plans for today."

My eyebrows shot up. "What's up?"

"My brother and his wife showed up this morning for a surprise visit. I think we need to push off the art stuff so Rosalee can spend time with them."

My stomach sank. Caven aside, I treasured my time with Rosalee. The disappointment was stifling. "Oh. Yeah. I understand. Maybe I can come over and see her on Monday after they leave?" Monday. Damn, that was a long time away.

His lips twitched. "Monday's fine. But then you're going to miss your party that she's been working on all morning."

I bit my bottom lip, smiling around it. "She's been working on it all morning?"

"Yep. And she's been hiding behind the couch, waiting to surprise you since you pulled up."

"Are you sure you don't mind me interrupting your family time with your brother?"

He placed his hand on my arm, giving me a gentle squeeze. "It's fine. Rosalee's excited. Trent wants to meet you anyway." He gave me a head-to-toe body sweep. "I wouldn't mind eye-fucking you for a few hours in that dress, either."

My cheeks heated with every color on the red spectrum.

He chuckled. "We're planning to grill out after the birthday extravaganza, so if you want to stay for that too, I'm sure Rosalee would love it."

Oh. My. God.

I was invited to the family cookout. *Caven* had invited *me* to the family cookout.

My nose started stinging.

I would not cry.

I would not cry.

I would not....

"You're going to cry, aren't you?"

"No!" I croaked, looking off to the side.

He laughed, giving my arm a tug, dragging me into his chest. "Relax. Trent sucks on the grill but insists he's in charge. You'll have plenty of time to cry later while you are eating rubber."

I barked a laugh and miraculously managed to keep my tears at bay when the scruff on his jaw brushed my cheek.

"I have good news," he rasped, his warm breath fluttering across the sensitive skin at my neck. "This morning when I made a food run, I found one grocery that had somehow made it through the apocalypse. I got into a brawl with another man and nearly got eaten by a zombie on my way out, but I managed to secure enough condoms for tonight."

It was funny, and I wanted to laugh, but the word *tonight* held so much promise that my breath hitched and my nipples hardened. Fisting the front of his shirt, I breathed, "Caven."

"Mmm," he hummed. "Good answer." He suddenly backed out of my reach. "Now, come on. Rosalee is probably collecting dust bunnies behind the couch at this point. Act surprised, remember."

I peered up at him, thrilled beyond words. I wanted to say thank you again in every way I knew possible. But I liked it when he smiled, so I went with, "I'm glad you didn't get eaten by a zombie."

He winked and opened the door, muttering, "You and me both."

The house was quiet as we walked inside. Streamers had been twisted and strung above the doorways, and the paper flowers we'd made together were taped on either side of a banner with scribbled words that possibly said *Happy Birthday Hadley*, but it just as easily could have said *Hot Pocket Harley*. I caught sight of a huge, pink balloon floating behind the couch, the kind that had a teddy bear and confetti stuffed inside.

My chest filled with warmth as I took in everything she'd done—with Caven's help, of course.

"Sorry, Hadley. Rosalee isn't here today," Caven announced loudly. "She went on a safari to Africa."

"What?" I replied, playing along. "All by herself?"

He flashed me a playful smile. "Yep. She said she was going to start collecting guinea pigs for her farm. And what better place to do that than Africa?"

"Well, obviously. I sure will miss her though."

"Surprise!" she yelled, jumping out from behind the couch with the balloon in her hand.

But that wasn't why my heart stopped.

Or why my lungs seized.

Or why the blood drained from my face and my head got light.

No, that was because a smiling, blond woman walked out from a hiding spot behind the curtain with Caven's father, Malcom Lowe, at her side.

It wasn't him. I'd watched Malcom die. I'd seen his dead body.

But this guy… He was too familiar.

I reached back and caught Caven's hand, praying that I

stayed in the present as my mind took the slow route to making sense of what I was seeing.

"Happy Birthday!" Rosalee sang, oblivious to my panic, and just the reminder that she was so close to that man set me on edge that much more.

"Come here," I choked around the fear.

She smiled up at me as I all but dragged her to her father.

"Jesus," the man muttered, looking down at the floor.

It wasn't his voice.

It wasn't Malcom's voice.

I'd never forget that voice, and this one wasn't his.

I didn't know if it was the trembling in my hands or the shake of my legs that gave me away, but Caven curled me into his front.

"Relax. It's Trent. It's *just* Trent."

Right. Trent.

His brother.

That he'd told me was there.

With his wife.

Trent.

Malcom's *other* son.

Who had clearly gotten his father's looks.

But he was not Malcom.

Because Malcom was dead.

And had been dead for a long time.

I tipped my head back to look at Caven. His arm was locked around my hips, and his eyes blazed with concern and… Shit. More guilt. After sucking in a deep breath, I held it in, willing my heart to calm and reminding my memories and my nervous system where I was and where I *wasn't*. Caven's strong hold on me did wonders to ease my racing mind.

"It's okay," I breathed, not yet trusting my voice. "I'm okay."

"Aw, man, did I scare you again?" Rosalee asked. "Please don't leave."

I swallowed hard. I could do this.

It was Trent.

We were all safe.

I didn't move out of Caven's arms. I wasn't quite there yet, but I finally found my voice. "I'm not leaving. I promise."

"Yay!" She clapped before handing me the balloon. "It's Hadley Posie Day, so you get to eat sweets all day! And guess what? Daddy said as long as I eat my hot dog later, I can eat sweets with you!"

I smiled down at her as my heart resumed a non-marathon pace. "That sounds amazing."

She tapped her fingers one at a time as she counted off. "We got cake and cookies and candy. Oh oh oh! Daddy bought lots of ranch for you too. And I made you a present."

"I cannot wait to see it."

"Hey, baby," Caven said. "Can you run out to Alejandra's and tell her that Hadley is here and see if she wants to join us for lunch?"

Rosalee cocked her head to the side. "I thought she was going to Ruby's house?"

"Just…do me a favor and go check. Okay?"

She shrugged and looked back at me with a big smile. If she noticed that I was currently glued to her father's hip, she didn't mention it at all. "I can't wait for you to see your cake. I put rainbow sprinkles all over it."

I feigned excitement for her sake. "Ohhh. I can't wait, either."

"I'll be right back." She took off at a dead sprint that, given her clumsy Banks genes, looked more like a speedy flounce.

As soon as we heard the door shut behind her, Caven put his lips to my ear. "You okay?"

"Yeah...I, uh." I peeked over my shoulder and found Trent eyeing us with suspicion.

The moment our gazes collided, his whole demeanor softened. He wasn't as tall or as big as Caven, but they shared the same olive skin and dark hair. The most notable difference between the two men were their eyes, shape and all. While Caven's were perfect ovals of sparkling blue, his brother's were dark brown and deep set, the kind that always look contemplative and cynical.

"I'm Trent," he said. Not taking a step forward. Not extending his hand. Just standing there with his wife tucked into his side. His face was unreadable, but the sag of his shoulders told me he hated this just as much as I did.

"I'm Hadley."

He gave me a weak smile. "I didn't mean to scare you. I can't do much about the face though."

"Don't be silly. No need to apologize. I was...surprised. That's all."

He tipped his head to the pretty woman at his side, his arms wrapped securely around her much the way Caven was holding me. "This is my wife, Jennifer."

I offered her a brisk nod. "Nice to meet you."

"*Incredible* to meet you too," she replied, and it looked like her smile was going to swallow her face.

"Don't say it, Jenn," Caven warned. "Just don't say it."

"What?" she drawled innocently.

Trent cleared his throat. "Come on, Jenn. Let's warm up the grill?"

She shot him an incredulous look. "Why do you need me for that? I haven't been allowed to touch a grill in ten years."

"I don't. But you're coming anyway."

She huffed, following him out to the backyard, pausing for one last giddy glance before closing the door.

Caven shook his head and looked down at me. "Talk fast. Rosie will be back any second and then I'm going to lose you for the rest of the day. You going to be okay with Trent? I can make up an excuse if you want to duck out."

I rested my hands on his pecs, my giant balloon nearly hitting him in the face. "I'm good. Really."

"He's not Malcom, Hadley."

"I know. It was a gut reaction. I'm fine. I promise."

He searched my face for several seconds, his concern doing some seriously warm things in my chest. "That changes and you find yourself *not okay*, I want to know. Right away. No dry-heaving in the bathroom without me."

I cut him a side-eye. "What? Who said anything about dry-heaving?"

He chuckled. "On a different note, I think my brother and Jenn might be onto us."

"Well, he's not Ian, Beth, or Rosalee. So I guess it could be worse."

"Clearly, you do not know Jennifer."

Rosalee's voice echoed through the room long before she entered it. "Ale's going to Ruby's house!"

With one last squeeze, Caven set me away and walked to the kitchen like nothing had happened.

I knew better though.

And I knew it would be happening again later that night, and that thought alone made the hum in my veins deafening.

He wasn't wrong. As soon as Rosalee got back, he lost me for the day. That little girl never left my side. We ate more sweets than I had in years, and I laughed when she explained to me that Caven had bought me some gross burgers at the store. I was assuming they were veggie burgers, but I made a mental note to check with him before lunch.

Jennifer joined us when Rosalee insisted on starting the tissue paper mosaics while the guys grilled. I liked her. She doted on Rosalee like she was her own. And even when she was not-so-subtly prying about my "friendship" with Caven, she was doing it with hearts in her eyes rather than the contempt we were going to get from Beth and Ian if they ever found out. I did what I could to avoid her interrogation in front of Rosalee. This included airing the sordid details about Rosalee's blooming romance with Jacob the love expert.

Trent kept his distance from me at first, but there was something eerie about the way he was always watching me out of the corner of his eye.

Or maybe I only noticed because I was always watching him out of the corner of my eye too.

As I'd listen to him and Caven laughing and telling embarrassing stories about each other over dinner, I'd come to piece together that Chief of Police Trent Hunt was nothing like his sociopath father.

But an hour later after Caven had sentenced me to the back deck while he and Rosalee put the final touches on my birthday cake, I realized Trent was nothing like his little brother, either.

"Mind if I join you?" he asked.

I forced a smile and waved a hand to the Adirondack chair beside me. "Please do."

He kicked his long legs out in front of him as he sipped on a beer. "I don't like it."

"What's that?"

He stared off into the distance, refusing to look at me as he spoke. "This thing. You. Caven. You coming back thinking you have any right to that little girl. I don't like it. Any of it. But most especially, I don't like *you*."

Ohhhhh-kay. Blunt. To the point. Rude as hell. But it definitely explained the eerie glares.

Straightening in my chair, I turned to face him. "I know it's an unusual situation, but I swear to you that I'm not here to—"

"My brother's got a fucking bleeding heart. He's been carrying Malcom's shadow like a noose around his throat for a lot of years. He's a strong man. A good man. But one mention of Watersedge and he's on his knees."

The hairs on the back of my neck stood on end as his dark gaze turned my way.

"There are people out there who might think to take advantage of that."

"I can assure you—"

He once again spoke over me. "Yeah. Yeah. Yeah. Not you, I'm sure. So, that being said, I hope you don't mind that I did some digging into your past."

A surge of panic blasted through my system, but I showed him nothing. "No. Not at all. I totally understand. He's your brother."

He leaned toward me, one side of his mouth hitching. "I didn't find much."

Relief fell like raindrops over the fire of my anxiety. "Sorry to waste your time. I guess I'm a pretty boring person."

"Nobody's *that* boring."

"You'd be surprised." Ready to find Caven and then immediately start dry-heaving, I started to push out of my chair, but his hand wrapped around my wrist, stilling me.

"I'm sorry to hear about your sister." He grinned. "Must have been hard to lose her, what with you two being twins and all."

My pulse spiked as I attempted to yank my arm out of his grasp. "I think losing a sibling, twin or not, is always devastating. But thank you for your condolences."

His fingertips bit into my skin as he refused to let go. "You want to know something I learned about twins when I was looking into your boring past?"

Adrenaline hit my system like a bolt of lightning illuminating the night sky. "What I want is for you to get your fucking hands off me."

"Identical twins have the same DNA." His arrogant grin grew. "But different fingerprints. Isn't that some shit?"

I tugged at my wrist again. "Let me go or, swear to God, I'll scream for Caven."

He gave me a rough pull toward him, the arm of the chair painfully digging into my side as my panic swirled to a new high. "No, you won't. See, I've got a theory on you, Hadley Banks." His eyes flared wide, that slimy smile never faltering.

I held his unwavering stare. "Is your theory that I'm going to have you arrested for assault if you don't let me go right fucking now?"

He shrugged and casually released me. "I'm a cop. I know a scam when I see one."

I stood up, rubbing my wrist, and backed toward the door. My chest was heaving, and my heart was in my throat. "You might want to talk to your brother before showing up here to rescue him from the clutches of a woman you know nothing about. I have more than enough money to ever need to scam a single cent off your brother."

He set his beer on the ground and then stood up, keeping his distance this time. "Now, that I'll agree with. Which honestly was the most confusing part of all. But while you may have money, you don't have much else. After losing your sister, you don't even have a family left. Let me ask you this: Why didn't the police find your prints in Caven's apartment?"

I stood up straighter. "I don't know."

"I mean, you were there that night, right? Or at least somebody with your DNA was there that night, because Rosalee exists."

Curling my lip, I shook my head. "We're done here. I get that you're trying to be a protective older brother and look out for Caven. But putting your hands on me and making wild allegations is quite honestly sick." I turned again, starting for the door, but he stopped me in my tracks.

"Your sister, Willow, died in a car accident in upstate New York. At the time, her home of record was Puerto Rico."

"She was visiting—"

"A friend. I got it. A buddy told me your girl Beth Watts was hysterical when they delivered the news. Apparently, you and your sister had been staying with her for a few days. You two got into an explosive argument where you both flew off the handle and then took off like bats out of Hell. Explain to me how Willow died on the exact route she would have taken to get to the cabin you two shared. Meanwhile, you, *Hadley,* flew back to Puerto Rico."

I spun to face him, my whole body trembling. "We were dissolving the business. I went to clear my stuff out of her studio."

His eyes flashed dark. "Could be. Or the city could have declared the wrong Banks girl dead and you've come back to reclaim the only family you have left. It could be that you aren't Hadley Banks at all. Isn't that right, Willow?"

Eighteen years earlier...

"Just try to breathe," the paramedics said as they poked and prodded at my side.

It hurt.

It hurt more watching my hero fall apart.

He was a wreck of sobs and adrenaline, screaming at the paramedics to help someone else. He was determined to stand on his own two feet but unable to remain upright, falling from one wall to the other. The wounds on his stomach and his side had soaked through until his entire shirt was red, which left blood pouring down the legs of his pants.

Nobody could lose that much blood. He was going to die if he didn't let them help him, and that terrified me all over again.

"Calm down," I choked out. He couldn't hear me beneath the oxygen mask the paramedics had placed over my face, so I tugged it down and gathered whatever strength I had left to shout, "Please just calm down!"

His head snapped to mine immediately and I could see the fight and despair turn to panic all over again.

"Let them help you," I pleaded.

His chin quivered as he stared at me. "I'm sorry. I'm so sorry."

Tears I should have long since run out of filled my eyes, and I stretched my hand out toward him. "What's your name?"

He stared at it for a beat before he lowered himself on flimsy legs to the floor beside me, taking my hand. "Caven."

"Kevin?"

"Caven."

"Gavin?"

His face crumbled, rivers of tears pouring from his eyes as an unlikely half smile snuck out. "Caven. But close enough."

"Okay, Caven. I'm scared."

He folded both hands around mine. "No. No. No. Don't be scared. It's over. He's dead. He can't hurt us anymore."

"But I'm scared *you're* going to die now."

"I'm fine," he lied, the pallor of his face growing grayer by the minute. "Really."

It was such a war zone that the paramedics and police were racing around in and out of the kitchen. They didn't have the time to fight with a fifteen-year-old boy who claimed he was okay while dozens of other people lay dying only yards away.

"You saved my life. Now, it's time to save yours."

"There are other people who—"

My entire body exploded in pain as I shouted, "There's you!"

"I'm sorry," he repeated for the millionth time, and even with as much pain and shock as I was in, it pissed me off.

"Fine. If you want me to forgive you, let them help you. You owe me that. Your dad did this to me." It was the lowest of low blows. But I was desperate.

His eyes got wide, and seeing the shame slash through

those crystal blues was more painful than anything else. I just wanted him to be okay, even if it broke my heart.

"That's not fair."

"Neither is you dying. Let them help you, Caven, and I'll forgive you. I promise. I will."

A pair of black boots entered my peripheral vision, and the paramedic who had been helping me said, "Son, listen to the girl. I need you to lie back now. We need to get you both out of here."

I gave his hand a squeeze and whispered, "Please."

He screwed his eyes tight, his resolve crumbling alongside his failing body. "I won't be able to forgive myself."

"But I will."

He broke into another round of sobs, sliding down to the side to rest his forehead on my hand.

He put up no more fight as they rushed in, cut his shirt off him, and went to work on the gaping hole in his abdomen.

He winced and cried.

He held my hand.

And he profusely apologized until his voice could no longer carry the words.

Just as they were moving me to carry me out to an ambulance, his hand slipping from my grip, he opened his eyes and, in a voice so slurred and filled with gravel, called out, "Wait! What's your name?"

It was the last word I would ever say to Caven *Lowe*.

"Willow."

To be continued in…
Written with You
coming June 13, 2019

OTHER BOOKS BY ALY MARTINEZ

THE RETRIEVAL DUET
Retrieval
Transfer

GUARDIAN PROTECTION AGENCY
Singe
Thrive

THE FALL UP SERIES
The Fall Up
The Spiral Down

THE DARKEST SUNRISE DUET
The Darkest Sunrise
The Brightest Sunset

Across the Horizon

THE TRUTH DUET
The Truth About Lies
The Truth About Us

THE WRECKED AND RUINED SERIES
Changing Course
Stolen Course
Broken Course
Among the Echoes

ON THE ROPES
Fighting Silence
Fighting Shadows
Fighting Solitude

Savor Me

ABOUT THE AUTHOR

Originally from Savannah, Georgia, *USA Today* bestselling author Aly Martinez now lives in South Carolina with her husband and four young children.

Never one to take herself too seriously, she enjoys cheap wine, mystery leggings, and baked feta. It should be known, however, that she hates pizza and ice cream, almost as much as writing her bio in the third person.

She passes what little free time she has reading anything and everything she can get her hands on, preferably with a super-sized tumbler of wine by her side.

Facebook: www.facebook.com/AuthorAlyMartinez

Facebook Group: www.facebook.com/groups/TheWinery

Twitter: twitter.com/AlyMartinezAuth

Goodreads: www.goodreads.com/AlyMartinez

www.alymartinez.com

Made in United States
Troutdale, OR
07/17/2025

32993713R00166